ANGEL'S CAGE

MOLOTOV OBSESSION: BOOK 2

ANNA ZAIRES

♠ MOZAIKA PUBLICATIONS ♠

Copyright © 2021 Anna Zaires and Dima Zales
www.annazaires.com

Published by Mozaika Publications, an imprint of Mozaika LLC.
www.mozaikallc.com

Cover by The Book Brander
www.thebookbrander.com

Photography from The Cover Lab
www.thecoverlab.com

ISBN: 978-1-63142-645-2
Paperback ISBN: 978-1-63142-646-9

1

CHLOE

I'm back. Back in the devil's lair.

The thought loops through my pain-dazed mind as the car rolls to a stop in front of Nikolai's ultra-modern mountain mansion. A man and two women in hospital scrubs—presumably the medical team Nikolai mentioned—are waiting for us on the driveway with a gurney. Behind them is Alina, Nikolai's sister, her beautiful face pale and worried.

I register all this only in passing. All my senses are consumed by the man holding me possessively on his lap.

Nikolai Molotov.

The devil himself.

His powerful arms are wrapped around me, securing me against his large body, and even though I've just seen him kill two men, I can't help but derive comfort from his touch, his warmth, his familiar cedar-and-bergamot scent. His taste lingers on my tongue, my lips throbbing from his kiss, and as much as I want to deny it, dread isn't the only emotion filling the pit of my stomach at the thought of him keeping me here against my will.

"Just a few seconds longer, zaychik," he murmurs, smoothing back my hair, and a shudder ripples through me as my eyes meet his tiger-bright gaze.

I can see the monster underneath his beautiful façade. It's now clear as day.

Pavel jumps out of the car first, opening the door for us, and a wave of dizziness crashes into me as Nikolai climbs out, holding me clasped against his chest. Though he's careful, the movement sends a stab of nauseating pain through my arm, and the distant mountain peaks spin in a sickening circle in my vision as he gently places me on the gurney.

Squeezing my eyes shut, I focus on breathing and not passing out as I'm wheeled inside the house, with Nikolai barking orders to the medical team in between speaking Russian to Alina and Lyudmila. I presume he's explaining what happened, but I'm in too much pain to care either way.

I've never been shot before, and it's not fun.

When I open my eyes next, I'm in my bedroom, with the doctor and his team bustling around my gurney. Within seconds, an IV is taped to my left arm, and I'm hooked up to several monitors. I have no idea where all this medical equipment came from, but my bedroom appears to have been transformed into a hospital room.

The doctor, already in scrubs and a surgical mask, asks if I'm allergic to latex or any medication as he pulls on a pair of gloves.

"No," I croak out, and one of the nurses attaches a bag of liquid to the top of the IV stand. Immediately, a pleasant lassitude spreads through me, making my lids heavy.

The last thing I see before the world fades away is Nikolai standing in the corner of the room, his golden eyes trained on me with fierce intensity. There's still a dark smear on his cheekbone—blood from the man he tortured to get answers—but with the sweet relief of anesthesia spreading through my veins, I can't help the loopy smile that curves my lips.

I'll keep you safe, he said, and as the darkness claims me, I believe him.

He'll keep me safe from everyone except himself.

2

NIKOLAI

My sister intercepts me as soon as I step out of Chloe's room. She must've been standing in the hallway the entire time.

"How is she?"

"She'll live, no thanks to you." My tone is harsh, but I don't give a fuck.

It's Alina's fault we're in this mess. She told Chloe I killed our father. She gave her the car keys, enabling her to flee.

At my words, Alina flinches but stands her ground. Her face is still pale and puffy, but her green eyes are clear and she no longer smells like a drug cocktail. "I mean, what's her condition? What did the doctor say?"

I sigh, raking a hand through my hair. "She got lucky. The bullet went straight through her arm, just barely grazing the bone. She's lost a good amount of blood, but not enough to require a transfusion. She also has a sprained ankle. Other than that, she's just bruised and scraped all over."

"Kolya…" My sister looks as miserable as I've ever seen her. "I'm really sorry. I didn't know about the—"

"Stop." I'm not in the mood to listen to her apologies and justifications. She might not have known about the killers hunting Chloe, but that doesn't excuse what she did. Nor does the fact that she was high on her meds. Before I say something I'll regret, I ask, "Where's Slava?"

"Lyudmila took him to visit the guards. I asked her to keep him out of the way for now, given… you know." She waves toward Chloe's door.

"Good thinking." I know I shouldn't mollycoddle my son, but I'm oddly reluctant to expose him to the brutal realities of our life, the way our father did with me. Hunting and fishing is one thing—I'm happy to have Pavel teach Slava that, along with other key life skills—but I'd rather not have him see his tutor covered in blood.

He'll learn what it means to be a Molotov eventually, but not yet.

Alina looks relieved at my praise. "So what happened?" she asks, following me as I head to my room. "Who sent the assassins after her?"

"It's a long story." One I'm still digesting myself. "Suffice it to say, she's still in danger."

Alina grabs my sleeve, bringing me to a halt. "So you didn't…?"

"I did." I put a bullet in the brain of one of the

assassins and wounded the other badly enough that he died shortly after—but not before I got a name out of him.

A name I'm still trying to come to grips with.

My sister peers at me with a frown etched into her forehead. "But you think there are more coming."

"I'm sure of it."

"Why? Who is she, Kolya?"

"That's what I intend to find out."

Pulling out of her hold, I step into my room and close the door.

———

Though Chloe is still under, I'm anxious to get back to her, so I quickly shower and change. Then I fire off a message to Konstantin, updating him on what I've learned and asking his team of hackers to look into the man the assassin named as their employer.

Tom Bransford.

The presidential candidate who may be Chloe's father.

She doesn't know that last part yet, and I don't know if I should say anything regarding my suspicions until I have more concrete proof. Right now, the evidence is circumstantial at best, and if I'm wrong, Chloe will have even more reason to think I'm a twisted monster.

Which I am. I just don't want her thinking that way about me.

My chest tightens as I picture the sweet, radiant smile she gave me before the drugs in the IV took hold. I want more of that, not the blank, terrified look she'd worn in the woods when I came toward her, gun in hand, having killed one of her assailants and wounded the other.

I never want to see that look on her face again.

Alina is gone when I emerge into the hallway and hurry back to Chloe's room. I know she's fine with the doctor and the nurses watching her, but I can't help the anxiety that gnaws at me each moment she's out of my sight. She came so fucking close to dying. If I'd shown up a few minutes later, if Konstantin's team hadn't been able to hack into the NSA satellite to pinpoint her exact location, if the bullet had pierced her body a few inches to the left—there's an infinite number of ways this could've turned out differently.

An infinite number of ways I could've lost her.

"She should be coming to in a few minutes," the doctor informs me when I step into her room. He's one of the best trauma surgeons in the state; Pavel had him and his team flown in on a chopper from Boise for an exorbitant fee that buys both their services and their discretion.

"Good. Thanks." Ignoring the stares from the two female nurses, I approach Chloe, a painful ache squeezing my ribcage as I note the grayish tinge of her bronzed skin. They've washed the blood and dirt off her face and arms and dressed her in a hospital gown, but her hair is still matted, with a couple of twigs and leaves caught in the golden-brown strands.

I remove the debris, dropping it onto the small table next to her gurney. I hate seeing her like this, so small and fragile and wounded. I'd give anything to have been able to take that bullet for her, or better yet, to have woken up a few hours earlier, so I could've stopped her from leaving.

Reaching over, I tenderly stroke my knuckles over her finely shaped jaw. Her skin is soft and warm. Unable to help myself, I rub my thumb over her slightly parted lips. Plush, doll-like lips, the upper slightly fuller than the lower. Sinful lips that could seduce a saint—not that I am or ever have been one.

Pulling my hand away before my body can react inappropriately, I go to a chair in the corner of the room and settle in to wait as the doctor disappears into the bathroom. The nurses pack up the supplies; as soon as Chloe regains consciousness and is stable, they'll be leaving.

True to the doctor's promise, only a few minutes pass before Chloe stirs, a faint noise escaping her lips as her eyelids flutter open. I'm immediately on my feet, crossing the room toward her.

"Hi," she murmurs sleepily, blinking up at me. "Did they already—"

"Yes, zaychik." I gently clasp her left hand, being careful not to dislodge the IV in her arm. Her delicate fingers are cold in my grip despite the sheet covering her up to her chest. "How are you feeling? You want something to drink?"

She blinks again, still clearly dazed, so I press a button to lift the head of her gurney to a half-sitting position, and then I bring a cup of water with a straw to her lips. She sucks on it greedily, making me smile.

The doctor bustles over and I step back, letting him and his team do their thing. The nurses put Chloe's right arm in a sling while he asks her a few questions and takes her vitals; then they remove the IV and all the monitoring equipment.

She's been deemed awake and stable.

"Take this for pain as needed," the doctor tells her, setting a bottle of pills on the table. "And take care not to get the bandage wet. It'll need to be changed every twenty-four hours." He glances toward me, and I nod.

I have a fair amount of experience with gunshot wounds and would be more than happy to play the role of Chloe's nurse. What I'm not happy about are the painkillers, but I know she'll need them.

Her injury may not be life-threatening, but it'll still hurt like hell.

"Here, I got this," I say as the nurses move to lift Chloe, presumably to transfer her to her bed. Shooing them away, I carefully pick her up and carry her over there myself—not a difficult task, as she's barely heavier than Slava. Though she's been eating like a lumberjack during the week she's been here, my zaychik is still much too thin from her month on the run.

She winces as I lay her down, and I feel it like a stab to my stomach. I've never been so viscerally attuned to another person before, to the point that I experience her pain as my own. If there'd been any doubt in my mind about what she means to me, it disappeared the moment I saw her Toyota gone from the garage.

I'd never known such rage and terror as when I learned the assassins were in the area—when I thought I might not find her in time.

My guts twist, and I shove the thought away before I'm tempted to strangle Alina. The important thing now is that Chloe is safe here with me. I've already told Pavel to beef up our security, in case the assassins had figured out who hired Chloe and conveyed that information to their employer before I found them. I doubt it—the one I tortured seemed to have no idea who I was—but I'm not taking any chances.

Besides, there's always the threat of the Leonovs. Alexei will be even more pissed now that we've stolen the lucrative Tajik nuclear reactor contract from his family's Atomprom.

Pushing that thought away as well, I focus on propping up Chloe on a couple of pillows and covering her with a blanket while the doctor and his team wheel the gurney and all their equipment out of the room.

A minute later, we're finally alone.

I sit on the edge of her bed and pick up her small hand. "Are you comfortable, zaychik?" I ask, rubbing her chilly palm. "Can I get you anything? Something to drink, to eat? I imagine you must be hungry."

She swallows and nods. "Some food would be great." She looks more alert now, her big brown eyes distinctly wary. Her fear has a double-edged effect on me, making my chest ache even as it arouses that primitive, twisted part of me that wants to chase her down and mark her, to claim her in the most brutal way possible.

Suppressing the dark instinct, I lift her hand to my lips and kiss her knuckles. "I'll bring it to you. Do you want something to entertain you while you wait? A book or—"

"I'll just watch some TV."

I smile and hand her the remote. "Okay. I'll be right back."

Leaning over, I drop a quick kiss on her forehead and hurry out of the room.

3

CHLOE

Heart beating unevenly, I watch the door close behind Nikolai's tall, broad-shouldered figure. My forehead still tingles where his lips touched my skin, even as my mind replays the raw, agony-filled screams of the man he tortured.

How can a ruthless killer act so caring and tender?

Is any of that real, or is it just a mask he wears to hide the psychopath within?

I'm not actually hungry—the anesthesia has made me somewhat nauseated—but I need a few minutes alone. Everything happened so fast I haven't had a chance to formulate my questions, much less attempt to come up with any answers. One moment, one of my mom's killers was straddling me, lust gleaming in his flat, dark eyes, and the next, his partner's brains were all over the forest floor and Nikolai was slicing open my attacker and threatening to remove his intestines.

Swallowing a surge of nausea, I push aside the

recollection. As brutal as Nikolai's interrogation methods were, they did yield some results, and with the worst of the shock wearing off and my mind clearing from the haze of anesthesia, I can finally think about the implications of what I've learned.

They were there to kill you both, Nikolai had told me in the car before asking if the name *Tom Bransford* means anything to me.

Which it does.

Because it's been all over the news lately.

With an unsteady hand, I lift the remote and power on the TV, tuning in to a news channel.

Sure enough, they're covering the primary debates, which Bransford appears to be winning, putting him ahead in all the polls.

My insides roil as I study his image on the screen. If Nikolai is telling me the truth, this is the man responsible for my mom's murder.

Youthful and trim at fifty-five years of age, the California senator oozes charm and charisma. His thick, golden-blond hair is barely touched with gray, his eyes are a brilliant blue, and his smile is bright enough to light a warehouse.

No wonder they're comparing him to JFK; he could be the dead president's even more handsome brother.

I search for signs of evil on his evenly featured face and find none. But then again, why would I? However good-looking Bransford is, he can't hold a candle to Nikolai's darkly magnetic appeal, and I know what *he's* capable of. I'm not the only one dazzled by Nikolai, either.

Even woozy from anesthesia, I couldn't miss the covetous looks the nurses surreptitiously cast toward him.

I've never been out in public with my employer, but I imagine panties drop left and right when he walks down the street.

A bizarre pang of jealousy strikes me at the thought, and I realize I'm getting distracted from the key question.

Why?

Why would a leading presidential candidate want to kill me and my mom?

It makes no sense. None whatsoever. Mom couldn't have been further removed from politics if she'd lived in the Amazon jungle, and God knows I don't follow the stuff. As embarrassing as it is to admit, I didn't even vote in the last election, being too busy with starting college and all. Nor have I ever met Bransford in any capacity; I have a good memory for faces, and his is more memorable than most.

Maybe Mom had encountered him somehow? At the restaurant she'd worked at, perhaps?

It's possible, theoretically. The upscale hotel the restaurant is attached to is frequented by all sorts of VIPs. Maybe Bransford had stayed there during a visit to Boston, and Mom witnessed him doing something he shouldn't have.

But then why would he want to kill me as well? Unless... was he afraid Mom had told me whatever it was she knew about him?

Holy crap. *Maybe she hid some kind of evidence at her apartment, and he thinks I know where it is.*

Excited, I sit up, only to fall back onto the mound of pillows with a groan. The anesthesia is definitely wearing off because that movement *hurt.* A lot. It felt like hot knives plunging into my arm, and the rest of my body isn't doing much better.

It's as if I've been knocked off my feet by an actual truck, instead of an assassin the size of one.

Before I can catch my breath and refocus, the door opens and Nikolai walks in, holding a tray of covered dishes.

My heart launches into a sprint, and what little breath I did recover evacuates my lungs.

Without the veil of shock dulling my senses and the distraction of the medical staff bustling around me, his effect on me is devastatingly, terrifyingly potent. I've never known a man who could make my body react by merely walking into a room. And it's not just his looks; it's everything about him, from the raw animal intensity in his striking amber-green gaze to the aura of power he wears as comfortably as one of his custom-made suits.

Right now, he's dressed more casually in a pair of dark jeans and a light-blue button-up shirt with the sleeves rolled up to his elbows. He must've changed and showered while I was under, I realize; not only are his clothes different from what he'd worn in the car, but the smear on his cheekbone is gone and his raven's wing hair is slicked back wetly, exposing the sharp symmetry of his striking features.

Greedily, my eyes trace over his face, from the thick black slashes of his eyebrows to the full, sensuous shape of his mouth. For once, it's not curved in that dark, cynical way of his; instead, the smile on his lips is warm, tinged with unsettling tenderness.

"I had Pavel warm up some leftovers and prepare a selection of different snacks," he says, crossing the room toward me as I reflexively power off the TV. His deep, rough-silk voice is like a caress to my ears, so much more pleasant than the newscaster's strident tones. Placing the tray on my nightstand, he takes a seat next to me and begins uncovering the dishes one by one. "I figured you might be dealing with some nausea, so I have some plain toast here as well."

Wow. Could he be any more considerate? If I hadn't seen him kill and torture with my own eyes, I would've never believed him capable of such cruelty—even with that dark, dangerous vibe I kept getting from him.

"Thank you," I murmur, trying not to think of his hands wielding a blade that sliced open a man as he extends the tray toward me, letting me pick what I want. There's everything from cut-up fruit to stuffed blintzes to cold cuts and various cheeses, but I *am* still nauseated, especially with the gruesome images refusing to leave my mind, so I just grab the plain toast and a handful of grapes.

He watches me eat with an approving half-smile, and I try not to think about how warm that smile makes me feel—and not just in a sexual way. It's an illusion, this feeling of safety and comfort he gives me, a leftover from when I thought he was a good man who just had trouble connecting with his young son.

I was beginning to fall for that man.

No. I'm lying to myself. I *did* fall for him, so much so that even with Alina's terrifying revelations ringing in my ears, I had turned my car around and was heading back here when the assassins ambushed me.

His own sister told me he was a monster, and I didn't believe her. I didn't *want* to believe her.

I still don't.

"Where's Slava? How is he?" I ask, choosing the most innocuous topic I can think of. There are so many things we need to discuss, from Bransford's motivations to whether or not I'm a prisoner here, but I'm not ready to go there yet.

That last question, in particular, is too disturbing to contemplate at the moment.

"He's just returned from a walk with Lyudmila," Nikolai replies. "Alina had her take him away before our arrival."

"Ah, good." I was worried the child might've seen us from his window. "What will you tell him about... you know?" I wave at my sling with my left hand.

"We'll just say you fell on a branch." His jaw tightens. "I'd rather he didn't know you left him."

"I didn't—" I stop, because I did. I was coming back, but Nikolai doesn't know that. Nor am I planning to tell him.

I don't want him to know how easily he'd fooled me, how even now, a part of me refuses to believe that he's a killer as ruthless as the men who'd murdered my mom.

His tiger eyes narrow with speculative interest. "You didn't what?"

"Nothing." The word comes out unconvincingly fast. I scramble to cover it up. "I just meant, I didn't leave *him*."

It's as if a thundercloud passes over Nikolai's face, blocking out all light and warmth. His gaze turns shuttered, his magnificent features taking on a statue-like hardness. "Right. You left *me*. Because of what Alina told you."

I swallow hard. I'm not sure I'm ready to go there either, but it looks like I have no choice. Ignoring the throbbing pain in my arm, I push up to a more upright position. "Did she lie?" My voice wavers slightly. "Did she make it all up?"

He stares at me, the silence stretching into painfully long seconds. "No," he finally says. "She didn't."

Something inside me withers. Up until this moment, I'd still held out hope that his sister was wrong, that despite what I saw him do to the two assassins, he's not guilty of the horrific crime of patricide. But there's no room for doubt now.

By his own admission, the man in front of me killed his father.

"What happened? Why—" My voice cracks. "Why did you do it?"

He doesn't respond for another long, nerve-racking moment. His face is that of a stranger, dark and closed-off. "Because he deserved it." His words fall like a hammer, heavy and brutal. "Because he was a Molotov. Like me."

I dampen my dry lips. "I don't understand." My heart pounds against my ribcage, each beat echoing in my ears. A part of me wants to shut this down and run away screaming, while another, infinitely more foolish part longs to curve my palm over the harsh, uncompromising line of his jaw, offering comfort with my touch.

Because hidden underneath that hard, emotionless façade is pain.

There has to be.

He opens his mouth to reply when someone knocks on the door. The sound is quiet, tentative, but it kills the moment as surely as a gunshot.

Springing to his feet, Nikolai strides over to the door to open it.

"Konstantin is on the phone," Alina says from the doorway. "His team has found something."

4

CHLOE

My stomach is in knots by the time Nikolai returns, the toast I've eaten sitting inside like a rock. I know Konstantin is his older brother, the tech genius of the family, and I strongly suspect that the "something" his team has found relates to my situation.

Now that I've had a chance to think about it, Konstantin is probably how Nikolai had known all those things about me from the beginning—like the fact that I hadn't posted on my highly private social media during my month on the run. And he's also how Nikolai got access to the police files and discovered that they'd been altered to make my mom's murder look even more like a suicide.

Konstantin and his team must be the "resources" Nikolai mentioned during the car ride here, the advantage he has over Bransford.

Sure enough, Nikolai's face is grim as he takes a seat on the edge of my bed and clasps my left hand in his strong palm. His touch both warms and chills me. "Chloe, zaychik..." His tone is worrisomely gentle. "There's something you should know."

My heart, which was already galloping in my chest, does a backflip. His gaze is no longer that of a stranger; instead, there's pity in his golden tiger stare.

Whatever he's about to say is awful, I can tell.

"How much do you know about the circumstances of your conception?" he asks in that same gentle tone. "Did your mother ever talk about it?"

It's as if an icy wind sweeps through my insides, freezing every cell on the way. "My conception?" My voice sounds like it's coming from some other part of the room, some other person.

He can't mean what I think he's saying. There's no way Bransford is—

"Twenty-four years ago, your mother lived in California," Nikolai says quietly. "In San Diego."

I nod on autopilot. Mom had told me that much. She'd lived all over southern California, in fact. After the missionary couple who'd adopted her from Cambodia were killed in a car accident, she'd gone from one foster home to another until she emancipated herself at seventeen—the same year she'd given birth to me.

"She wasn't the only one who lived in San Diego at the time," Nikolai continues. "So did a certain brilliant young politician whose local campaign she volunteered at to get extra credit for her American History class."

The icy wind inside me turns into a winter gale.

"Bransford." My voice is barely a whisper, but Nikolai hears it and nods, squeezing my hand gently.

"The one and only."

I stare at him, simultaneously boiling over with emotions and numb. "What are you saying?"

"Your mother tried to commit suicide when she was sixteen. Did you know about that?"

My head nods of its accord. When I was a child, Mom had always worn bracelets and bangles around her wrists, even at home, even while cooking and cleaning and bathing me. It wasn't until I was almost ten that I walked in on her changing and discovered the faint white lines on her wrists. She sat me down then and explained that when she'd been a teenager, she'd gone through a difficult time that had culminated in her trying to take her own life.

"She said it had been a mistake." My throat is so tight each word scrapes it on the way out. "She told me she was glad she'd failed because soon after, she learned she was pregnant. With me."

His eyes turn opaque. "I see."

He sees? Sees what? Suddenly enraged, I yank my hand out of his grasp and sit up all the way, ignoring the accompanying wave of dizziness and pain. "What exactly are you trying to tell me? What does her suicide attempt have to do with Bransford? Did he try to kill her that time too? Is that his freaking MO?"

"No, zaychik." Nikolai's gaze fills with that disconcerting pity again. "I'm afraid that attempt

22

wasn't staged. But there's reason to believe that Bransford *was* responsible. According to the hospital records my brother's team dug up, your mother had been to the ER twice that year: once for the suicide attempt, and two months earlier as a rape victim."

A rape victim? I stare at him, black flecks dotting the edges of my vision. "Are you saying Bransford *raped* her?"

"She never filed any charges nor named her attacker, so we can't know for sure, but her first ER visit coincided with the last day of her volunteering at the campaign. She never went back after that—and nine months later, almost to the day, she gave birth to a baby girl. You."

The black dots multiply, taking over more of my vision. "No. No, that's not... No." I sway as the room blurs in my vision.

Nikolai's strong arms are already around me. "Here, lean back." I'm guided back onto the mound of pillows. "Take a few deep breaths." His warm palm smooths my hair back from my clammy forehead. "That's right, just like that," he murmurs as I attempt to obey, dragging shallow inhales into my unnaturally stiff lungs. "It's okay, zaychik. Just breathe…"

The dizziness recedes, slowly but surely, and by the time Nikolai pulls back, my brain is functioning again —and beginning to process what he's told me.

Mom had been raped.

Nine months later, I was born.

I want to throw up.

I want to scrub my skin raw and boil my DNA in bleach.

"She never..." My voice falters. "She never talked about my father. Not even once. And I asked, repeatedly."

Nikolai nods, watching me with that same unsettling pity.

The words keep coming out of my mouth, like water leaking from a faulty pipe. "She told me it had been a difficult time in her life. She dropped out of high school. Got a job as a waitress and applied for legal emancipation, on account of the pregnancy and all."

He nods again, letting me work it out on my own—and I do. Because for the first time, so much about my mom makes sense. It had always puzzled me how she'd gotten pregnant because as far as I knew, she'd been the polar opposite of a wild teen. Though Mom had rarely talked about herself, I'd gleaned enough to know she'd been a straight-A student prior to dropping out, too quiet and introverted to go out to parties and flirt with boys. Nor had she displayed any interest in dating as an adult; she'd never brought home a single boyfriend, never left me with a babysitter to go out and have fun. As a kid, I thought that was normal, but as I got older, I realized just how strange it was for a beautiful young woman to close herself off like that.

It was as if she'd taken a vow of chastity... *or never recovered from the trauma of rape.*

"Do you think..." I swallow the sour bile in my throat. "Do you think he knew? About her pregnancy? About... me?"

I always thought my father had simply walked away from the responsibility, though Mom had never said that outright, only implied it. I figured he'd been a teenager himself, someone who just wasn't ready to be a parent. But this—this changes everything. Mom might not have even told him of my existence. Why would she have, if he'd raped her?

Except... he has to know now.

Because he killed her and tried to do the same to me.

Oh God.

I barely hold back a surge of vomit.

My biological father is not only a rapist—he's a murderer.

Nikolai takes my hand in his again, his touch shockingly warm on my icy skin. "I think he had to know," he says, echoing my thoughts. "Maybe not from the beginning, but later on, for sure."

"Because he tried to kill us."

"Yes—and because of the scholarship you got."

I blink, not comprehending at first. Then his words filter through. "You mean... *he* paid for my college?"

"Konstantin is tracing the exact source of those funds, but I'm almost certain about what he's going to uncover." Nikolai's eyes are somber on my face. "It was a private scholarship, zaychik, intended for only one recipient: you. Remember how you told me that your friend applied for it and didn't get it, despite being even more qualified than you? That's because it was never meant for her. That money was yours all along."

Fuck. He's right. My friend Tanisha had been our class valedictorian with perfect SAT scores, but she didn't get this full-ride scholarship to Middlebury—I did. I even told Nikolai how strange that was. Except...

"I don't understand. Why would he do that? Why would he pay for my education if he hated me and my mom? If he... planned to kill us?" I can barely utter the last words.

Nikolai squeezes my hand. "I don't know for sure, but I have a theory. I think your mother contacted him at some point and told him about you. And I think she threatened him. It was likely something along the lines of 'if you don't provide the funds for our daughter's education, I'll go public with my story.'"

"You think she blackmailed him?"

At Nikolai's nod, I sink deeper into the pillows, shaking my head. "No. No, you're wrong. Mom wouldn't have done that. She's not—she wasn't..." To my shame, my eyes flood with tears, my throat closing as a wave of crushing grief catches me off-guard.

"A criminal? A blackmailer?" Nikolai's deep voice is gentle as his thumb massages my palm in soothing circles. Tactfully, he waits until I get myself under control, then says quietly, "You have to remember, zaychik, she was a mother first and foremost. A single mother who worked as a waitress, whose earnings couldn't have covered even a fraction of the exorbitant costs of college education in this country. What would *you* have done to ensure your child's future?"

I would've done whatever I had to—and most likely, it had been the same for Mom.

"If that's true, why did he wait?" I ask in desperation. Some childish part of me is still hoping that this is all a huge misunderstanding, that my biological father isn't a total monster. "Why pay for all four years of my schooling and then try to kill us? If he'd already spent the money—"

"It wasn't about the money. He's rich enough to have paid for ten illegitimate daughters." Nikolai's tone hardens. "It's about his career. His run for president."

Of course. The stakes are infinitely higher now, and while some politicians thrive on scandal, Bransford is an all-American icon of middle-class morals and values, with a squeaky-clean reputation that won't survive this kind of hit.

Still, assuming all of this is true, there's something that doesn't fully make sense. I can see how Mom was a threat to him, since she could go public with her story at any point. But why try to kill me?

How villainous do you have to be to send assassins after your own child? Especially if she knows nothing about you?

Then, in a burst, it comes to me.

"I'm walking proof of his crime, aren't I?" I say, staring at Nikolai. "A single DNA test, and he's toast.

Even if he tries to claim it was consensual, Mom was still underage at the time of my conception. Sixteen to his thirty-plus."

Nikolai nods. "At the very least, he's guilty of statutory rape. It's the rare case where it's not his word against hers. No matter how he tries to spin it, what he did is a criminal offense."

"And he probably doesn't know that Mom never told me about him. As far as he's concerned, I can pop up at any moment, publicly claiming him as my father."

"Afraid so, zaychik." He tilts his head, studying me intently. "Are you okay?"

I start to nod on autopilot, then shake my head. "No. No, I'm not. I need a minute." Or ten thousand minutes. Or the rest of my life.

My biological father is a rapist and a murderer who's trying to kill me.

I don't know how to even begin processing that.

Gaze filled with understanding, Nikolai squeezes my hand again, then curves his palm over my jaw and leans in, stroking my cheek with the edge of his thumb. "I'll let you rest, zaychik," he murmurs, his breath warm and subtly sweet against my lips. "We'll talk more when you're feeling better."

Closing the small distance between us, he kisses me. His lips are gentle on mine, tender, yet I can sense the hungry possessiveness underneath the restraint. It terrifies me nearly as much as my body's instinctive response.

I may evade Bransford with his help, but there will be no evading *him*.

There's no escape from the devil.

NIKOLAI

Closing the door behind myself, I make a mental note to install some cameras in Chloe's room, the way I have in Slava's. Not because I feel compelled to watch her every moment of every day—though that need is definitely there—but because I'm worried about her.

I've had my entire life to come to terms with my fucked-up heritage, and there are days when I'm still tempted to slit my own throat. That or get a vasectomy, so the mistake I'd made that night with Ksenia can never be repeated. I wasn't even aware that the condom was faulty, but it must've been.

That's the only explanation for the existence of my son.

I was planning to go to my office, but my feet carry me to his room instead, propelled by the same compulsion I'm experiencing with Chloe.

Daddy, he called me when I returned home last night. I'd been too distracted by everything related to

Chloe to take it in fully, but now I can't help thinking about that word and the way my ribcage had filled with a strange, piercingly sweet ache. And it's all because of her.

Chloe Emmons had not only discerned my deepest, most secret wish regarding my son; she'd made it come true.

Quietly, I push open the door to Slava's bedroom and step in. As usual, he's on the floor, diligently working on his LEGO castle. Lyudmila told me once that my son has a remarkably long attention span for a child who's not yet five, and I suppose that must be true. From what I can recall of my younger brother, Valery, at this age, he was always running around and getting into trouble. Slava, on the other hand, is quiet and focused, much more the way Konstantin was as a child. I wonder if Slava has inherited my older brother's aptitude for math and programming as well. I should probably introduce him to these subjects and find out.

At my entrance, his eyes—my eyes in miniature—shoot up to my face, the look in them equal parts quizzical and wary. My chest tightens with the usual discomfort, but I ignore the urge to back away, distancing myself from the unsettling feeling. Instead, I crouch in front of my son, giving his LEGO creation my full attention, the way I've seen Chloe do.

"That's a very nice castle," I say in Russian, studying the carefully assembled building blocks in front of me. Though Slava's English skills are rapidly improving under Chloe's tutelage, he's far from fluent in the language of our adopted country. "Did it take you long to build it?"

He blinks at me for a couple of moments before a shy smile blooms on his face. "You like it?"

"I do." I mean it, too. The castle displays admirable symmetry and complexity, especially given the fact that it was put together by such tiny hands. Even if math and computers turn out not to be Slava's strengths, he might have a future in architecture and structural design.

That is, if he doesn't take after me and Valery—and every other Molotov before us.

My mood darkens, but I force myself to maintain a calm, inquisitive expression as I ask again how long it'd taken him to build the castle.

"I worked on it in the morning and again after I came back from the woods," Slava says, visibly more comfortable with me now. He's still nowhere near as chatty and animated as he is with Chloe, but I consider this progress. Before, he'd reply to most of my questions with just a word or two, or stay completely silent.

For the next few minutes, he shows me all the ins and outs of the castle—there are turrets and towers and big windows, the latter similar to the ones in our house —and then he shyly asks where Chloe is and why he hasn't seen her all day.

"She's resting," I tell him. "A branch injured her arm, so we had to have some doctors come out here and fix it. She's all better now, but she'll be staying in bed for a couple of days while it heals."

As I speak, his eyes grow wide with worry. "Chloe is hurt?"

"Only a little bit. She'll be better soon."

He still looks concerned. "She won't die, like Mama?"

It's like a shard of glass goes through my chest. "No, Slavochka. I won't let that happen." Alina told me he occasionally asks her about Ksenia, but this is the first time I've heard him talk about his mother—and I hate it.

I hate her for hiding him from me all those years, and I hate even more that she got herself killed in a car crash, leaving him with her vile family.

At my words, Slava brightens. "Can Chloe stay with us forever?"

Now this is a question I'm happy to answer. "Yes." I look my son square in the face. "She can, and she will."

No force on earth is powerful enough to take Chloe away from me now that I have her back. I will do whatever it takes to keep her—both for Slava and for myself.

She's asleep when I stop by her room on the way to my office, so I let her rest. That's what she needs now. Her physical injuries will heal in a matter of weeks, but the emotional wounds are a different matter. I contemplated not telling her what Konstantin uncovered about Bransford and his relationship with her mother, but I decided it was important that she know—that she understand the full extent of the danger she's in.

I didn't tell her everything, though—like the fact that her teenage mother slit her wrists *after* she'd learned she was pregnant. Or that after that unsuccessful suicide attempt, she visited an abortion clinic twice, only to chicken out both times. None of that is important. What matters is that after Chloe was born, Marianna was able to power through her trauma and become the caring mother Chloe had known and loved.

The first thing I do upon stepping into my office is call Pavel and tell him to come up. The second is videocall Valery.

"I need you to send a dozen of your best men here," I tell my younger brother in lieu of a hello. "I need them right away."

"On it," Valery says, as coolly emotionless as always. Konstantin must've already briefed him on my situation. "Anything else? Weapons? Explosives?"

"Yes. Everything." I already have a large stash here at the compound, but more won't hurt. "Also, send over some pharmaceuticals."

"You got it."

He hangs up just as a knock sounds on my door.

I walk over to let Pavel in.

My right-hand man's gunmetal eyes are unblinking. "War?"

"War," I confirm grimly.

I'm not waiting for Bransford to send more assassins after Chloe.

Now that we know who her enemy is, we're taking the fight to him.

CHLOE

My eyes pop open as I wake with a gasp, my heart racing and my hospital gown soaked with sweat. Only the throbbing pain in my arm and the paralyzing soreness throughout my body keep me from reflexively sitting up. Instead, I force myself to lie still and take in the stunning view of the sun descending behind the distant mountain peaks outside my floor-to-ceiling window.

Slowly, I begin to calm.

A nightmare.

It was just another nightmare.

Unlike the vivid, horror-movie-style dreams that have been tormenting me since Mom's death, this one was more of a jumble of images and impressions. The whine of a bullet past my ear, branches hitting me in the face as I run through the woods from some kind of beastly creature, a heavy weight knocking me down—it doesn't take a psych degree to know that my mind was replaying my encounter with the assassins in an attempt to deal with the lingering terror.

A quiet knock distracts me from the gorgeous view. Before I can say anything, the door swings open and Nikolai steps in, a warm smile curving his sensual lips as he sees me awake.

My heart rate kicks up again, but with an emotion far more complex than fear. He's changed yet again, this time into one of the perfectly tailored suits he favors at dinnertime. A crisp white shirt and a skinny black tie complete the formal outfit, setting off his masculine beauty in a way that should be illegal—not that he'd care about something as trivial as legality.

Given what I saw him do earlier today, my captor is not exactly big on the rule of law.

At least I suspect he's my captor. We still need to have *that* conversation.

"How are you feeling?" he asks softly, stopping next to my bed. Before I can reply, he feels my forehead with the back of his hand and frowns, then pulls out a thermometer from the inner pocket of his jacket.

Huh. I guess I do feel a bit feverish.

"Open," he instructs, bringing the thermometer to my lips, and I obey, feeling incongruously like a child as he sticks it in my mouth and orders me to hold it. A few seconds later, the thermometer beeps, and he glances at the small screen on the side.

"Ninety-nine point two," he says, looking relieved as he hides the device back in his pocket and sits on the edge of the bed. "The doctor warned you might run a low-grade fever before the antibiotics kick in."

"Really? Is that a thing? I've never been shot before."

His white teeth flash in a dazzling grin. "It is—I know from personal experience."

My unruly heart picks up pace again, and my skin warms in a way that has nothing to do with the low-grade fever. "Great. I guess we each have our war stories now."

"I guess we do." His smile fades. "How are you feeling, aside from the fever?"

"Like someone's used me as a tennis ball in a match with Serena Williams," I say without thinking, only to regret it as his expression darkens, his jaw going dangerously taut.

"Those motherfuckers. If only I'd gotten there sooner..." His fingers flex menacingly on his thigh.

"No, don't." Instinctively, I reach over to cover his hand with mine. "If it hadn't been for you, I wouldn't have—" I swallow, the jumbled images from the nightmare invading my mind. "I wouldn't have made it."

And it's one hundred percent true. I haven't had the chance to really think about it, but if he hadn't come after me, if he hadn't used his scary "resources" to track me down as quickly as he did, I would already be six feet under, after first suffering through a brutal rape.

Nikolai saved me.

However terrifying his methods, he saved my life.

His gaze drops to my hand for a second, and his

expression shifts again, the menace in his tiger eyes giving way to a dark heat that feels infinitely more dangerous. "Zaychik..." His voice grows softer, deeper. "I—"

"So thank you," I blurt, pulling my hand back. Savior or not, I can't let myself fall under his spell again, can't let myself forget what he is and what he's done. "I'm sorry I haven't said it before, but I'm so, so grateful. I know I owe you my life and more. You didn't have to come after me, but you did, and I hugely appreciate it. If you hadn't been there, I—"

He presses two fingers to my lips, stopping my rambling. "You don't need to thank me." He leans over me, propping one palm on the pillow beside me and curving the other over my cheek. His gaze is darkly intent, his tone grave. "I will always protect you, zaychik. Always."

I stare up at him, my chest ballooning with a contradictory mixture of emotions. Relief and worry, gratitude and fear, joy and pain—it's like a pendulum inside me, swinging back and forth between the two extremes, the two versions of Nikolai that exist in my mind.

The one before Alina's story and the one after.

The caring lover and the brutal killer.

Which one of them is real?

With effort, I curtail my spinning thoughts and blink to break the hypnotic pull of that golden gaze. The most important thing right now is to figure out where we stand.

"You don't have to protect me," I say, injecting my tone with a confidence I'm nowhere near feeling. "Mom's killers are dead, and even if Bransford sends others, there's no guarantee they'll find me. I can just leave the country, disappear and—"

"No." The word is filled with harsh finality as he straightens and pulls back his hand. His beautiful face is set in hard, uncompromising lines. "You're not going anywhere."

"But you're in danger with me here. Your family's in danger."

I've made this argument before, and it's as ineffective now as it was then. Nikolai's expression hardens further, a savage intensity entering his gaze. "You're not leaving. The guards will stop you if you try."

So it is true then. I didn't misinterpret his refusal to let me out of the car. I *am* his prisoner.

The knowledge fills me with equal parts dread and relief. It's out in the open now; we're done pretending. Of course he's not going to let me go. I know his family's awful secret. I've seen him kill with my own eyes. The crimes he's committed would land an ordinary man in an electric chair, but Nikolai Molotov is too rich, too powerful—and more importantly, too ruthless—to ever have to pay for what he's done.

Whatever his intentions had been toward me before Alina's revelations, there's only one thing he can do now.

Detain me. Keep me where I can never reveal what I

know.

At least I hope that's the only course of action he's considering. Because there's a much more efficient way to ensure my silence, the one my biological father appears to have chosen.

But no. It might be naïve of me, but I can't bring myself to believe that Nikolai would kill me. Not with the potent, emotionally charged connection that sizzles between us. Not when he's gone to so much trouble to save my life.

And that's the thing, I realize, staring at his implacable expression. That's why, in a twisted way, it's a relief to know I can't leave. I should want to leave. I should want to run as far as possible from this dangerous man and the fixation he seems to have on me. But I don't want to. Not deep down, where it matters—and it's not just because of the stupid crush I've developed on him.

The truth is, I'm not brave and strong. I learned that today when I came face to face with death, when I felt the bullet tear through my flesh and looked into the assassin's empty eyes. I'd come close to dying before— the time I'd hidden in Mom's coat closet after finding her body, the night I'd woken up to scratching sounds at the door of my Airbnb, the couple of times the assassins had nearly run me over with their car, and the time they'd shot at me in Boise—but I had never known such prolonged, nauseating terror as when I was driving my rickety Toyota on that pothole-ridden dirt road with the bullets whining past my ears.

I don't want to die. I'm nowhere near ready to die—and I know that however ruthless of a killer Nikolai is, he doesn't wish me dead. The opposite, in fact.

He's promising to protect me.

To keep me captive and protect me.

I swallow to moisten my dry throat. "May I please have a sip of water? I'm thirsty."

The fierce expression on Nikolai's face eases. "Of course, zaychik. And you must be hungry, too. I'll get you dinner in a moment." Leaning over me, he arranges the pillows in a mound and gently props me up against it.

My breath catches at his nearness, even as my arm throbs harder at the movement, making me glad I didn't attempt this on my own.

I must've grimaced anyway, because he smooths my hair off my face, looking concerned. "Do you want a painkiller?" he asks, and I shake my head as he brings a cup of water with a straw to my lips.

The pain is not unbearable, and I want to keep my wits about me for now.

I suck down the entire cup, and when I finish, I become aware of another pressing need. "Um…" My face burns as I force myself to sit up, ignoring the spike of pain accompanying the movement. "I actually need…"

"The bathroom? Of course." He scoops me up and carries me to the adjoining bathroom, where he carefully sets me on my feet in front of the toilet. "Do you want some help here?"

"I've got it, thank you." I could've walked here on my own too—or at least limped—but it's probably best that I rest my injured ankle. Besides, some weak, needy part of me is enjoying his tender care, reveling in his nearness, his strength, his obvious worry for me.

He can't be a complete psychopath if he cares for me like this, can he?

"All right," he says, though his gaze is still filled with concern. "Don't lock the door and call me if you need anything, okay?"

At my murmured agreement, he drops a light kiss on my forehead and walks out, closing the door behind him.

I do my business as quickly as I can—which isn't quick at all, as I only have one arm to work with—then I limp over to the sink to wash my hands. The reflection in the mirror makes me wince. I can't believe Nikolai wanted to kiss me earlier. I look like a hot mess, all scratched up and bruised, my hair limp and matted. And... is that a *twig* by my ear?

I look at the shower stall, then at the sling holding my right arm immobilized against my side. Could I manage a shower? Maybe not a full-blown hair washing, but at least a quick rinse...

A rapping on the door ends my musings. "Zaychik, you done? Can I come in?"

"Yeah, okay." I try not to cringe in embarrassment as he approaches me, all clean and well-dressed and stunningly handsome. In comparison, I'm in a hospital gown that I've sweated through during the nightmare,

43

looking—and probably smelling—like I haven't showered in weeks.

I must glance longingly at the stall again because Nikolai asks, "Would you like a bath?"

A bath? That sounds even more heavenly than a shower. Just the thought of submerging my bruises and aching muscles in hot water makes me want to moan out loud.

Nikolai reads the answer on my face. "I'll prep it for you while you eat," he says with a smile and scoops me up to carry me back to bed, where a tray of covered dishes is already sitting on the nightstand.

Carefully depositing me on the mattress, he arranges me against the mound of pillows and uncovers one of the dishes. A rich, savory aroma fills the room, making me salivate. It's Russian-style garlic potatoes with mushrooms, the ones I'd happily stuff my face with every day if I could.

While I'm drooling in anticipation, he uncovers the rest of the offerings on the tray, including a Greek salad with crispy lettuce and plump black olives, a platter of roast duck with poached pears, and buttered baguette slices with black caviar.

It's official: Pavel is back in the kitchen. His wife's cooking is nowhere near as fancy or good.

What amazes me is that Nikolai managed to assemble everything and get it up here while I was in the bathroom. He must've flown downstairs and back, Superman style.

"Pavel brought this up," he says, once again picking

up on my thoughts. It's uncanny how he does that—how he's always been able to do it. From the moment we met, I've had the unsettling sensation that he can see straight into my brain, viewing my most private fears and desires.

It's as if we really are joined by those threads of fate he's talked about, connected on a level that's far deeper than the short length of our relationship should allow.

But no. I'm not buying that—especially not now that I know what kind of man he is. It's bad enough I can't extinguish the sexual chemistry that burns between us like wildfire, nor forget the crush I'd developed on him before I learned the truth. To believe that we're somehow meant for each other, that this can be something lasting and real, would be beyond foolish.

There's no such thing as fate, and even if there were, I can't be fated to love a monster.

"Here, zaychik," the monster in question says, setting a plate filled with a little bit of everything on my lap and handing me a fork. His gorgeous mouth curves in a warm smile. "Start eating while I run you a bath."

My chest squeezes tight as he gently brushes his fingers over my ear, extracting the twig I'd noticed earlier, and walks out of the room—presumably to draw me a bath in his bathroom, where there's an enormous tub. We took a bubble bath there last night after he'd worn me out with the hottest, most intense sex of my life.

A wave of scorching heat moves through me at the memory, adding to the aching tightness in my chest. I close my eyes, willing the feeling away, but it's futile.

The arousal that electrifies my body is nothing compared to the desperate craving in my heart.

By the time Nikolai returns a few minutes later, I've gotten myself under control and am working on devouring all the food on my plate. It's a little awkward, eating with my left hand, but I'm so hungry I'd eat with my feet if I had to.

"Here, zaychik, let me help you," Nikolai says, taking the fork from me after I drop a piece of mushroom onto my chest. Ignoring my objections, he feeds me as if I were a clumsy toddler—which, to be fair, I might as well be right now—and when I'm so stuffed I can't swallow another bite, he pats my lips with a napkin, carries the tray away, and returns a couple of minutes later with the announcement that the bath is ready.

To my surprise, Lyudmila comes into my room behind him, her face carefully neutral as Nikolai picks me up and carries me out past her. "She'll change the sheets while you're bathing," he explains, walking down the hallway with long, easy strides, as if my weight in his arms were nothing.

He's strong, this captor of mine.

So strong I should be far more terrified than I am.

Pushing open the door to his bedroom with his back, he carries me past the king-sized bed where he'd taken me so many times last night. At least some of the soreness in my body must be from that, I realize with a flush. Nikolai was insatiable, and so was I.

I lost count of how many orgasms he'd given me.

The memories are still playing in my mind in an X-rated reel when he sets me on my feet in front of the tub and reaches for the tie of my hospital gown. Those memories must be why I stand there like an obedient child, letting him pull the gown off me, baring my body to his hooded gaze—and why I don't voice a single objection as he picks me up again and deposits me into the hot, bubble-covered water, being careful to drape my bandaged arm over the side of the tub to keep it dry.

I can feel the tension in him as his hands brush over my naked skin, the same tension that coils inside me, making my skin burn and my pulse thunder in my ears.

Killer. Torturer. Monster. The damning words float through my mind, but they do nothing to cool the fire raging in my blood. Having experienced the devastating, addicting pleasure of his possession, my body craves more, needs more. It doesn't care that the hands running the soapy sponge over my chest and shoulders had taken two lives mere hours ago, that I'm not his lover but his captive.

"Sink in a little deeper," he murmurs, his voice a low, sensual rasp, and I mindlessly obey, reveling in the feel of his strong fingers on my skull as he cradles the back of my head, keeping my face above the water while soaking my hair.

I must still be under the influence of whatever drugs were used for the anesthesia because this doesn't feel entirely real, especially when I close my eyes to protect them from stray drops of water. It's as if I'm in a dream, one in which nothing matters but the warm pleasure of his touch, the soothing comfort of his tenderness. Everything about this should feel wrong, repellent, but instead, I feel like a pampered pet as he lifts my head out of the water and applies shampoo to my wet strands, then rubs the lather into the roots, his fingers exerting just the right amount of pressure as his short fingernails gently scratch my skull.

It's the best head rub I've ever gotten, and it's all I can do not to beg for more when, after a few blissful minutes, he deems my hair sufficiently lathered and guides my head back into the water.

Thankfully, it's not over. He applies conditioner to my hair next and rubs it into the roots as well. I'd tell him that's the wrong way to do it, but I'm enjoying the experience too much to care that my hair will lie flat tomorrow and will get greasy faster. The latter might even be a plus if it incentivizes him to do this again soon.

"Dip your head back in," he orders huskily, and I oblige as he runs his fingers through my strands, rinsing off the conditioner and detangling them in the process.

He's good at this, so good he's either a natural or he's had some practice.

A sharp stab of jealousy catches me off-guard. I open my eyes, the warm lassitude engulfing me fading as I glare up at him, my head still half-submerged in the water.

How many women has he done this with?

How many have known the bone-melting pleasure of his ministrations?

"What's wrong, zaychik?" His dark eyebrows pull together as he helps me sit up. "Did I hurt you?"

"No." I know I shouldn't say anything, but I can't help it. "You've done this for a lot of women, haven't you?"

He looks taken aback for a second. Then a wickedly sensual smile spreads across his face. "Not a lot, no. You're the only one, in fact."

"Oh." Now I feel like an idiot. "Never mind then. I just…"

I'm about to close my eyes and slide back into the water to hide my mortification when he gently grasps my chin, forcing me to meet his gaze.

"But even if that weren't the case," he says softly, "every other woman is in the past. You're the only one for me going forward. Just keep in mind, zaychik"—he leans in so close I can see the forest-green flecks in the rich amber of his irises—"I'm the only one for you now as well. No other man will ever touch you. You're mine as much as I'm yours."

I stare into those hypnotic eyes, enthralled and

terrified by the possessive intensity in them. He means it, I can tell. For whatever reason, he's decided we belong together, and there's nothing I can say or do that will alter that conviction—a conviction that would be dangerous even if the man himself weren't the embodiment of darkness.

It's as if he's obsessed with me... and not in an entirely healthy way.

He holds my gaze for a few beats longer, then leans in and presses a kiss to my forehead. The gesture should feel tender, paternal even, but instead, it's an imprint, a brand. His lips linger on my skin for a couple of seconds too long, his grip on my chin tightening to hold me in place. *You're mine*, that kiss says, and when he finally pulls back, the same message is repeated in his eyes, then echoed in his touch as he picks up the sponge and resumes washing me, his hands traveling over my body with a platonic restraint that only emphasizes the hunger he's keeping so carefully leashed.

He thinks that hunger is dangerous, I realize. Too dangerous to give in to while I'm weak and hurt.

With effort, I push the thought away and close my eyes, letting myself simply enjoy the moment. Tomorrow, I'll worry about the future and what Nikolai's obsession with me means—what the cost of his care and protection may turn out to be. Tonight, I'll just revel in the fact that I'm his prized possession.

That I'm as safe in the devil's arms as anyone can be.

7

NIKOLAI

It's two o'clock in the morning and I'm still wide awake, staring at the dark ceiling above my bed. Partially, it's because my body is still on Dushanbe time, but mostly, I'm just too wired, my thoughts cycling between my plans for Bransford and the adrenaline-spiking recollections of yesterday. The latter are especially intrusive, filling my chest with all sorts of violent emotions.

Chloe ran from me. I almost lost her. Another few minutes and—

Fuck. Enough is enough.

I jackknife off the bed and stride to the closet to pull on my running shorts. I already ran this evening. As soon as I finished bathing Chloe and tucked her in for the night, I laced up my sneakers and headed out. But I need another run. That or a nice, hard sparring with Pavel or the guards. Or better yet, a run *and* a sparring, since I need to work off some serious sexual frustration as well.

Touching Chloe's wet, naked body without fucking her had required all of my willpower and then some.

Before exiting the room, I pull up a video feed of Chloe on my phone. I had Pavel install a small camera on the TV above her bed while I was bathing her, so I'd be able to keep an eye on her without coming into her bedroom and disturbing her sleep.

As expected, my phone screen shows her tucked under the covers in the darkness, with only the sound of her even breathing filling the silence. Unlike me, she's sleeping peacefully, and I'm glad. She needs good rest in order to recover—which is why I have to keep my hands off her, no matter how much it kills me.

I'm stronger than the savage beast inside me.

At least I hope I am.

Leaving the phone in my room, I head downstairs, and my chest expands as soon as I step outside. The night is dark and cool, the mountain air crisp and pure.

I set off for the woods, running down the mountain and into the forest, as is my custom. But this time, instead of returning to the house after I've worked off most of my restless energy, I head to the north side of the compound, to the guards' bunker.

I'm not surprised to find Pavel there, playing cards with Arkash and Burev by a campfire. Like me, he must be wound too tight to sleep, even with Lyudmila by his side.

Seeing me, he jumps to his feet, and so do the

others. "All good," I say, motioning for them to relax. "Just need a workout is all."

"You got it," Pavel says, eyes gleaming with eagerness. "Knives or not?"

"Knives, of course."

The guards provide the weapons, and for the next forty minutes, my mind is blissfully free of all except the primitive goal of survival, of avoiding getting sliced into pieces by Pavel's ruthlessly wielded blade. Twice, I'm nearly disemboweled; three times, I narrowly miss having my jugular sliced through. Pavel pulls no punches, and by the time I finally get the sharp edge of my blade against his throat, we're both covered in stinging nicks and cuts.

Panting, I step back and return the knife to Arkash, who claps me on the shoulder in congratulations. None of the guards are good enough to go up against Pavel with a blade and win, but then again, none of them have been trained by him since they were my son's age.

Leaving them to their duties, Pavel and I head back to the house together. At first, we're both too tired to talk much—the fight was as draining as I hoped it would be—but when the house appears within view, Pavel says quietly, "You really should forgive her, you know."

I glance at him in surprise. "Chloe? I already have." As much as it upsets me that she ran, I understand why she did it. What my sister told her would've frightened anyone, not just a vulnerable young woman who'd already seen the worst of humanity.

"No. Alina." Pavel shoots me a sidelong look. "She's upset. Lyudmila caught her crying."

Fuck. I should've known he'd take my sister's side in this. "She should be upset. She fucked up, big time." My words come out harsher than I intended. I've been trying not to dwell on Alina's role in all of this, but the fact of the matter is, Chloe almost *died*.

I don't know if I'll ever be able to forgive Alina for that.

"She knows she fucked up," Pavel says evenly. "But she's still your sister."

"And blood is thicker than water, right?"

He ignores my sarcasm. "It's not good for her, to be so upset. The headaches—"

"I know all about her fucking headaches." I take a steadying breath. "Look, I'm not sending her away or punishing her in any way. We'll still do her birthday celebration Friday, as planned. But you can't expect me to just forgive and forget. High or not, Alina knew what she was doing when she opened her big mouth and handed Chloe those car keys."

"But she didn't know." Pavel's expression is grim as he steps in front of me, blocking my way. "You hadn't told her Chloe was in mortal danger. And don't forget *why* she was high last night."

My molars grind together. "Get out of my fucking way. Now." He might be my friend and mentor, but if I had my knife to his throat right now, I wouldn't care—

not with the dark memories surfacing in my mind, filling my stomach with a toxic brew of rage, horror, grief, and guilt.

Alina's need for medication *is* my fault, I know.

However big her fuckup, it can't hold a candle to mine.

Pavel must realize he's gone too far, because he wisely steps out of my way and drops the topic. We cover the remaining distance to the house in tense silence, all the benefits of our sparring undone by this short exchange.

There's no way I'm falling asleep now.

Not when I can once again feel my blade sinking into my father's stomach and see the monster that is me in his dying eyes.

8

CHLOE

I'm about to consume the forkful of scrambled eggs Nikolai is holding to my mouth when I hear voices in the hallway, followed by a knock on the door. My gaze jumps to Nikolai's face, and my cheeks flame at the amused gleam in his eyes.

We both know I'm not incapacitated enough for him to be spoon-feeding me; it's just a peculiar, slightly kinky dynamic we've fallen into. I didn't even try to eat with my left hand this morning when he brought me breakfast—he just started feeding me and I let him.

Even his four-year-old eats without help, yet here I am, with one arm completely functional, acting as if I can't hold a fork on my own.

My embarrassment deepening, I snatch the fork from Nikolai and set it down on the tray sitting on the nightstand. "Come in!"

I was expecting Pavel or Lyudmila, but it's Alina

who steps into my room, Slava's tiny hand clasped in hers.

The child's eyes brighten when he sees me. "Chloe!" Letting go of Alina, he dashes toward me, babbling excitedly in Russian.

"He's been worried about you," Nikolai translates, smiling wryly as Slava jumps onto my bed with the boundless energy of a puppy. "Even though I told him you won't die like his mother, he feared you might, so he's been asking to see you ever since he woke up this morning. Which was forever ago because—and I quote —you slept *so, so late*."

"Oh, no, darling, I'm totally fine." I pat his back with my left hand as he wraps his arms around me in as fierce a hug as his childish strength allows. "It's just my arm that's hurt, see?" I show him the sling when he pulls back.

He frowns and rattles out a question.

"He's asking why you're in bed if it's just your arm," Alina says, and I look up to find her standing next to the nightstand. Her strikingly beautiful face is again fully made up, her slender figure clad in a sleeveless yellow dress that looks like it came off the runway. No trace remains of the tormented, broken woman who'd confronted me yesterday morning with terrifying warnings about the man sitting at my side.

I give her a cautious smile before shifting my attention back to Slava. "It's because my ankle hurts a little too," I tell him, and Nikolai translates my words. I notice he's avoiding looking at Alina; he hasn't acknowledged her presence at all, in fact.

Slava peers at my blanket-covered feet and asks another question.

"He wants to know how you hurt your ankle," Nikolai says. "I'm going to tell him you twisted it when you fell on the branch."

"Makes sense."

While he speaks to the boy, I glance up at Alina and give her a bigger smile. She's probably worried that I'm mad at her, but I'm not. I'm grateful, in fact. I don't know what would've happened if I hadn't run, but I'm guessing that, at best, it would've delayed the clusterfuck I now find myself in. The assassins would've located me eventually, and either then or at some point later, I would've learned what Nikolai is capable of. By then, though, I might've been several weeks or months into an intense relationship with him, and it would've been that much more devastating to have my illusions shattered.

Or maybe, just maybe, he would've succeeded at keeping me in the dark, and I would've never found out that he kills and tortures as easily as other men cut grass. I would've slept in his arms and taken him into my body all the while convincing myself that my instincts are wrong, that the thread of darkness I've sensed in him is nothing more than my overactive imagination.

Ugh. Maybe I *should* be upset with Alina. That kind of ignorance does sound like bliss.

Visibly relieved, Alina returns my smile, and I push aside silly notions about how nice it would've been never to face the truth about Nikolai—or about Bransford and all the rest of it. If I were to indulge in that kind of thinking, I might as well wish for my mom to be alive, or better yet, for her to have never encountered my biological father in the first place.

I wouldn't exist in the latter case, but it would be worth it to have her alive and happy in a life that hadn't been derailed when she was a teen.

Realizing I'm again spiraling into useless what-ifs, I look up at Nikolai and say brightly, "How about Slava and Alina stay with me for a while? I don't want to monopolize your time. I'm sure you have work to do, and I can teach Slava from my bed as well as from anywhere."

Nikolai's face tightens at my clear hint that I want him gone, but he rises to his feet and says calmly, "All right. I'll see you in a bit. Don't forget to eat, okay?"

"On it." I grab the fork and bring the eggs to my mouth with exaggerated clumsiness. My goal is to make Slava giggle, and I succeed.

By the time I look over, Nikolai is gone.

Alina's face is somber as she sits on the edge of the bed, taking Nikolai's spot. "How are you feeling?" she asks quietly as Slava runs over to the window, apparently curious about the view from my room.

"I'm good. Already on the mend." I stuff a big forkful of eggs into my mouth to showcase how quickly I'm healing. I'm not lying, either. My arm still

59

hurts, but with the painkiller I swallowed upon waking, it's manageable, and I'm able to put some pressure on the ankle without it protesting too much.

Alina smiles hesitantly. "That's good." She takes an audible breath. "Listen, Chloe... I was in bad shape yesterday morning. Really bad shape. I might've said things that didn't make sense. Things that weren't... necessarily true."

I put down my fork, my appetite having vanished without a trace. I understand what she's trying to do, and I hate it. "You don't have to lie. He's admitted it. And I saw what he did to the men who attacked me."

A myriad of expressions flashes across Alina's face before it turns carefully neutral. "I see. And you're... okay?"

Okay? Does *not* jumping out of the window or running out the door screaming constitute okay? If so, I'm totally fine, or at least as fine as you can be after discovering that your biological father is a rapist and a murderer who's trying to kill you, and that you're being held captive by a man who might be even more ruthless than said father.

"I'm handling it," I say, and to my surprise, it's not a total lie. Maybe it's the month of living on the run, or the horror of finding Mom's body and hiding from her killers in the coat closet, but I'm not freaking out nearly as much as I would've expected. About any of it —but especially the fact that I'm Nikolai's prisoner. It's as if my mind has erected a wall between the present and the recent past, between what I'm experiencing and what I know.

Right now, I'm cozy and well fed, my safety ensured by the same security measures that would prevent me from leaving if I tried. And it's possible to focus on just that first aspect of it. Just as it's possible to forget Nikolai's true nature when he's being so caring and tender... when my blood turns to warm molasses at his touch.

Somehow, I'm able to put all the horror in a little box and pack it away, to pretend it isn't there.

"Good," Alina says. "I'm glad. But if you're ever having trouble dealing, or just need someone to talk to, I want you to know that you can always come to me." Jade eyes gleaming softly, she adds, "No matter what you're going through, I'd understand."

And she would, I know. My throat tightens as I take in the genuine sympathy in her gaze. I didn't know until this moment how much I'd longed for this: not an offer of friendship, precisely, but something that feels an awful lot like it. "Thank you," I say thickly. "I appreciate it—just as I appreciate what you tried to do before, what with warning me and all."

Maybe it's another illusion that's bound to be shattered, but it feels like I have an ally in Nikolai's sister. Like I'm not completely alone in this mess.

She smiles wryly and rises to her feet. "Yeah, well, that didn't exactly turn out how I'd hoped. I—" She stops as Slava exclaims something from his spot by the window and runs back to us, chattering excitedly in Russian.

"He says there's a family of raccoons on our driveway," Alina translates with a grin. "Apparently, they've just come out of the forest."

"Really? I want to see." I sit up straighter and, ignoring the pang of pain in my arm, swing my feet to the floor. Carefully, I stand up, mindful not to place too much of my weight on the sprained ankle.

So far, so good.

"Here, lean on me." Alina lends me her elbow, and with her help, I limp over to the window, where the raccoons—a mama and two babies—are indeed frolicking in plain sight.

Slava laughs in excitement as one of the babies playfully jumps on the other, and I ruffle his silky hair, my chest expanding as he gives me a beaming smile.

"Raccoons," I say, recalling my role as his English tutor. "Those are called *raccoons*."

He obediently repeats the word after me, and the three of us watch the animals until they disappear back into the woods. Then Alina helps me limp back to the bed, and I ask her to bring me a book that I can read with Slava.

"No problem," she says, already heading for the door. She returns a few minutes later with a stack of children's books that she sets on the blanket next to me. "Do you want me to take that away?" she asks, gesturing at the tray on the nightstand, and I nod as Slava gets comfortable at my uninjured side.

It'll be lunchtime soon, and I've eaten enough to tide me over until then.

She picks up the tray and heads out again. It's only when she's almost by the door that I realize I haven't asked her something important.

"Alina, wait," I call as she opens the door with one stiletto-clad foot.

She turns around, a quizzical look on her face.

"Will you come back in a bit? I'd like to know more about what happened." My voice turns unsteady. "With Nikolai and... and your father."

She stiffens, her face wiped of all expression.

"Please, Alina. I need to know."

I need to find out just how much of a monster I've fallen for.

She closes her eyes and takes a deep breath, then opens them again. "It's not my story to tell." Her voice is low and strained. "It never was. Nikolai's the one you should talk to."

And before I can plead with her further, she steps out and closes the door.

9

NIKOLAI

Unclenching my tightly balled fist, I click away from the camera feed of Chloe's room and open my inbox. I don't know what I would've done to Alina if she'd agreed to Chloe's request. Fortunately, my sister has recovered enough of her wits to realize she needs to keep her mouth shut.

It *is* my story to tell—and I'm not sure I want to tell it.

Yesterday, when Chloe asked me if what Alina had told her was true, I was tempted to lie, to tell her that Alina had made it all up—that she'd been delusional because of all that medication. But for some reason, as I looked into Chloe's soft brown eyes, the words refused to form in my throat. As much as I hate it that my zaychik sees me as evil, something deep inside me wants her to know the real me.

To know me and love me regardless.

Fuck. This is a problem—but not as big of one as the email from Valery that's just popped into my inbox.

LEONOV IN AMERICA, the subject line states in all-caps, and when I open the message, it informs me that my younger brother's US contacts have gotten word of Alexei Leonov's presence in New York City. What he's doing there is anyone's guess, but just the fact that he's on the same continent as my sister and my son is bad news. I haven't forgotten what he said to me in the restroom of that Tajik restaurant, the threat he made about holding Alina to their archaic betrothal contract. At the time, I figured he was just trying to piss me off—and I still suspect that's the case—but there's a chance he meant it.

Tell Alina it's time. I'm done being patient.

I grit my teeth, shutting out the memory of those softly uttered words. Whatever Alexei's agenda is, he's not getting anywhere near Alina. It's bad enough that my son spent almost two months in the tender care of the elder Leonov before I was able to get him out; the last thing I want is for my emotionally fragile sister to be pulled into that nest of vipers.

Alina and I may have our differences, but she's my responsibility, my cross to bear, and I will protect her from anyone who wishes her harm—especially her so-called intended.

Tamping down on the rage burning in my stomach, I reread the email. New York City—that's about as far from Idaho as it gets. Could Alexei's presence in the US so soon after our run-in in Dushanbe be a coincidence after all? I flew to Tajikistan on our private jet, and I know Konstantin's team put safeguards in place to prevent anyone from learning my flight plan, so it's possible Alexei is in New York for a reason totally unrelated to my family.

And it's also possible he's learned I'm in America, but he doesn't know where, so he's starting his search with the most logical place: the Big Apple.

Either way, it's a headache I don't need, especially with the *Mission Impossible*-level task of assassinating a presidential candidate already on my plate.

Switching my focus to that, I pull up the email that details Bransford's upcoming travel and public appearance schedule. Step one is to verify that he is indeed Chloe's father. For that, we need his DNA.

There are a dozen ways to go about doing this, but the most straightforward would be for me to attend one of his fundraisers under the guise of a potential donor and discreetly acquire a sample—say, by stealing his wine glass. The problem with that strategy is those events are far more public than I'm comfortable with, especially given Alexei's unexpected arrival in the States. Now, more than ever, I have to stay under the radar to avoid exposing our location—which rules out another simple solution: getting a one-on-one meeting with Bransford.

Given his status as the frontrunner in his party's primary race, I'd be thoroughly vetted, and my information would end up in some database that the Leonovs' hackers might access. Additionally, it wouldn't be wise to get on Bransford's radar. Even if the assassins hadn't made the connection between me and Chloe before I took them out, Bransford might know that she'd last been spotted in this area of Idaho, and if he somehow learns that this is where I'm residing, he'll get suspicious.

No, as convenient and satisfying as it would be, I can't get his DNA—or carry out the assassination—personally. Not without putting my family and Chloe in greater danger. As is, the clock is ticking. If the assassins told their employer that Chloe had inquired about my job posting at the local gas station, it's only a matter of time before some other hired guns of his show up at my door.

I have to eliminate Bransford as a threat, and fast.

Reaching a decision, I fire off an email directing one of Valery's new arrivals to pose as a waiter at the next event, so he can get Bransford's DNA from a used glass or a utensil. It's a formality at this point; I know I'm right about him—I can feel it in my gut. However, given the magnitude of what I'm planning, I need ironclad proof, and this is the best way to go about it. The only stronger evidence would be an outright confession of his guilt, and I don't see a way to get that short of kidnapping the man—a task even more difficult than killing him outright.

For now, I will proceed as if he's guilty, and plan out the hit. That way, as soon as the DNA test confirms his relationship with Chloe, I can pull the trigger—figuratively, if not literally. A sniper bullet would generate too much heat, so our best bet is to use one of our carefully crafted pharmaceuticals, or to stage some sort of accident.

Either way, he'll pay for killing Chloe's mother and trying to kill her.

Tom Bransford might not know it yet, but he's already dead.

———

I spend the next two hours working out various logistics, and then I check the camera feed from Chloe's room again.

She's still with Slava; he's camped out on her bed, his books and LEGO pieces scattered all over her blanket. They appear to be playing a game where she shows him something in a book, and he acts it out for her. As I watch, he jumps off the bed and hops around the room, imitating a rabbit.

"That's a *zaychik*, right?" she says, smiling, and Slava's eyes go wide before a huge smile takes over his little face.

"*Da!*"

"Yes," she corrects, her own smile widening. "We say *yes* in English."

My son vigorously bobs his head. "Yes, yes, yes!" He's jumping up and down now, too excited to stand still, and I make a mental note to teach Chloe some more words in Russian. That way, she can surprise him randomly like that again, and I'll enjoy listening to her cute, American-accented Russian.

Come to think of it, I should teach her some sex words as well, so I can hear her soft, husky voice crooning them to me when we're in bed.

My body hardens at the image, and I have to take a deep breath to control myself. I've already had her once—or rather, several times in one night—and it's nowhere near enough. I feel like a starving man who was allowed a single lick of ice cream.

I want more. I want to fuck her every night, to take her every hole and pleasure her in every way possible. I want to go to sleep holding her and wake up buried deep inside her. I want to do all sorts of dark, depraved things to her, and I want to cuddle her afterward as she comes down from the pleasure-pain high.

I want to possess her so completely she'll forget all about wanting to leave me.

Soon, I promise myself, shutting the laptop as I get up. She'll be better soon, and then I'll have her.

In the meantime, I have to do whatever it takes to keep her safe.

CHLOE

A few minutes before the official lunchtime of twelve-thirty, Lyudmila comes to take Slava downstairs.

"Nikolai come with food soon," she says in her thickly accented English, correctly surmising that the growling sounds from my stomach indicate hunger. I smile at her bashfully, but she's already hustling Slava out the door while speaking to him in rapid-fire Russian.

Sure enough, Nikolai appears with a tray at twelve-thirty on the dot.

"What's with the military-style adherence to specific meal times?" I ask as he sits next to me and places the tray on the nightstand before uncovering the delicious-smelling dishes.

It's something I've been wondering about for days but haven't had a chance to ask—and I figure this question is a lot easier to answer than the other ones I have prepared.

A wry smile lifts one corner of Nikolai's sensuous lips. "You said it: It's a leftover from the military. More specifically, Pavel's time in the military. He's been running our household ever since he got out of the army some thirty years ago, and this is one of his rules. I don't mind. I grew up this way, so I find it a comforting ritual."

"What about the formal wear at dinner? Is that also Pavel's thing?" That would be odd, given that I've never seen the bear-like Russian in anything resembling a suit or a tux, but there's a lot of weirdness in this household.

The tiny muscles around Nikolai's eyes tighten, though the smile remains on his lips. "Not exactly. That's something my mother insisted on. She said we needed something beautiful in our lives to cover up all the ugliness."

"Oh, I see." My pulse speeds up with anticipation. This is the first time he's spoken of his mother to me—of either of his parents, really. All I'd known before Alina's terrifying revelations was that both of their parents were dead.

"Here," Nikolai says, bringing a piece of French bread slathered with butter and caviar to my lips. "Open up."

I obediently bite into the gourmet offering like the invalid we're both pretending I am. My mind isn't on our strange little game, though; it's churning with all the questions. There's still so much I don't know about my dangerous protector, and I need to know.

I need to know everything, because some small, irrational part of me is still hoping that the darkness in him is not as pitch-black as it seems.

I let him feed me some of the other appetizers on the tray, as well as the flaky white fish with lemon sauce and scalloped potatoes that is the main dish, and when he switches over to dessert—poached pears with black currants and honeyed walnuts—I steel my spine and launch into my planned interrogation.

"So," I say in as casual of a manner as I can, "are you guys mafia?"

I'm pretty sure I already know the answer to this, but might as well hear it from the horse's gorgeous mouth.

To my surprise, instead of flattening in offense or anger, said mouth twitches with amusement. "No, zaychik. At least not the way you imagine it. We don't do illegal drugs or weapons or anything along those lines—that's more of the Leonovs' province. The vast majority of our businesses are legal and above board, and the small portion that are not fall within Konstantin's domain—dark web, hacking, social media bots, all that high-tech jazz."

I blink at him in disbelief, the image of the gun in his hand crisp and clear in my mind. There's no way a regular wealthy businessman, even one with military training, would be able to kill and torture as casually as he had. "But I saw you... And your men... And—"

"I didn't say we were angels. Open up." He brings a

forkful of currant-dotted pear to my lips and waits for me to start chewing before he continues. "In Russia, to gain and retain power, you have to be ruthless. You have to be willing to do whatever it takes. It's always been that way, since time immemorial."

I open my mouth to speak, but he just feeds me another bite of the pear and continues in a light, even tone, as if reading a bedtime story.

"My family has always understood that," he says, "which is why we've prospered since the times of the Mongols' rule. In fact, our first known ancestor was one of Genghis Khan's right-hand men—a nice, kind guy who looted, burned, and raped his way all across Siberia and into the Moscow region back in the thirteenth century. His children followed in his footsteps, and by the time Peter the Great was building his city, the Molotovs—or Nebelevskys, as we were known back then—were a fixture at the tsarist court, guiding and directing national policy from behind the scenes. We were also filthy rich and owned thousands upon thousands of serfs—which makes it extra ironic that during the Revolution, my great-grandfather was one of the ones putting the 'despicable nobles' and 'evil bourgeoisie' on trial for crimes against the common people. He even changed his name to Molotov, the root of which means "hammer" in Russian—a much more Communist-friendly last name than Nebelevsky. But that's how we roll." A hint of bitterness twists Nikolai's lips. "We do whatever it takes to stay on top: whether it's running the gulag labor camps during Stalin's era, or spearheading the propaganda machine of the Communist Party in the fifties and sixties—or jumping on the oil and gas vouchers during the Perestroika and then diversifying to retain the resulting billions in wealth. We're like cockroaches—except the kind that know not just how to survive but how to rule their corner of the world."

I'm both disturbed and fascinated, so much so I forget to chew the next bite of dessert before asking, "So you're not actual mafia?"

My mouth is so full the words come out jumbled, but Nikolai understands and smiles. "No—but that doesn't mean we shy away from getting our hands dirty. Staying on top in Russia is like building a house on a sandy ocean beach: The ground underneath washes away with every tide, and a storm is always brewing on the horizon. My late grandfather, for example—my father's father—was nearly executed back in the fifties when a high-ranking Party rival falsely accused him of disloyalty to the Communist regime. He spent two years in one of the Siberian gulags he'd been overseeing, and when he made his way out, the first thing he did was plant evidence on his rival and get *him* sent away to the gulags while having the government transfer all of his property to himself. Then, later on, my father—" He stops, his expression darkening.

I sit up straighter. "Your father what?"

Nikolai's face turns impassive. "Nothing. The nineties in Russia were just a particularly corrupt and volatile time, so my family had to be extra vigilant and ruthless."

"Specifically, your father." I'm not about to let him drop this topic, not when I'm finally getting some answers.

"And his brother, Vyacheslav—my uncle. His son, Roman, is now nearly as rich as we are."

"Uh-huh." At any other time, I'd jump at a chance to learn more about Nikolai's extended family, but right now, I'm solely focused on his father. I let him feed me a couple more forkfuls of dessert, and after I swallow, I ask cautiously, "So what kind of things did your father have to do to stay on top in the nineties?"

Nikolai's eyes turn a greener shade of amber. "Nothing worse than any other oligarch of his generation: a lot of bribery, some blackmail and racketeering, a little physical coercion, and—when required—forceful elimination of obstacles. Tactics you might think of as falling into the organized crime domain, except they were standard business strategies in Russia at the time. And it wasn't just the oligarchs— the government used the same toolbox. That's still the case to some extent; lawfulness and criminality are highly flexible, constantly evolving concepts in my country, each with a lot of room for interpretation."

I do my best to keep my expression neutral, even as my arms prickle with a chill. *Physical coercion* and *forceful elimination*—those are obviously euphemisms for torture and murder. And this is what he's been raised to view as standard business strategies?

The Molotovs might not be mafia in the formal sense of the word, but in some ways, they're even more dangerous.

"Is that why you brought Slava here? Because Russia is such a lawless place?" I ask, unable to help myself. This is another mystery that's been gnawing at me, and though I intended to keep this interrogation focused on his father, I can't pass up a chance to get some answers on this front.

After what he's just told me about his home, I can't blame him for wanting to raise his son as far away from Russia as possible.

"No, zaychik." His beautiful mouth takes on the cynical curve it wears so often. "I'm not that good of a father, I'm afraid."

"So why *are* you here? You promised you'd tell me." Actually, he promised no such thing. All he said on the videocall where I'd questioned him about this was that it was a long story.

He must remember that too because his eyes gleam with amusement. "Nice try." He glances at the now mostly empty tray. "Are you full, or would you like anything else?"

I'm so full my stomach is on the verge of exploding, but I don't want him to go yet. Not when we're just getting to the things I'm dying to know about. "I'd love some fruit," I say hopefully. "Maybe some berries if you have them? And coffee. I'd love some coffee."

He looks even more amused but rises to his feet without arguing. "All right. I'll be right back."

Dropping a kiss on my forehead, he picks up the tray and walks out.

11

NIKOLAI

I'm still smiling when I step into the kitchen. My zaychik is so wonderfully transparent in her attempts at manipulation. *You promised me.* It was all I could do not to grab and kiss her on the spot—especially since as she said it, she pushed out her bottom lip in a small pout, like a wheedling child.

I love that she's less afraid of me now, that instead of horror, there's curiosity in her pretty brown eyes. I've been doing my best to keep the beast inside me leashed in her presence, to make her feel comfortable and secure, and it looks like I'm succeeding—which makes all the restraint worth it. So what if my hands all but shake with the need to touch her, to press her to me tightly as I drive myself deep into her slick, warm body?

I can be patient.

I can be gentle.

I can care for her like a fucking eunuch if that's

what it takes to wipe the memory of my sister's tale from her mind.

Not that it's likely to happen. I know where Chloe was leading with all her questions. She wants to know the full story, and I can't blame her. The coffee, the berries—that's just a pretext. What she wants is more time with me, more time to probe, and I have to decide how much of the truth I'm willing to give her, if any.

"How is she?" Lyudmila asks as I place the tray on the counter, and I fill her in on Chloe's condition—namely, that she's doing better. I changed her bandages this morning, and the wound looked like it was healing nicely. I also surreptitiously counted the pills on her nightstand, and it seems she's only taken a couple so far—another good sign.

Rationally, I know Chloe isn't likely to spiral into addiction from a few painkillers, but after witnessing Alina's struggles, I can't help but worry.

"It's good that she has such an appetite," Lyudmila says after I convey Chloe's requests to her. "Better if she were to drink tea, though."

"Agreed. But let's give her the coffee she wants."

Lyudmila grunts in agreement and prepares a tray of artfully arranged strawberries, raspberries, and blueberries, along with a cup of steaming-hot coffee. I thank her and hurry back upstairs, where my zaychik is waiting.

I've decided there *is* a question of hers I can answer today, a portion of the truth I can give her.

Her eyes are brightly inquisitive as I walk into her

room and take my seat on the edge of the bed, placing the tray on its spot on the nightstand.

"So," she begins, "about the—

"Open," I order softly, picking up a strawberry by its stem, and when her plump lips part obediently, I push the juicy berry in and watch her white teeth sink into its flesh—the way I want to sink my teeth into hers.

The jolt of lust is so sudden, so strong, I have to tense every muscle in my body to prevent myself from acting on the urge. There's something almost cannibalistic in the way I want her, the way my mouth waters at the thought of tasting her smooth, bronzed skin and licking the droplets of sweat off her naked body after I fuck her to exhaustion once again. I remember how her nipples felt on my tongue, the salt-and-berry essence of her, and the control I was just priding myself on suddenly feels as thin and frayed as an ancient rope.

She tenses too, her eyes locked on mine, her slender body stiff with the primal awareness of prey. A trickle of strawberry juice escapes her mouth, and I instinctively catch it with my thumb, my heart hammering violently at the feel of her warm skin, the plushness of her bottom lip, all glossy red and sticky from the juice. Holding her gaze, I bring my thumb to my mouth and suck it clean, the way I'd suck on those sweet, berry-sticky lips of hers if I could trust myself to stop there.

Her eyes widen, her breath hitching at my action as her gaze drops to my lips for a beat before meeting my eyes again. She's as turned on as I am, I can see it, and the scorching tension simmers in the air between us, heating the room until my very bones feel like they're on fire, my cock so hard the zipper is going to leave an imprint on its length. I can all but feel her supple flesh under my palms, can all but taste those glistening, red-tinted lips—

A distant peal of childish laughter brings me to my senses, and I realize I was leaning toward her, my hand already fisting in her blanket. *Fuck.* Unclenching my fist, I jackknife to my feet and stride over to the window. Dragging in deep, cleansing breaths, I take in the sight of my son running around the driveway with Arkash chasing him. He's laughing so hard I can hear him even through the bulletproof glass, and the sound further clears the fog of lust enveloping my brain.

Fucking fuck. I thought I had a handle on myself—I was sure of it after I bathed her yesterday while maintaining rigid self-control. I wanted her, yes, but I could distance myself from that want and focus solely on her well-being, on the fact that she was just out of surgery and needed me to be her caretaker. Today, though, she's better—and my self-control is a thousand times worse.

"Um, Nikolai…" Chloe's tone is uncertain, her voice soft and slightly husky. Hearing it makes me shudder with hunger once again. This time, though, she's not right there, and it's easier to pull myself together, reining in the savage need.

Smoothing out my expression, I lock my hands

together behind my back and turn to face her. "Yes, zaychik?"

Her delicate throat ripples with a swallow. "What's Slava doing out there?"

"Playing a game of tag with one of my guards." I walk back to the bed and sit at the foot of it, about as far away from her as I can be while still occupying the same piece of furniture. "Pavel must've asked him to watch Slava while he cleans up after lunch."

Her small white teeth worry her bottom lip. "Right. Right." Watching me intently, she picks up the coffee mug and blows on the hot liquid. I can guess what's going through her mind—she's debating the best way to approach the topic of greatest interest to her—so I decide to help her out.

I'm not ready to talk about my father, but I can tell her the truth about my son.

Holding her gaze, I say evenly, "Five years ago, my brother Valery celebrated his twenty-second birthday at a nightclub in Moscow. It was the party of the year; everyone who's anyone in our part of the world was there—including, as I learned later, Ksenia Leonova, the reclusive daughter of our family's long-time enemy and rival."

Chloe frowns in confusion. "Leonova? As in, the Leonovs you mentioned earlier? The actual Russian mafia family?"

"They would reject that label also, but yes. They fish in a much dirtier pond. In any case, unlike her brother Alexei, Ksenia had always stayed out of the public eye, so I had no idea who she was when she approached me." I take a breath to control the familiar rage kindling inside me. "I thought she was just another socialite or model wannabe, so we danced, downed a few shots, and then went to a hotel to fuck."

Chloe flinches slightly, the coffee mug wobbling in her hand. I move swiftly, grabbing it from her and placing it back on the tray before any of the dark liquid can spill. Then I sit closer to her.

The good thing about remembering Ksenia is that it kills my libido dead.

"I wore a condom, as I always do," I continue, and Chloe's eyes widen. She must realize where the story is heading. "Yes," I say before she can ask, "it broke. Either that or she tampered with it somehow—I still don't know which it is. I didn't notice anything at the time. I'd had a few drinks, and the night wasn't especially memorable. In fact, I'd forgotten all about it until a little over eight months ago, when I got a call from a friend of Ksenia's telling me that Ksenia had died in a car crash, leaving behind a son—*my* son, according to her diary."

"Oh my God," Chloe breathes, looking horrified. "So Slava's mother was—"

"Someone I wouldn't have touched in a hazmat suit if I'd known who she was, yes. The relations between our families had been strained for decades, to say the least."

"Decades? Why?"

"Remember the story I just told you, about my grandfather being sent away to the gulag?"

Chloe nods and cautiously picks up her coffee again.

"The man who accused him of disloyalty to the Party was Matvey Leonov, Ksenia's grandfather."

She freezes, the mug midway to her mouth. "Oh. Wow."

"Yes. He was a poisonous snake, like all the Leonovs —but especially Ksenia." Despite myself, my voice drips with bitter hatred. "To this day, I don't know if she'd planned to fuck me over all along, or if it was an accident that she'd gotten pregnant. Either way, she didn't tell me that I had a son. Was probably never going to tell me. If she hadn't died, I might not have ever learned of Slava's existence—at least not until he was old enough to appear in our circles. At that point, the resemblance would've clued everyone in to his Molotov heritage, if not necessarily his actual paternity." My mouth twists. "You haven't seen my brothers or my cousin, but we all look very much alike."

Chloe puts the coffee back on the nightstand without so much as taking a sip. "Why do you think she approached you that night? She must've known who *you* were, right?"

"Of course she did." Unlike her, I was well known among Moscow's high society. "As to why, I still have no clue. Maybe she planned the whole thing, right down to the broken condom, or maybe she was just young and stupid and wanted to flirt with danger. I don't even know why she was at the party or how she got in—certainly, none of the Leonovs had been invited. Either way, the end result is the same: I have a son I didn't know about until eight months ago. A son who's half Leonov."

Chloe sucks in a breath. "Wait a sec. Is that why you're—"

"Here?" At her nod, I smile humorlessly. "You guessed it, zaychik. His mother's family didn't exactly hand him over to me. I learned about Slava's existence a week after Ksenia's death, and by then, he was already living with Boris Leonov, Ksenia's father—a man known for his cruel and violent proclivities. I never wanted children, never planned to have them, but I couldn't leave my son in his clutches, couldn't abandon him to grow up in that vipers' nest."

"So you what? Stole him from them?"

I nod. "It took my brothers and me almost two months to figure out a way to breach their security, but we got him out and I brought him here, where nobody knows who we are and can't report to the Leonovs that I suddenly have a child."

Her smooth forehead knits in confusion. "I don't understand. Why didn't you just go through the legal channels? You're Slava's father. Couldn't you have gotten custody with a simple paternity test?"

"I could've—and would've—if it had been anyone but the Leonovs. They hate our family as much as we hate theirs, and they'd do anything to thwart us... to thwart *me*. The moment I filed for custody—the moment they realized I knew of Slava's existence—he would've been spirited away, hidden someplace we would've never found him. Maybe his death would've been faked for the sake of the courts—or maybe they would've actually killed him. Anything to deprive me of a chance to raise my son."

Chloe gasps in horror. "You think they would've…?"

"I wouldn't put anything past the elder Leonov." Or Alexei and Ruslan, Ksenia's equally ruthless brothers.

Chloe looks horrified. "That's terrible." Then her eyes widen, and she gasps again. "Grandpa Duck! Oh God… do you think Ksenia's father hurt Slava while he was living with him?"

"I wouldn't be surprised." I try to keep a level tone, but dark rage seeps into my voice, making it hard and guttural. "Slava has never talked about his time with his grandfather, but the way he'd acted around me and Pavel at first… the way he still acts around me, to a certain extent…" I stop, my throat closing on a surge of fury.

The vague suspicions I'd harbored about Boris Leonov's treatment of my son had crystallized into near certainty when Chloe told me about Slava's odd reaction to Grandpa Duck in the children's story. The only reason Ksenia's father is still alive is that Konstantin's team has uncovered the carefully concealed fact that he has late-stage pancreatic cancer and is not expected to last longer than a couple of agony-filled months.

Killing him would be a mercy I'm not willing to extend.

Chloe places her hand on my knee. "I'm so sorry, Nikolai." Her soft brown eyes are filled with sympathy, and an echo of the same rage that burns inside me.

She, too, would like to tear apart anyone who's hurt Slava, I can tell.

With effort, I tamp down on my fury. Nature has already devised the most exquisite torture for Boris Leonov, and I have to be content with that. The only thing ordering a hit on Ksenia's father would achieve is shortening his suffering and triggering an outright war between our families. Right now, we have, if not precisely a truce, then at least a détente: No blood has been spilled in a number of years, despite constant friction on both business and personal levels.

That will change if I kill Boris—or if they learn that I'm behind Slava's kidnapping. They may harbor some suspicions on that front now—Alexei certainly dropped some hints during our encounter in Dushanbe —but they won't act on those suspicions unless they're sure. Not only because doing so would mean starting that war, but because if they're wrong and I don't know about Slava, their attack might clue me in, opening up the entire ugly, wriggling can of worms.

On my end, I've done my best to ensure that doubts are all they have. I left Russia three weeks before we extracted Slava from their compound, so the timelines wouldn't match too closely, and Ksenia's friend, the one who called me after finding the diary, has been relocated to New Zealand with a million dollars and a new identity—and a promise that should she contact any of the Leonovs to relay our conversation, her family in Russia would pay the price.

I don't go into all those details with Chloe now. There's no need; she can draw her own conclusions from what I've told her. Instead, I cover her hand with mine and say gravely, "Thank you, zaychik." Her sympathy and her anger on Slava's behalf cool my rage, the warmth from her small palm seeping into my skin despite the thick material of my jeans.

She swallows and pulls her hand back, averting her gaze. She's afraid of this, I realize with a pang—afraid of emotional intimacy with me. It's both disheartening and encouraging. Disheartening because I want us to be past this, to go back to the way things were before Alina's revelations. And encouraging because it tells me there's hope for us… that no matter how much she'd like to be repulsed and terrified by me, her feelings are more complex than that.

Reining in my frustration, I wait for her to look back at me, and when she does, I pick up the coffee and hand it to her. "Here, zaychik." My tone is calm and bland. "You should drink this before it gets cold."

I'll let her hide from the truth for now, allow her to put up her shields and defenses. They won't save her from me. Nothing will.

Whether she likes it or not, I will own her.

Heart, mind, body, and soul.

CHLOE

Despite downing the full cup of coffee, I fall asleep right after lunch and nap until Nikolai brings me dinner. I think it's the painkillers that make me so drowsy—that or my brain is using sleep as a way to process the most recent revelations while hiding from the anxiety-inducing unanswered questions.

They kidnapped Slava, stole him from his mother's family. I suppose I should be shocked, but I'm not. I think I suspected something like that on some level; it was part of the wrongness I was picking up on, that unsettling vibe I kept getting from this family— especially my darkly mesmerizing captor.

I want to condemn his actions, but instead, I can't help but applaud them. To extricate his son from a potentially abusive situation, Nikolai has completely upended his life, leaving his home country and giving up his role as the head of the Molotov conglomerate.

Not every father would do that for his child, especially a child he didn't know about.

A child he claims never to have wanted.

My chest squeezes as I recall that admission, thrown out so casually, so offhandedly, as if it doesn't matter. He didn't explain, didn't go into details, but I could read between the lines.

It wasn't a desire to live for himself, or travel, or prevent overpopulation—or any other reason people typically give for choosing not to have children. In Nikolai's case, he didn't want to be a father because he didn't think he'd be a good one… and because he didn't want his line to continue. There's a part of my captor that despises himself, either because of what he's done or what he is.

A Molotov.

I've been thinking about the story he told me, about his family's history and the way he was raised. He didn't say much about the latter, but his omissions were as telling as the details he did include. It was obvious that he was taught to view life as a never-ending battle for survival and dominance, a fight that only the most ruthless can win.

I'd bet anything that his upbringing at his father's hands wasn't far from the way his Mongol ancestor might've raised *his* son back in the thirteenth century, torture skills and all.

I try to probe deeper during dinner, but Nikolai is no longer in the mood to talk about himself. Instead, as he feeds me wine-poached venison with mushroom gravy and sweet potato mash, he keeps the conversation focused on me: my food likes and dislikes, my favorite movies, my friends in college. And he does it so skillfully that I find myself talking to him without reservations, smiling and laughing as I describe the time my roommate's cat peed on my bed and how one of my guy friends mistook my mom for one of the students and hit on her during our freshman-year orientation.

It's as if we're back to our video chats, as if everything that's transpired since his return has been nothing but a terrible fever dream.

It's not until dinner is done and he kisses me goodnight, his lips soft and cool on my forehead, that I realize I've missed the opportunity to get the answers for the rest of my burning questions.

The pattern repeats the next morning, when Nikolai brings me breakfast. He skillfully avoids my attempts to bring the conversation around to his father—or *my* father. Instead, as he feeds me *grechka*—the roasted buckwheat kasha Alina likes in place of oatmeal—we discuss Slava's progress and the next lessons I have planned. Then he helps me shower, changes my bandage, and, at my insistence, dresses me in a pair of yoga pants and a soft T-shirt.

My ankle is feeling better, as is my arm, so I intend to be up and about.

"Don't overdo it," he warns me as I determinedly limp over to Slava's room instead of letting him carry me there. "You still need time to heal."

"I'll take it easy, don't worry," I say, plopping on Slava's bed—much to the boy's delight. "We're going to read some books, build some castles... Nothing strenuous, I promise."

Nikolai still looks concerned, so I give him a bright smile. "I'm all better, I really am. Didn't even need a painkiller this morning." The latter is not entirely true —I could definitely use a painkiller for the dull, nagging ache in my arm—but I decided against taking one, to see if I can tough it out on my own.

Either way, my reassurance works as intended. Nikolai's face clears. "All right then," he says, and with a few words in Russian to his son, he leaves us to our lessons.

By mid-morning, my arm is aching harder—Slava accidentally bumped against the sling while climbing onto my lap—so I limp back to my room to take the painkiller after all.

In the hallway, I run into Lyudmila, who's carrying a huge bouquet of flowers, everything from lush roses to sunflowers and tulips. "Alina birthday," she informs me when I ask what it's for. "Big one. Twenty-five today."

Oh, shoot. Alina did mention that her birthday is

this week when we smoked pot together. I had no idea it was today, though.

Thinking fast, I ask Lyudmila, "Where's Nikolai?"

I need some kind of gift, and the only thing I can come up with is a bouquet of my own—wildflowers gathered in the forest nearby. During my hikes, I spotted a few places where they grow in abundance.

The trick will be getting to one of those places with my ankle misbehaving, but that's where Nikolai hopefully comes in.

Lyudmila nods toward his office. "He working."

Brushing past me, she continues on to Alina's room, and I bite my lip, eyeing Nikolai's closed office door. Do I dare interrupt?

A trill of feminine laughter and animated Russian chatter coming from Alina's room decides it for me.

I can't not get at least *something* for Nikolai's sister.

I limp over to Nikolai's office and quietly knock.

"*Da*," his deep voice replies—*yes* in Russian.

I take a deep breath. "It's Chloe. I was just wondering if—"

The door swings open, and the words die on my lips as stunning green-gold eyes meet mine, stealing my breath and spiking my heart rate.

Dammit.

Will my body ever stop responding to him so strongly? At this point, we've fucked and he's bathed me several times, yet his masculine beauty still blindsides me each time we've spent a couple of hours apart.

"What is it, zaychik?" he asks, dark eyebrows pulling together as he gives me a swift, concerned once-over. Before I can reply, he grips my hands. "Is everything okay?"

"Yeah, everything's fine. I just..." I throw a quick glance over my shoulder. The hallway is empty, but I still lower my voice, just in case. "I need a gift for Alina."

"Ah. Come in." He shepherds me into his office and guides me to a chair, which I gratefully sink into. I might've overdone it with all the walking today—my ankle is better, but it's definitely not completely well. Neither is my arm.

That painkiller is becoming more necessary by the minute.

"Here," Nikolai says, pulling open a drawer in his desk. He takes out a small black box and hands it to me. "You can give this to her."

Confused, I open it—and gape at the diamond-studded bracelet inside.

What the hell?

My gaze jumps to his face. "What do you mean, give it to her?"

"It can be your gift," Nikolai says matter-of-factly. "I'll give her another piece of jewelry."

Is he serious?

"Of course it can't be my gift," I say when I've recovered my powers of speech. "*You* got it for her, not me. I can't afford a single stone in that bracelet, and Alina knows that."

He shrugs. "So what? She'll enjoy it regardless."

Oh my God. I take a breath and count to three. "No, she won't. Because I'm going to give her something else —something that's actually from me."

"Such as?"

"Flowers. I'd like to put together a bouquet for her. I saw some really pretty ones blooming not far from here."

His eyebrows draw together again. "There's no way you're going for a hike with that ankle."

"It's not far. I can make it. Especially if you come with me and help."

A peculiar gleam appears in his tiger eyes. "You want me to take you flower-picking?"

Now that he's said it, I realize how ridiculous it sounds—and how big of an ask it is. What the fuck was I thinking? He's not my boyfriend; he's my captor, a powerful, dangerous man who has far more important—

"All right," he says before I can backpedal. "Give me a minute to finish up here, and we'll go."

13

NIKOLAI

Ignoring Chloe's claims that she can walk "just fine," I carry her to her room and return to finish the message I was writing, instructing Valery's newest arrival on how and where I want the DNA sample collected. It's not a man my brother is sending for this job, but a woman—which is even better.

It opens up some interesting possibilities in regard to getting close to Bransford.

I then answer a few more urgent messages and go get Chloe for our flower-gathering expedition.

My heart pounds with anticipation as I approach her room. Maybe I'm reading too much into this, but I feel encouraged that she's actively sought me out, that she wants to spend time with me, even if it's under this bullshit pretext.

My strategy of being nothing more than her patient, platonic caretaker is working. Slowly but surely, my zaychik is losing her fear of me, letting down her shields. And that's good—because I don't know how much longer I can remain patient.

The better she feels, the harder it is to control the beast inside me, to stop myself from claiming her as my instincts demand.

She's watching the news as I walk into her room. Seeing me, she powers off the TV and stands up, a radiant smile on her face. "I'm ready."

Something deep inside my chest simultaneously expands and contracts. "Let's go get those flowers, then."

I let her walk toward me on her own, just to see how well her ankle is healing. As soon as she reaches me, though, I pick her up, once again ignoring her objections. I can't watch her limp—it hurts me too much—so the only way this hike is happening is with her in my arms.

"You're not seriously planning to carry me all the way there," she says as we exit the house.

I smile down at her. "Why not, zaychik?"

I love holding her, feeling her pressed against me. Until her ankle is healed, I intend to carry her around as much as possible—and maybe afterward as well.

"For starters, it's at least half a mile to the spot I have in mind," she says with utmost seriousness, as if half a mile is any sort of real distance. "If you just lend me your elbow, I could walk there at a slow pace."

"That's not happening."

"But I'm heavy. There's no way—"

"You're kidding, right?" I grin into her small,

indignant face. "Zaychik, I've carried backpacks heavier than you for a day straight."

She blinks. "You mean... when you were in the army?"

"And now. Pavel and I frequently train with the guards to keep fit."

"Uh-huh. But still—"

"How about this? I promise I'll let you walk if I get tired." Or rather, if I drop dead. That's the only way she's hiking through these woods on that ankle of hers.

She huffs. "Fine. Be all macho, see if I care when your arms fall off. The flowers are that way." She points to a small dirt path leading into the woods to the east of us, then lays her head on my shoulder, as if planning to take a nap.

I laugh and head down the path she indicated, being careful to protect her from low-hanging branches and shrubs. I can't remember the last time I felt so light, both physically and mentally. Instead of tiring me, her slight weight in my arms buoys me, the feel of her body against mine evoking not only the usual carnal hunger but also something warm and pure... something almost like joy.

It's as if the dark clouds that have hung over me for the past several years have lifted for a moment, revealing a sliver of sunlit sky.

The sensation persists the entire way to our destination, aided by her occasional grumbling about foolish macho men and their egos. I'm sure she means to be insulting, but all I feel is amusement mixed with relief. I like her snarky and grumpy; it means she's feeling safe with me, forgetting the things she's heard and seen me do.

Forgetting that I'm a monster.

When we get to a small, wildflower-dotted meadow, I put her down to let her gather the flowers. Despite the sling, she's quick and efficient in her task, her nimble fingers plucking the straggly plants and arranging them into something beautiful. By the time she's done, I have to admit that it *was* a good gift idea— my sister will love this unusual, forest-scented bouquet.

"I'm ready for my ride home," she says with faux haughtiness, and I laugh as I pick her up, careful not to crush the flowers she's holding. Their aroma mingles with the fresh, intoxicating scent of her hair, and my body ignites with a surge of arousal, my cock hardening as she lays her head on my shoulder, her nose brushing my neck.

"Harder uphill, isn't it?" she says gleefully as I start up the path leading back to the house. Raising her head, she places her palm over my chest and grins. "Your heart is beating faster already."

So it is—but not for the reason she thinks. It's all I can do not to pin her against the nearest tree and drive deep into her tight little body. The feel of her, the smell of her, that mischievous sparkle in her eyes—it all adds fuel to the fire burning inside me, to the violent hunger I've been trying so hard to suppress.

My pace slows as my gaze falls to her lips, so pretty

and plush, so temptingly curved in that bright, teasing smile.

Don't do it.

My thudding heartbeats intensify to a roar in my ears.

Don't fucking do it.

My vision turns tunnel-like, the world around us blurring out of focus. All I can see is her smile, as brilliant and warm as the sun; all I can feel is the carnal heat scorching my veins.

Do not fucking do it.

Her smile fades, a wary look entering her soft brown eyes as I stop completely, staring at her. "Nikolai, I didn't mean—"

My lips cover hers, swallowing the rest of her words. *Fuck, she tastes good.* Like apples and berries and flowers, something wholesome and wild and fresh. The heady flavor feeds the dark hunger inside me, adding to the ferocious need thrumming under my skin.

Her lips part under the pressure of mine, and my tongue invades the slick, warm depths of her mouth, seeking every bit of that flavor, of the sweet, clean essence of her. Greedily, I breathe in her panting exhales, reveling in the moan that vibrates her throat as I tug on her lower lip with my teeth, nearly breaking the fragile skin in the process.

Mine. She's fucking mine. I want to consume her, devour her, brand her... take her, savage her, destroy her. No, not destroy—possess, though with my being a Molotov, it's basically one and the same. My need for her is obsessive and dark, dangerous to her and to me. But I refuse to think of that now, refuse to remember my parents' fights and my grandmother's warnings. Fate has brought Chloe to me, and fate will determine our path. For now, she's mine to claim, mine to own.

Ravenously, I deepen the kiss, and she responds with equal ardor, her tongue dueling with mine as her left arm loops around my neck. My arms tighten around her, crushing her against my chest—and wrenching a pained cry from her throat.

Fuck. Her sling.

What am I doing?

With superhuman effort, I tear my mouth away and set her down on her feet. Breathing hard, I back away as she stares at me, eyes wide and kiss-swollen lips parted.

Shocked. She's shocked by what happened, and so am I. Shocked that I let her go, that I found the strength to release her when the beast inside me is howling and raging, demanding that I take her here and now, no matter how hurt and fragile she is.

"Nikolai, I..." She swallows hard, bringing her left hand to her chest. The bouquet she's holding is damaged, some flowers torn and bent in half. "I don't think it's a good idea. I mean, you and me—"

"I know what you mean." My tone is as sharp as the blade-like hunger twisting inside me, whittling away at my self-control.

I came so close to fucking her. Another minute, and

I would've been plunging deep inside her tight, wet heat, having forgotten all about her injuries.

It's official. I'm a fucking savage.

There's no longer any doubt in my mind.

She chews on her plump lower lip, making me want to do the same. "I'm not—"

"You should fix that." At her blank look, I growl, "The flowers. They're crushed."

She blinks and glances down, as if only now realizing they're still in her hand. "Right." She steps back unsteadily. "Let me do that."

She kneels to gather the few straggly flowers that grow along this path, and I turn away, taking deep breaths. By the time she calls my name again, I have myself under control. *Mostly.*

Turning back to face her, I smooth out my expression. "Let's go."

She starts toward me with a limp, and I grit my teeth as I swoop in, lifting her off her feet. Self-control issues or not, I'm not letting her hike back on her own.

Holding her tightly against my chest, I lengthen my stride until I'm almost running. She stays silent, though she must hear my breathing pick up from exertion. There's no more teasing about macho men, no more protests about how she can walk by herself. She doesn't want to draw attention to herself, and it's just as well.

My restraint is hanging on by a thread.

It's only when we're approaching the house that she speaks. "Thank you," she says quietly, forcing me to meet her gaze—something I've avoided the entire trip back. "I really do appreciate it."

"Of course. Happy to help." My tone is casual, calm, as if we're discussing taking her to gather the flowers. But we both know we're not.

What she's grateful for is the fact that I didn't fuck her—that for now, she gets to keep her walls up and pretend.

14

CHLOE

As soon as Nikolai deposits me in my room, I go looking for Alina. I find her in the kitchen, chatting with Lyudmila, and I give her the flowers, along with the birthday congratulations.

"Thank you." She accepts the bouquet with a beaming smile. "Where on earth did you get these? They're so pretty."

I smile back. "Oh, just around here."

"Really? With your ankle this way?"

My cheeks heat at the memory of what almost happened in the forest. "Nikolai might've helped."

Her smile dims slightly, but she doesn't say anything to me. Instead, she turns to Lyudmila, who's chopping up some veggies by the sink, and speaks a few words of Russian to her. The blond woman bustles off to fill a pretty vase with water, and Alina arranges the flowers in it before taking it out to the dining room, where it joins the other bouquet decorating the table.

"How are you feeling?" I ask, following her there. The table is already set with a variety of appetizers; it looks like it's going to be an extra-fancy lunch today. "Any more headaches?"

"I should be asking you that." She faces me, her jade eyes gleaming. "How's your arm? Your ankle?"

"All better." The ankle not so much right now—I've definitely overdone it today—but I keep quiet about that.

"I'm glad." She hesitates, then asks quietly, "Have you spoken to Nikolai?"

My pulse quickens. "He's told me about Slava and the Leonovs." Is she about to tell me more? Has she decided to reveal the full story after all?

Her face takes on a sphinxlike expression. "I see."

I guess the answer is no. I'm tempted to press her, but I don't want to bring up a traumatic topic on her birthday—though it could be argued she's just brought it up herself.

"Do you want to hang out tonight after dinner?" I ask impulsively. "Maybe play some board games, grab a couple of beers? Obviously, Lyudmila's welcome too."

My offer is only partially motivated by my desire to probe for more information. Mostly, I just want to get to know Alina better, as I'm starting to really like her.

She looks startled but quickly recovers. Flashing me a warm smile, she says, "That sounds great. Let's see how long the dinner lasts, and then we'll decide what to do."

Since I'm already downstairs, I join everyone for lunch instead of having Nikolai feed me in my room. Not only am I feeling well enough to resume being a functional adult, but after what nearly happened in the forest, being alone with Nikolai feels like a dangerous undertaking—especially next to a bed.

I'm certain he only stopped because he was worried about hurting my arm, something that would be way less of a concern if it were comfortably arranged on a pillow.

My heart hammers faster at the thought, and I sneak a glance at him from under my lashes. I can still feel his lips devouring mine, can still taste his warm, minty breath. My nipples feel overly sensitive, and my lower lip throbs where he'd bitten it, the pulsations echoing deep into my core.

I want him. And not in a casual, would-be-nice-to-have way. Even knowing what he is, I crave him so desperately it's like a sickness, an addiction as unhealthy and dangerous as a heroin user's dependence. I have no willpower around him, no ability to resist his touch. By all rights, he should terrify and repulse me, but instead, I'm drawn to him as much as, if not more than, before.

It's twisted. It's wrong. I know that, but I can't help it.

My body and heart refuse to sync with my head.

He catches my gaze on him, and his tiger eyes grow hooded, filled with unmistakable dark heat. My pulse spikes further, my breath hitching as I look away. However much I want him, he wants me even more. And his desire is not of the soft and sweet variety. I felt the savage urgency in him today, the need to dominate and conquer. If not for my injuries, he would've taken me right then and there, on the leaf-strewn dirt. And he wouldn't have been gentle, either.

When we have sex again, it will be devastating for me, both physically and mentally, and the only way to prevent it from happening is to stay out of his reach—an impossibility in my current situation. Even if I were willing to risk an encounter with a new set of Bransford's goons, Nikolai won't let me leave.

For the first time, I allow myself to think about the future and what it holds. Will Nikolai ever let me go? And if he does, will I ever be safe? If Tom Bransford does indeed want me dead, what's to stop him from coming after me again and again? Judging by the polls, he's most likely going to be his party's nominee. If he then wins the general election, there will be almost no limits to his power—not that there are many limits now.

Raised voices pull me out of my dark ruminations. It's Alina and Nikolai, having what sounds like an argument in Russian. I was so lost in my thoughts I didn't notice the strained atmosphere at the table, but there's no missing it now.

Brother and sister are clearly at loggerheads, and Slava is watching them, his golden eyes wide with curiosity—and more than a hint of worry.

I tug on his sleeve. "Hey. What do we call this in English?" I point at the tomato on his plate.

He blinks up at me.

"We just learned it this morning, remember?" He still looks clueless, so I decide to give him a hint. "It's a vegetable that we call the to—"

"Tomato!" he exclaims, beaming up at me.

"That's right." Grinning, I fluff his silky hair. My goal was to distract him from the adults' argument, but it looks like my interference has ended the argument altogether, with Alina and Nikolai turning their attention to us instead.

"He's learning so fast," I say, and Slava proudly puffs out his chest as Alina gives him a warm smile and says something that sounds like praise in Russian.

"We should speak English to him." Nikolai's tone still holds a bite. "At least when Chloe is around. He'll learn even faster that way."

Alina's lips tighten, but she nods. "As you wish. He's your son."

I'm beyond curious to know what their argument was about, but I don't think it's a good idea to go there. Instead, I ask Alina how she normally celebrates her birthday, and she entertains me with descriptions of trips to exotic locales and lavish parties in Moscow, the latter attended by all sorts of glitterati.

"Wait, back up," I say when she casually mentions how one movie star passed out on her yacht during a birthday bash in Mykonos. "You know Hollywood celebs?"

She laughs. "Not all of them, obviously, but some. They're people too, you know. Nothing special in the grand scheme of things."

Not special to *her*, maybe, but I'm fascinated. I make her tell me all about her famous friends and acquaintances, and before I know it, we're wrapping up the meal. Which is good—because even *TMZ*-worthy stories about misbehaving celebs haven't lessened my awareness of Nikolai and his intent, unwavering focus on me.

Throughout the entire meal, he's been watching me with the lethal patience of a predator, one who knows it's only a matter of time before he consumes his prey.

Our eyes meet as we get up from the table, and I look away again, my skin tingling as my pulse jumps uncontrollably.

This is bad. I've been counting on at least a few more days of Nikolai restraining himself, but I don't think I'll get nearly that much time. Another day, maybe, if I'm lucky.

If not, I'll end up in his bed tonight.

"Let's go to your room," I tell Slava, trying to ignore

the flush heating my entire body. "We can play Batman and Robin—or Batman and Superman."

The child eagerly grabs my hand, and we walk out of the dining room together as Nikolai and Alina start what sounds like another argument in Russian.

NIKOLAI

"I'm telling you, you cannot keep her in the dark," Alina says again as Chloe and my son disappear from view. "It's her father. She deserves to know what you're planning."

Fucking Pavel. He's told Lyudmila about Bransford, and she, naturally, couldn't resist spilling the beans to my sister—who's again determined to have a say in a matter that doesn't concern her.

I glare down at her. "You need to stay the fuck out of it. This is between me and Chloe, understand?"

Alina's green eyes blink up at me, all wounded innocence. "I wasn't going to interfere. I'm just saying that if you want a chance at a real relationship with her, you have to—"

I scoff. "What do you know about real relationships?"

She takes a breath and squares her shoulders. "Look, I was wrong to interfere before. I can't apologize enough for that. But the fact remains: Chloe is not like us. No matter what Bransford's done, he's still her biological fa—"

"He's her mother's rapist, nothing more." I can't even bring myself to call him a sperm donor. That's what *I* was to Slava for the first four years of his life, but as soon as I learned of his existence, I couldn't imagine harming a hair on his head, much less ordering a hit on him... not even if he one day orders one on me.

Alina flinches at my sharp tone. "I know. I'm not saying she views him as family or anything. But she still deserves to be consulted."

"Why? So she can have his death on her conscience?"

"What if she doesn't want him dead?"

"That's not her decision." There's no way I'm letting the fucker live, not even if Chloe begs for it.

"But it should be," Alina says in frustration. "If it were me—"

"I wouldn't place that burden on you either." I'd carry it myself, the way I'm doing now.

Her eyes darken. "Kolya..."

"Don't." Our father's death is not a topic I want to discuss with her. Ever. "Just stay the fuck out of my relationship with Chloe, understand?"

And before she can aggravate me further, I stride away.

I spend the afternoon catching up on business—even with my brothers assuming most of the responsibility for our family's conglomerate, there's plenty for me to do—and then I turn on the video feed from Chloe's room, where she should be getting ready for dinner.

Sure enough, I catch her emerging from her closet, already dressed in an evening gown. For a second, I wonder how she managed to change without assistance —I was planning to go help her in a minute—but then my sister steps into the camera's view.

"Stand here," she tells Chloe, guiding her to the window. "Since your arm is out of commission, I'll do your makeup."

I lean back in my chair, watching with amusement as she begins to paint Chloe's face with the various tubes and brushes she takes out of a small bag. I remember her painting her dolls much the same way when she was little; I guess she's never outgrown it. I don't mind. Chloe doesn't need any makeup—she's beautiful without it—but this is something women do when they dress up, and I like my zaychik dressed up. Or dressed down. Or better yet, completely naked.

My body hardens at the thought, and I have to take a few deep breaths to control my accelerating pulse. I can't have her. Not yet. No matter how much it physically hurts to deny myself.

For now, I can only watch and plan what I'll do to her once she's completely well.

CHLOE

To my relief, the atmosphere at dinner isn't strained in the least, partially because Pavel and Lyudmila join us instead of staying in the kitchen. Their presence adds to the festive feel of the meal nearly as much as all the exotic, colorful dishes populating the table.

Pavel has outdone himself today; it's more like a gourmet wedding celebration than an at-home birthday.

Aside from the gorgeously arranged, delicious food, there's plenty of alcohol, everything from wine to vodka and cognac. Every few minutes, either Pavel, Lyudmila, or Nikolai proposes a toast to the birthday girl, and we drink—or in my case, take a sip of wine. There's no way I can keep up with the copious amounts of hard liquor the Russians are consuming. Well, everyone except Slava. He's guzzling orange soda —a treat for special occasions, I'm guessing, as it's the first time I'm seeing the child drink anything but water.

As the meat course comes out, the volume and frequency of toasts go up until it feels like someone is raising a glass to Alina's health, beauty, smarts, or future success nonstop. The conversation is a boisterous mix of Russian and English, the latter likely solely for my sake. There's plenty of laughter too, along with jokes that don't always make sense when translated from Russian—"anecdotes," Nikolai calls them. They're something along the lines of "a donkey and a horse walk into a bar," but way more creative and elaborate. He explains that telling these funny anecdotes at social gatherings is a tradition in his country, and that just about every self-respecting Russian has a repertoire that they constantly replenish by scouring the internet and buying special books.

By the time Pavel disappears into the kitchen and emerges with a tea tray and a three-tier, candle-studded cake, I'm laughing so hard I'm convinced I've managed to get drunk despite my precautions. Nikolai out to amuse is not something I've seen before, and I have no defense against his dry, witty charm. Neither does anyone else at the table, it seems. Slava, hopped up on sugar and adult merriment, forgets all about keeping his distance from his father and climbs on his lap, while Alina drunkenly loops her arm around Nikolai's neck and gives him a big smooch, leaving a lipstick imprint on his cheek—the first time I've seen her act like a playful younger sister.

It makes me realize how reserved she and everyone else in this household usually are, how little of a normal family dynamic I've seen between them.

The realization brings me back to my senses, reawakening my caution, but then Alina blows out the candles among loud cheers and I forget that I'm not at a typical birthday celebration, that the gorgeous, sharply dressed man laughing with his family is as much my captor as my protector.

Nikolai is dangerous, and not just because I've seen him kill with my own eyes.

It's because he's so much more complex than a man without a conscience should be.

As I observe him closer, I realize that unlike everyone else, he doesn't seem drunk. There's a certain calculated quality to his laughter and jokes, to the charming, light-hearted façade he's assumed. It makes me recall Alina's assertion that her brother does nothing by accident, that all his actions are planned.

Still, even this can't keep my heart from squeezing with tenderness when I notice the genuine softness in his eyes as he carefully embraces his son—who's now giggling and bouncing on his lap while chattering away in Russian. I catch the word "Papa" in the rapid stream of words, and my chest swells with an emotion so intense tears prickle behind my eyelids.

Daddy, Slava called him in Russian, unprompted.

They're finally bonding as father and son.

Blinking back the burning moisture, I look down at my half-eaten dessert—only to feel the back of my neck tingle with familiar awareness. Sure enough, when I glance up, Nikolai's gaze is trained on me, his tiger eyes filled with unnerving intensity.

I was right. He's not drunk in the least. If anything, the alcohol has made him sharper, more focused.

"You don't like the cake, zaychik?" he murmurs, his voice too low to carry to the rest of the table, where Pavel and Lyudmila are loudly toasting Alina yet again. "Or are you simply too full?"

My face warms. Why does that simple question feel like a sexual innuendo? It shouldn't, not even with that seductive, intimate edge to his tone.

He's holding his son, for fuck's sake.

"I'm stuffed," I say, only to immediately want to take the words back as his mouth curls in a wicked half-smile.

It's Slava who comes to my rescue. "Daddy," he says loudly in English, twisting his little body to wrap his arms around Nikolai's neck. "*My* daddy."

Nikolai's gaze shifts to his son, and the wicked gleam in his eyes disappears, replaced by an expression so achingly tender my heart all but dissolves in my chest. This is so much more than the child casually dropping a "Papa."

Slava is officially claiming Nikolai as his father, embracing him with all the possessiveness in his little Molotov heart.

I force the words out through the growing lump in my throat. "Yes, darling. That's *your* daddy. Good job." The stupid tears are back to burning my eyelids, and I realize my joy at witnessing this is bittersweet, tinged with envy.

As a child, I dreamed of meeting my father—and embracing him exactly this way.

Fortunately, Nikolai is not looking at me. All his attention is on his son. Murmuring something in Russian, he gently smooths back Slava's hair… and my throat threatens to close completely as I catch a tiny tremor in his strong, callused hand.

What I'm seeing on Nikolai's face is just the tip of the emotional iceberg. The powerful, ruthless man in front of me is completely undone by his son.

Swallowing thickly, I force myself to look away before I also come undone. It's bad enough my body melts for him; now my heart is joining in as well. There's no way I can label him a psychopath going forward, no way for me to pretend that the ruthless killer I've fallen for is incapable of genuine emotions.

Whatever Nikolai might or might not feel for me, he's deeply in love with his young son.

1 7

CHLOE

The dinner party lasts late into the evening, so I don't get a chance to hang out with Alina afterward. By the time Nikolai carries me up to my room and helps me shower and change, I'm so drunk and exhausted I all but pass out in his arms.

It's not until the next morning that I realize that, contrary to my fears, I didn't end up in Nikolai's bed. Once more, he'd been the perfect nursemaid, taking care of me without demanding anything in return. Even the copious amount of alcohol hadn't undermined his self-control—though I'm guessing the fact that I was more or less comatose when he brought me upstairs helped his resolve.

After that scene with his son, I turned to wine to manage my unruly emotions, and between that, the painkiller I took earlier in the day, and my still-healing body, I was basically a humanoid log.

Fortunately, I don't have much of a hangover, so I

make it to breakfast on time. To my relief—and more than slight disappointment—Nikolai isn't there.

"On a call with Russia," Alina explains. Like me, she doesn't seem to be overly affected by the late-night festivities, and after breakfast, she joins me and Slava in our play lessons, even going so far as to chase her nephew in a game of tag despite wearing her usual uniform of a fancy dress and high heels.

"I have no idea how your toes don't fall off," I say, eyeing her stilettos, and she laughs, explaining that she's so used to wearing such shoes that sneakers feel weird to her.

"Russian women pride themselves on being able to tolerate all sorts of discomfort in the name of beauty," she tells me wryly. "It's our long-suffering, masochistic nature. So while leggings and such have made inroads in my home country, you'll have to pry our high-heeled shoes from our cold, dead feet."

I laugh and drop the topic. I really do like Alina. Her beauty was so intimidating at first that it took me a while to see past it. Now that I have, I realize that a lot of her initial reserve was a form of self-protection. With her family the way it is, she needs her glossy, prickly façade to conceal her vulnerability—and the trauma she's still recovering from.

Over the next few days, my wish of getting to know Alina better is fulfilled, partially because Nikolai has delegated much of my care to her. It's now she who helps me get dressed and shower, though he's still the one who changes the bandage on my arm when necessary.

I suspect it's because as I'm getting better, he doesn't trust his restraint to hold.

I don't mind. Not only does this enable me to maintain some semblance of emotional equilibrium when I do see him, but Alina and I are developing a real rapport. With my ankle quickly improving and my arm finally out of the sling, we go on short hikes near the house—during which she does swap her stilettos for stylish boots—and we spend a lot of time with Slava, whose English is progressing with lightning speed.

I think it helps him to listen to me talk with Alina; he's starting to pick up words and phrases I haven't formally taught him.

The only fly in the ointment is Alina's refusal to talk about what happened with her father—or in general expound on her family and her past. No matter how much I probe and pry, she discloses nothing, and with Nikolai avoiding me except during bandage changes and mealtimes, I'm no closer to getting answers.

In a way, I don't mind this either. As much as I'm dying to understand how a man who's becoming so openly affectionate with his son could've committed the terrible crime of patricide, not knowing all the details forces me to put it out of my mind. Same goes for the situation with Bransford; without any updates coming my way, I can go for hours, even days, without dwelling on the danger my biological father poses and what my future may hold.

These calm, easy days feel like an interlude out of time, a respite from the terrifying reality that is my life.

A respite that ends when the mystery girl arrives.

18

CHLOE

Slava and I are in front of the house, observing three squirrels chasing one another from tree to tree, when the black pickup truck rolls up the driveway. The windows aren't as darkly tinted as those of the deceased assassins' vehicle, but I still freeze in place, ambushed by a flashback so intense I break out in a cold sweat.

"Chloe? Chloe, who is it? Who is it, Chloe?"

I blink at Slava, who's tugging insistently at my sleeve, and force down the gruesome recollections of my Toyota getting smashed against the tree. I thought I was getting over what happened—even my nightmares have eased during these halcyon days—but I guess I was fooling myself.

I'm no more recovered from my trauma than Alina is from hers.

"Who is it?" Slava demands again, rocking back and forth on his heels as the truck comes to a stop some dozen feet from us. As both his English skills and his relationship with Nikolai have improved, he's become much more of an assertive—and occasionally annoying—little boy, much to my delight.

I manage a warm smile in his direction. "I don't know, darling. Let's see."

The two of us stare intently at the car as the driver's side opens and a petite young woman dressed in a pair of jeans, a tight-fitting white T-shirt, and scuffed hiking boots bounces out of the seat. Small-boned yet subtly curvy, with delicate, symmetrical features and thick blond hair piled up high in a messy bun, she looks to be seventeen or eighteen, and reminds me of a cross between Saoirse Ronan and Marilyn Monroe—if either were hopped up on speed.

Like a whirlwind, she descends on us. "Hey there! You must be Chloe." Before I can reply, she grabs my hand and pumps it enthusiastically. Then she drops down to her knees and beams at Slava. "*A ti Slavochka, da?*"

Her sudden switch to Russian catches me off-guard; she'd spoken to me in pure American English. Slava seems taken aback as well. None of the adults around him are usually this bubbly and energetic.

"Hi," I say as she jumps back up to her feet. Literally jumps, like a child. Maybe she's even younger than I thought? "I *am* Chloe. And you are?"

Her wide grin is dimpled, her gray eyes sparkling appealingly. "You can call me Masha."

"Nice to meet you, Masha. Are you—"

"Where's Nikolai?" she interrupts. "I'm here to see him."

Something pinches deep inside me, an ugly suspicion stirring in my mind. "He should be in his office. Do you want me to take you there?"

"No need," she says breezily and runs up to the house.

The pinching sensation transforms into an outright churning in my stomach. This girl is pretty—more than pretty. She's dazzling, even in her casual clothes. Put her in one of Alina's dresses, and she could strut her stuff down the runway—or at least on the red carpet, since she's not even my height. And while she's young, she's far from childlike; in fact, her self-assured manner makes me think she might not be a teenager at all. As I watch her disappear into the house, I can't help recalling that prior to meeting me, Nikolai was in the habit of flying in all sorts of beautiful women—which, for all I know, included this Masha.

How else does she seem to know where to go? Or has heard about Slava?

Or me?

That last bit doesn't fit this theory, I have to admit. If she's Nikolai's hookup, present or past, why would he tell her about me? Unless, of course, they have some weird friends-with-benefits situation going on, and, unlike me, she doesn't have a jealous bone in her body.

"Have you ever seen her before?" I ask Slava, doing my best to keep my tone casual. "I mean, prior to today?"

Slava blinks up at me. He understands some of what I say now, but not everything.

Heaving a sigh, I grab his hand and lead him to the house. I don't understand why I'm so anxious to find out who this young woman is—if Nikolai is losing interest in me, it can only be for the best. Yet no matter what my rational mind says, the mere thought of him with Masha makes me want to break every bone in her tiny, Marylin Monroe-like body.

19

CHLOE

Leaving Slava with Lyudmila in the kitchen, I head over to Nikolai's office, my ribcage tight as I go up the stairs.

It's stupid to be jealous. Irrational. But I can't help the green monster clawing at my chest. What if I have completely misinterpreted Nikolai's avoidance of me over the past two weeks? Maybe instead of fighting his desire for me, he's simply stopped wanting me. After all, taking care of my injuries could've made him view my body in a different light.

I've never been particularly insecure about said body, but I've also never been in a relationship with a man as wickedly gorgeous as Nikolai.

Wait, no, we're not in a relationship. That might've been happening before, when I thought he was a normal, law-abiding—albeit obscenely rich—man. I don't know what to call it now. If the person you've slept with is holding you captive while also protecting you from someone who wants to kill you, does that constitute a relationship? At least of the non-Stockholm syndrome variety? Not to mention, he's still technically my employer—the cash envelopes have been arriving in my room every Tuesday like clockwork.

Shelving those ruminations for now, I approach his office door. It's closed, and when I press my ear to it, I can hear voices speaking Russian. As I listen, I can discern the new arrival's bright, feminine tones, along with Nikolai's deep, smooth, dangerously seductive ones.

"What are you doing?"

Startled, I whip around to face Alina, who's standing in the hallway, head cocked inquisitively. "Um…"

Amusement glimmers in her eyes. "Are you spying on my brother?"

"No, of course not." I can feel my face burning as I scramble for a good explanation. "I was just—"

"Come." She grabs my elbow and tugs me down the hallway to her room, where she all but pushes me inside before turning to face me. "Okay, now tell me. What's going on?"

"Nothing."

She arches an eyebrow, looking disconcertingly like her brother.

I cave. "Okay, fine. There's this young woman who's just arrived, and—"

"You mean Masha?"

My heart sinks. "You know her?"

"She's Valery's newest find." At my uncomprehending look, she says, "My youngest brother collects people with various useful skills. I have no idea what hers are, but I ran into her briefly at his place before we left Moscow, and unlike his other pets, she introduced herself."

"His pets?"

She nods. "That's what I call them. He inspires almost pathological loyalty in these people."

Huh, okay. Maybe she's not Nikolai's hookup—or at least not only that.

"Has Nikolai met her also? Like back in Moscow? Or—"

"Chloe..." Alina hesitates, then says gently, "I don't think you have to worry about her in that way."

My face heats again. "I'm not—"

"You are, and I get it. She's unusually pretty. But she's not here to warm Nikolai's bed."

"So you know what she's here for?" My relief is quickly eclipsed by anxiety-tinged curiosity. For some reason, this Masha's arrival feels portentous, like a bad omen.

Alina hesitates again, then shakes her head. "Not really. You should talk to Nikolai about all this."

"All what? Is it connected to your father?"

Her flinch is nearly imperceptible, as is her quickly hidden surprise. "I can't say," she says, her expression carefully veiled. "My brother is the one with all the answers."

I stare at her, my mind churning. If this isn't about her father... "Does this have something to do with *me*?"

She sighs. "Just talk to Nikolai, Chloe. Please."

And before I can press her further, she shepherds me out of her room.

I don't get a chance to talk to Nikolai until later that evening. He spends the entire afternoon in his office with Masha—I know because I walk past his door dozens of times. At some point, Pavel joins them, and the murmur of two voices becomes three, with the bear-man's growl easily identifiable.

By dinnertime, Masha leaves—Slava and I watch her pickup truck depart through his bedroom window —but a family meal is not a good time to drill Nikolai about a potentially combustible issue, so I swallow my burning questions and wait.

My moment arrives after dinner, when Lyudmila clears the table and everyone gets up to go to their rooms. All dinner long, I have felt Nikolai's intense tiger gaze on me, have sensed the speculation in his stare.

Whatever's going on does concern me. I'm almost certain of it now.

As if wise to my plan, Alina grabs Slava and disappears up the stairs with record speed, leaving me and Nikolai alone in the dining room.

"Can we grab a nightcap?" I ask as he turns to leave

as well. My voice is steady, even as my heart beats unevenly. This is dangerous in more ways than one. Not only am I risking an end to the peace and calm that's reigned in my life over the past two weeks, but my gunshot wound is almost fully healed.

If Nikolai is still interested in me in that way, there's little to stop him from acting on that desire.

He turns back to face me. His jaw is taut, his eyes gleaming like ancient amber. "A nightcap? I thought you weren't big on digestifs, zaychik."

I swallow against the dryness in my throat. "I'm in the mood for a little cognac."

If nothing else, I could use it to bolster my courage.

Nikolai's voice roughens. "All right. Give me a minute." He disappears into the kitchen and emerges with a tray of crystal decanters surrounded by drinking glasses. Pavel must be off server duty tonight —that or Nikolai also wants privacy.

As he pours us each a drink, I sit back down, surreptitiously wiping my damp palms on the skirt of my evening gown. It's made of a silk material in a coral-peach hue that, according to Alina, makes my complexion look "all golden and glowy." I wonder if Nikolai thinks that too, or if all he sees when he looks at me now is his son's tutor.

Which would be fine. Amazing, really. I shouldn't want such a dangerous man fixated on me, making all sorts of unnerving claims about threads of fate and—

"What did you want to discuss, zaychik?" Nikolai's voice is once again brushed velvet as he sinks into the seat across from me. Swirling the cognac inside his glass, he regards me over the rim, lids at half-mast. "I'm assuming you're not here because you're suddenly craving my company."

My skin flushes all over. I actually am craving his company, as reluctant as I am to admit it. Ever since our flower-picking expedition, we haven't spent much time together—at least not by ourselves. At mealtimes, Alina and Slava serve as a buffer, and Lyudmila and Pavel are always around in the background. Even the bandage changes, the one time he'd enter my room by himself, stopped once my wound scabbed over and no longer needed to be covered.

The truth is, I've barely interacted with him in recent days, and I've missed it. I've missed our conversations, his unwavering focus on me... even the way he makes me feel like a mouse being toyed with by a scary-hot cat. Of course, I can't have him know this. Not when I still have a shred of hope that someday my life will go back to normal—a normal that won't involve dangerous men who torture and kill.

Taking a breath, I launch right into it. "Why was she here? Who is she?"

He's silent for a few moments, studying me in that intense way of his while the cognac goes untouched in his hand. "She's an asset," he finally says. "My brother Valery sent her over when I explained your situation."

My heart leaps, and my mouth goes dry. After my conversation with Alina, I wondered if this might be the case, but to hear it confirmed so bluntly... Shakily, I reach for my cognac and take a sip, letting it light a path of fire down my esophagus. "What kind of asset?" I ask when the urge to cough subsides.

"Originally, the government kind. Now ours."

A spy then, or some other kind of operative—and not nearly as young as I thought if she has this kind of background. I suppose I can see it. If I'd met Masha on the street, I would've never suspected her of being any sort of "asset," but that's probably the point. That bubbly, youthful exterior makes for an effective mask.

Before I can ask what exactly her role is in my situation, Nikolai speaks again. "Zaychik…" His tone is once more disconcertingly gentle. "It's confirmed. Bransford is your biological father."

My heart rate spikes further, a chill prickling the skin on my arms. "You mean…"

"Masha obtained a DNA sample from Bransford. It matches yours."

Matches mine. My stomach twists nauseatingly, the chill spreading to engulf the rest of my body. I've known this had to be the case ever since Nikolai told me what his older brother had uncovered, but a part of me must've been still holding out a sliver of hope.

A hope that's now crushed and ground to dust.

"Why did you—" I stop to clear the hoarseness in my throat. "Why did you want to confirm it?"

I don't want to think about how this Masha obtained Bransford's sample, or mine. Actually, the latter must've been easy: my toothbrush, a few loose hairs on my pillow, a cup I drank from… A presidential candidate with all the accompanying security, though—

"Because I needed to be certain."

I blink, realizing I've let my thoughts wander away from the key question. "But why? I mean, don't get me wrong, I'm grateful." At least I think I am. Is it better to know you're the offspring of a murdering rapist, or to just suspect it strongly?

Nikolai sets his glass down, the liquid inside still untouched. "I promised to protect you, zaychik."

The chill ripples over me again, my mind venturing down a path I wish it wouldn't go. "You did. You have. I'm safe here, aren't I?" At least from Bransford.

He leans forward, his big, warm palms covering my frozen hands. "You are. And you'll be even safer once he's no longer a threat to you."

I stare into his hypnotic irises, that rich, deep gold speckled with green. "Not a threat how?" I've avoided thinking about the future for this very reason: because I can't imagine one where Bransford *won't* be a threat. Like a turtle, I've been content to hide inside my shell, taking it one day, one hour, at a time, all the while telling myself that eventually, I'll get it figured out and bring Mom's murderer to justice.

Not Nikolai, though. He hasn't been hiding from reality—he's been planning. And it's the nature of those plans that makes icy fingers dance down my spine.

I have a feeling Nikolai's idea of justice differs drastically from mine.

He smiles as if I were a naïve child. "You don't need to worry, zaychik. I'm handling it."

For a brief, cowardly moment, I'm tempted to do just that: not worry, leave the matter in his capable, ruthless hands... the ones holding mine so possessively, so gently.

The same hands that had taken two lives in front of me without hesitation.

It's that memory, that vivid recollection of the tortured assassin's screams, that decides it for me. I may have developed a knack for avoiding reality, but even I can't close my eyes and pretend to be blind.

"What are you going to do to him?" My voice is as unsteady as my pulse. "Nikolai, please, I have to know. What are you going to do?"

The tiny muscles around his eyes tighten—the only change in his expression. "Nothing he doesn't deserve."

I draw back, pulling my hands out of his grasp. "You can't kill him."

"Why not?" His voice is even, his tone as bland as if we were speaking of going to a party. Leaning back, he picks up his cognac again, and this time, he takes a leisurely sip before setting it down.

I stare at him incredulously. "Because he's a *person.*" How is this not self-evident? "An evil person, sure, but you can't just go about killing anyone who—"

"Who tries to kill you? I can, and I will."

My heart misses a beat. He means it, I can see it, and the realization fills me with all kinds of fucked-up emotions: gratitude overlaid with terror, hope edged

135

with dread, and most disturbing, a vengeful sort of glee.

I want Bransford dead for what he did to my mom. I want it so badly I can taste it. And I want it for myself as well. I want my life back, my freedom, my peace of mind. I want to sleep through the night without nightmares and walk down the street without fear. I want to stop seeing danger in every pickup truck, every unfamiliar face.

I want Bransford six feet under, and if Nikolai makes it happen, I'll be free... and as much of a murderer as he is.

It's that last thought that squashes my dark longing. As much as I want freedom and vengeance, we're talking about murder—cold-blooded, premeditated murder. It was one thing for Nikolai to dispatch the two armed assassins in the woods; as disturbing as it had been to witness, what he did is ultimately no different than what a cop in his situation might've done, minus the torture bit. What we're discussing now is a whole other level of fucked up, and though some part of me can't help but rejoice in Nikolai's willingness to protect me to this extent, I can't stand by and let it happen.

Since appealing to common-sense morality didn't work, I try a different tack. "Nikolai, please. Be reasonable. He's a prominent political figure. You can't just kill him. It would be an assassination, one with major global ramifications. The FBI, the CIA, the media—"

"I know. Which is why I had to be certain of his guilt."

Another chill runs down my spine. His face is implacable, his voice still disturbingly even. He's thought this through; this isn't some impulse on his part.

To protect me, he's going to take out a presidential candidate, and there's nothing I can do to change his mind.

I try anyway, if for no other reason than to protect *him*. "What about your family? The life you're building here with Slava? If they find out you're behind it—"

"They won't."

"How can you be so sure? There will be a global manhunt, the kind not seen since—"

"Zaychik..." Leaning forward, he covers my hands again, making me realize I've been wringing them on the table. His voice is soft, his tone eerily calm as his gaze holds mine. "I know what I'm doing. Bransford will die, and it will be of natural causes. His party will mourn, the nation will mourn, and then they'll move on to another shiny new thing, some other silver-tongued politician."

"Natural causes? At fifty-five?"

"A heart defect, hitherto undiagnosed. It will be properly tragic." He sits back, picking up his glass. "Where there's a will, there's a way—and us Molotovs excel at finding those ways."

20

NIKOLAI

She stands up shakily, staring at me, and I fight the urge to gather her into my arms. I fight it because underneath the need to comfort are darker, more dangerous urges, ones born of a hunger so deep and savage it scares even me.

Once I give in to it, once I unleash the beast snarling inside me, there will be no going back.

Two weeks I've given her. For two century-long weeks, I've done the impossible and stayed away. Well, not entirely. I've spent dozens of hours watching her through the cameras in Slava's room and in her bedroom, but that and our brief interactions at mealtimes have only added to my torment.

I've never thought of myself as a masochist, but I must be, because I've willingly embraced the exquisite torture of having her within arm's reach yet not allowing myself to possess her.

And tonight, it seems, is the ultimate test of my self-control. Because she's finally sought me out, though not for the reasons I wished. A part of me hoped that she'd miss me, that she'd come to me because she wants me with the same desperation I want her.

Because she's ready to be mine, with all that it implies.

"I should go to bed," she says, her voice unsteady, and I have to quell a surge of disappointment. What did I expect? She's shocked, and for a good reason. Few ordinary citizens realize how easy it is to make a murder look like something else—if that's the desired outcome. All the high-profile assassinations and radiation poisonings that make the news are meant to be newsworthy. They're a message, a warning to others who may try to go against the establishment.

For every exotic poison that screams of secret government involvement, there are dozens of health failures and routine accidents that clear away the obstacles in the paths of powerful, ruthless people... people like my family.

This isn't the first covert assassination I've had to plan.

Originally, I wasn't going to tell Chloe any of it. She would've learned about Bransford's death on the news, same as everyone else, and whatever suspicions she'd have harbored at that point would've been nowhere near as burdensome as the knowledge she's now carrying. But she came to me tonight demanding answers, and I couldn't bring myself to lie to her. In a way, my sister is to blame for that, too. Though Alina has kept her mouth shut around Chloe, she's been coming to me almost daily, insisting that Chloe has a right to know what I'm planning, that it should be her decision.

I strongly disagree about the latter, but I've come to see some merit in the former. I don't want my zaychik stressing about her situation, worrying that at any moment more assassins might show up on our doorstep. Not that they'd get through, but still, it has to weigh on her, the knowledge that someone out there wants her dead.

That her biological father wants her dead.

No, it's for the best that I've told her. Masha needs at least a few weeks to complete her mission, and this way, Chloe knows that I'm taking care of it and she doesn't need to worry.

Having lodged her objections, she can relax with a clear conscience. It's my decision, my sin, not hers.

Getting up, I smile at her, hoping she can't see the twisted hunger in my eyes, the dark need that bubbles in my veins like fresh lava. "Of course. If you're tired, go to bed, zaychik."

As much as I want to claim her, tonight is not the night. I'm too hungry, too close to the edge, and though her injuries are all but healed, she's still nowhere near where she needs to be to handle me.

She backs away, as if she's read my mind, but then

her shoulders pull back and her delicate chin comes up. "No," she says firmly, stepping around the table toward me. "I'm not leaving until you promise to find another one of those 'ways.'"

21

CHLOE

I know this is a bad idea. I also know that I can't be a coward and slink away like he hasn't just admitted to me that he plans to assassinate a man on my behalf. A terrible, awful man, but still a man... who happens to be my biological father.

Something dark flickers in Nikolai's eyes as he gazes down at me, and belatedly, I notice the dangerous tautness of his jaw.

"Zaychik..." His voice is a soft growl. "You should go. Now. While you still can."

My breath stutters to a halt as the realization of what he means crashes into me, ratcheting up my pulse and paralyzing my muscles.

He still wants me, badly, yet for whatever reason, he's restraining himself.

I should listen to him. I should back off and back away while he's giving me this chance. If I don't, it'll change everything, put an end to this interlude out of

142

time, bridge the distance between us that's kept me so safe.

Because the biggest danger to me is not out there.

It's here.

It's always been him.

I will my muscles to move, to obey the frantic commands of my brain, but I might as well be wishing to bench-press a car. All I can do is stare up at him, mouth dry and heart pounding as pulsing tension gathers low in my belly, peaking my nipples and painting my skin with swirls of heat.

I can see the savage storm brewing in his eyes, can feel the crackle of that electric charge in the air, yet I remain still, frozen and mute, the perfect prey for the taking.

"Chloe…" The hoarsely uttered word is equal parts warning and capitulation. Slowly, with exaggerated gentleness, he cups my face with both hands, the heat of his broad palms burning my chilled skin. His eyes are a hypnotic alchemist's gold as he whispers, "My sweet zaychik, it's over. You've lost your last chance to escape."

22

CHLOE

I'm still frozen in place when his lips descend on mine, as inevitably and violently as lightning striking a tree on a plain. The shock of it jolts my whole body, scalding every cell on the way.

There's no finesse to his kiss, no gentleness. He doesn't ask, he takes. With my head immobilized between his palms, he plunders every inch of my mouth, sucking me into a vortex of savage desire, a lust so dark and volcanic it scorches me from deep within.

He tastes like cognac and danger, like every twisted, secretive yearning of mine. The heady flavor intoxicates me, the sensual notes of his cedar-and-bergamot cologne making my head spin. Whatever thoughts of resistance I still entertained evaporate, my willpower dissolving like a grain of sugar in hot tea. With a helpless moan, I arch against him, my belly pressing against his groin as my hands clutch his sides.

He's fully hard, the thick bulge in his pants jutting

against my softness, reminding me of what it felt like to have him inside. The memory evokes both arousal and trepidation—it hadn't been easy, taking in something that size. But even that thought soon disappears, burned away by the fierce heat of desire, destroyed by the brutal seduction of his merciless kiss.

I forget where we are. I forget everything, so much so that I'm startled when he pulls away to scoop me up against his chest. It's only when he starts up the stairs, taking them two at a time, that my head clears enough for a sliver of rational thought.

What on earth am I doing? This isn't what I intended. It's the polar opposite, in fact. My goal was to talk to him, to convince him not to—

With a low growl, he pins me against the wall in the upstairs hallway and reclaims my mouth, as if he can't bear not to taste me all the way to his room, and I forget all about my goals. I forget that I exist outside of this moment, that there's anything out there but him.

We merge, or at least that's what it feels like. His mouth is fused to mine, his breath is in my lungs, his scent is in my nostrils. His powerful body surrounds me, all heat and hardness and raw, primal maleness. I'm vertical now, standing on tiptoes as he devours my lips, and his hands roam over my back, my sides, my ass, squeezing and kneading the latter, working the long dress up my thighs. Breathless, I grip the cool, silken strands of his hair as he lifts me up until my legs are wrapped around his hips and my pelvis is riding on his, my aching sex grinding against his erection.

We kiss, our tongues dueling, until we're completely out of air. Then his mouth trails over to my neck, raining hot, biting kisses over the tender hollow near my ear. Moaning, I arch my head back and grind harder against him, lost to everything but the dark, scorching pleasure. The tension inside me is coiling and building, my nerve endings so sensitized the movement of air feels like a touch on my skin.

I'm going to come from dry-humping him, I realize with distant surprise.

It's going to happen again.

And then it does, the release as startling as it is welcome. My fingers convulsively clench in his hair and my inner muscles spasm as ecstasy rips through my body, curling my toes and wrenching a cry from my throat. Only he doesn't stop; he keeps going, rocking his hips into my pelvis, intensifying the aftershocks blasting my core. Eyes squeezing shut, I cry out again, and like an animal claiming his mate, he bites down on my neck as his big, callused hand delves into my bodice, squeezing my naked breast as his thumb grazes over my—

"Chloe? Nikolai, what are you—oh fuck. Never mind."

Alina's voice wrenches me out of the heated delirium, and I stiffen, my eyes flying open. Sure enough, over Nikolai's shoulder, I see her backing away, her pale face uncharacteristically pink. Before I can say anything, or process the fact that this is the second time she's caught us nearly fucking, she spins on her heel and disappears back into her room.

Which is just down the hallway.

The public hallway where anyone could've seen us —and heard me coming.

My face, my body, even the roots of my hair feel as if they're on fire as Nikolai pulls back to stare at me. His golden eyes are heavy-lidded; his hair, with my hands still clenched in it, is mussed; his sensual lips are wet and swollen, parted in an expression of pure lust.

It's the way a fallen angel might look after committing his first sin—except this angel has never known an innocent existence.

He's been the devil all along.

I dampen my lips. "Your sister—"

"Fuck my sister."

Before I can address that furiously growled sentiment, he sweeps me up in his powerful arms and carries me to his room with long, impatient strides.

23

NIKOLAI

I should stop, or at the very least slow down, but I can't. Now that I've tasted her again, the hunger inside me is too strong, too feral. Like an alcoholic who's downed his first drink of the night, I can't even imagine moderation. The dark need pulses in my veins, a drumbeat of sexual desire and a deeper, less defined yearning, a craving that seems to emanate from my very soul.

With the fraying remnants of my self-control, I lay her down on the bed, careful not to hurt her arm. There's a scab there now, marring her silken, golden-hued skin. The sight of it feeds the savage beast inside me, filling my chest with equal parts possessiveness and rage.

She's mine, and I'll annihilate anyone who's ever hurt her.

No one will ever lay a finger on her… except me.

Already, without my willing it, my hands are on her

dress, ripping at the pretty, flimsy fabric, tearing it off her body in a furious campaign to bare it to my gaze. Her breasts pop out of her bodice first, two small, delicious globes tipped with erect brown nipples, followed by her narrow ribcage and flat belly, all covered by that glowing, bronzed skin that makes me think of captured sunshine, of warmth, light, and purity—all the things I hunger for, everything I want.

Her lower body is next, her barely-there thong all but disintegrating in my hands to expose a pussy that's as delicate and soft as I remember. My mouth waters at the recollection of her sweet, rich flavor, of how those tender folds felt on my lips, under my tongue, clenched on my fingers... fingers that can't help but grip her thighs, pulling them wide apart.

Her soft brown eyes meet mine, slumberous with desire, edged with that provoking wariness, and the last shreds of my self-control unravel. Like a starving animal, I fall upon her, burying my face between her thighs, lapping at her slickness, gorging on her salt-and-berry essence, on the warmth and sunlight that is her.

She gasps and grips my head, her fingers clenching in my hair as she arches underneath me, writhing at each greedy stroke of my tongue. Soon, my fingers join in as well, toying with her clit while I lick her opening, reveling in the wetness I find there. She's as delicious as I remembered, all silk and heat and molten honey, and though my cock is on the verge of bursting, I can't tear myself away from what I'm doing, can't stop until I feel her come again.

And come she does. With a choked cry, she bucks underneath me, her back bowing off the bed as her fingers tighten in my hair, all but tearing it out by the roots as more delicious slickness coats my lips and tongue.

The surge of satisfaction is as intense as it is brief, my lust having only sharpened with her orgasm. Hot blood pounds in my temples, my balls drawn tight and every muscle in my body tense with need. There's no gentleness left inside me, no patience, just raw, primal hunger to possess and claim, to bury my throbbing cock inside her heat.

Driven by a purely animalistic instinct, I flip her over and loop my arm under her hips, raising her shapely little ass toward me until she's standing on all fours. Her smooth cheeks are a little fuller, a little rounder than the last time I saw her naked, the rosebud of her sphincter a tiny, tempting dot, and my hunger intensifies to a knife's edge sharpness, my body tightening to an unbearable degree. I'm barely cognizant of my actions as I rip open my fly and free my cock, then line it up against her gleaming slit.

I have to have her. Now.

The drumbeat of desire grows deafening, drowning out everything, blurring the world around us. I'm no longer man; I'm nothing more than primal hunger, a savage, atavistic need.

Gripping her slim hips, I plunge inside, reveling in

the slick grip of her inner walls, in the delicious tightness of her narrow passage. She cries out, a sound of pain, but I can't stop, can't do anything but thrust even deeper, taking her, claiming her, satisfying the feral lust scorching me inside.

Mine. All fucking mine. My hips pump savagely, my heart pounding like a fist against my chest. Distantly, I'm aware that I'm being far too rough, but I can no more slow down than I can let her go. She's all silky tightness and wet heat, the closest thing to heaven a man can know. Her pleading gasps and cries only spur me on, heightening my lust, fueling the beast inside me.

I fuck her like there's no tomorrow, like nothing outside this moment matters. Maintaining my grip on her with one hand, I wind the other in her hair and pull, making her arch her back as I thrust in harder, deeper, imprinting my brand on her tender flesh. I can feel the orgasm boiling up inside me, my balls tightening until they're nearly as hard as my throbbing cock, and as she screams my name and spasms around me, the release crashes over me like a tsunami, sending ecstasy exploding through my nerve endings and painting the world around me bright white.

24

CHLOE

Dazed, I flop onto my belly as soon as Nikolai lets go of my hair and pulls out of my swollen, twitching flesh. Even with the orgasmic aftershocks still rippling through me, my sex feels battered, my insides sore. My thoughts are scrambled too, my mind as sluggish as if I were emerging from a deep sleep.

Despite that, when he gathers me against his side and begins murmuring sweet nothings, I again experience that unusual sense of peace, the one I've known only in his arms. My eyes drift shut, a floating sensation coming over me as he strokes and pets me, raining light, soothing kisses over my face and neck, massaging away the aches and bruises from his rough handling. Eventually, my disjointed thoughts coalesce into something coherent, and I force open my eyelids to find his mesmerizing eyes peering into mine, the gold-hued amber of his irises streaked with the darkest green.

"Zaychik…" His voice is soft, his expression hard to read as he curves his large palm over my cheek. "I didn't use a condom."

For a moment, the words don't make sense to me. Then, with a jolt of adrenaline, I become aware of a warm wetness between my legs and on my thighs.

A lot of wetness. Way more than I've ever felt.

My heartbeat spikes, the floaty feeling disappearing. Pulling back sharply, I sit up. "What do you mean? I'm not on anything. I ran out of pills weeks ago. I thought —I thought you always wore a condom." I dart a glance at the thick white liquid on my naked thighs, trying not to panic as I frantically count the days.

When was my period? Was it this week or last week? Why haven't I bothered to keep track? I know it's been several days since I've stopped bleeding, but maybe—

"I do." Nikolai sits up as well, the powerful muscles in his chest and arm flexing as he rakes his hand through his hair, mussing the black locks further. "At least I always have until today."

I finally recall when my period started: early last week, almost twelve days ago. Last Monday was when I had to ask Alina for supplies.

I'm roughly in the middle of my cycle.

I must look as panicked as I feel because Nikolai tilts his head, regarding me with that same indecipherable expression. "The timing is just right, isn't it? Or more precisely, wrong?"

I nod, my hand instinctively moving to my stomach.

"Why—" I stop to steady my shaking voice. "Why didn't you use a condom?"

The enigmatic gleam in his eyes deepens as he moves toward me. "Why don't we get cleaned up and then talk more?"

I must still be in shock because I don't voice any objections as he scoops me up and carries me to the bathroom. Instead, I let him take care of me in the shower the way he'd done when I was hurt. His touch is again gentle, soothing and tender, even as his cock grows harder with each stroke of his callus-roughened hands over my wet, naked body.

By the time he's done washing away the evidence of our mistake, he's fully erect, and his hands are moving over me with growing intent, cupping my breasts and playing with my nipples, venturing between my thighs to find my clit. It should be too much, too soon, but my body responds as if it hasn't just survived a cataclysmic upheaval of its senses, as if the savage fucking that's left me so overwhelmed had been nothing but a preview of the main event.

My breathing picks up, a tension gathering low in my stomach as his lips slant over mine in a deep, searching kiss, then venture over to my ear, my neck, my shoulder. Panting, I clutch at his shoulders as he wraps my wet hair around his fist and arches me backward over his powerfully muscled arm, lifting my breasts toward him like a sacrificial offering. His broad back shields me from the water spray as he bends over me, latching on to one nipple, then another, the hot, powerful suction of his mouth sending tugs of sensation straight down to my core, heightening my growing arousal.

Still, I'm sore inside, way too sore to feel pleasure as two of his fingers push into me, forcing apart the swollen, tender tissues. That is, until those fingers curve inside me, finding a spot that makes sparks detonate behind my closed eyelids and taking me over the edge so swiftly I can barely gasp out his name.

The spasms are still rippling through my body when he releases my nipple with a wet *pop* and guides me down to my knees while still shielding me from the shower spray with his body. Dazedly, I blink up at him, only to realize what he wants as he slaps the hard, massive column of his cock against my cheek, then drags the tip over to my mouth.

On instinct, I brace my hands on his muscled thighs and part my lips, taking him in as far as he'll go. I've given blow jobs before, but this feels different, nothing like those casual, playful times with my ex-boyfriends. I'm not in control—he is—and there's nothing playful in the merciless way he fucks my mouth. His hands grip my skull, holding me still for his deep, slow thrusts, and it's all I can do not to gag as he goes farther down my throat with each stroke.

It shouldn't be hot—he's using me solely for his pleasure—but something about being treated like a fuck doll sends pulses of heat directly to my clit. He's taking what he wants from my body, and it's both degrading and perversely liberating. There's nothing complicated in this exchange; I please him simply by existing, by being nothing more than a warm, wet mouth for his use. My eyes scrunch shut, tears leaking out the sides as he picks up pace, forcing his big cock down my aching throat, yet the urge to gag remains quiescent, even as my mouth floods with enough saliva to fill a lake. It drips down my chin, my neck, my chest, but none of that matters because I can sense the tension building in his body, can feel his thick shaft swelling in my mouth even more. With a groan, he thrusts in so deep I lose the ability to breathe, and warm liquid spurts down my throat as his fingers clench tightly in my hair, tugging on the roots hard enough to make me wince.

By the time he pulls out of my throat, I'm so desperate for air my nails are digging frantically into his thighs. Yet when I open my watering eyes and look up to meet his gaze, I shiver with pleasure at the warm possessiveness reflected there.

"Zaychik..." His voice is a dark, velvety rasp as he hooks his hands under my arms and lifts me to my feet, then steadies me until I regain my balance. Holding my shoulder gently with one hand, he rinses the cum and saliva off me with the other, then cups my chin, staring down at me with a peculiarly intent expression.

My pulse kicks up anew, a strange premonition tightening my stomach as he says softly, "You are everything to me, the source of my greatest happiness and pleasure. I want you with me for the rest of our lives, for as long as breath remains in our bodies. Fate brought you to my door, delivered you to me like the gift you are, and I couldn't be more grateful."

My heart is now in my throat, my breath coming so fast my vision is going gray. This can't possibly be heading where I think it's heading. There's no way he's—

"Chloe Emmons..." He frames my face with his broad palms, his tiger eyes filled with a fiercely tender light. "I want you to marry me. I want you to be my wife."

25

CHLOE

For a moment, I'm convinced I misheard him. Because there's no way he's proposing, not when we've known each other less than a month. Except there's no mistaking the intensity in his hypnotic stare, no hiding from the fact that he's just used the words "marry" and "wife."

My mind spins frantically as I clasp his powerful wrists, instinctively tugging his hands down from my face. The shower behind him is still running, filling the spacious stall with steam, but I'm all of a sudden freezing, goosebumps rippling over my wet skin.

"Nikolai, I…" I have no idea what to say, how to approach something so insane. Finally, I blurt, "You're joking, right?"

His gaze darkens. "Why would I joke about this?"

"Because… because we hardly know each other!"

He lays his hands on my shoulders and squeezes lightly, his tone remaining soft even as his jaw hardens dangerously. "I know everything I need to know about you."

"Well, I don't. Know about you, I mean." I back out of his hold and wipe a shaking hand over my face to rid it of the water droplets. My heart hammers unevenly, my stomach knotting at his rapidly darkening expression as I grope for the shower stall door. "Nikolai, please, don't get me wrong—I'm super flattered. It's just... this isn't a good idea right now." Or ever.

I may have fallen for this lethally gorgeous man, but I haven't forgotten who and what he is—or what he's about to do for me.

I'm not cut out to be a mafia wife, even if that's not the formal label.

He watches my retreat with narrowed eyes, steam billowing in the air behind his powerful body, and it's all I can do not to trip over the bathroom mat as I step out and grab a towel.

There's no need for me to be so freaked out.

He asked and I refused.

End of story.

"What do you need to know about me?" He steps out after me, his movements soft and deliberate. A predator following his prey. "What will it take for you to say yes?"

"Well..." I wrap the towel around myself, frantically searching for the least offensive answer. There isn't one, so I'm forced to opt for the truth. "Nikolai, I just can't marry you. We're too different. Our values, the

way we approach things… The truth is, I don't think—"
My heart jumps at the storm gathering in his eyes, but
I'm committed, so I plow ahead. "I don't think this can
work long term."

He stills, his hand halfway to his own towel. Then,
slowly and deliberately, he pulls it off the rack and
dries himself, his eyes trained on me the whole time,
his face now darker than a moonless night.

I swallow hard as the tense silence grows. "I should
go to bed. We can talk more in the morning."

He moves like the big feline he reminds me of. A
blur of explosive motion, and he's between me and the
bathroom door, chiseled muscles flexing as he stares
down at me, golden eyes in slits.

"No, zaychik," he says softly. "*We* should go to bed.
And tomorrow, you will marry me. No matter how you
feel."

26

CHLOE

I wake up bleary-eyed, my head pounding and my body aching all over. Suppressing a groan, I attempt to roll over onto my side, only to find that I'm pinned in place by a heavy arm slung over my torso.

Adrenaline floods my veins, clearing away the fog of sleep, and I realize where I am.

In bed with Nikolai.

My breath catches, and I carefully turn my head to look at him. I've only seen him asleep once before, the one other time we spent the night together, and I'm again struck by how beautiful and dangerously animalistic he looks in repose, with jet-black lashes fanning over his sharp cheekbones and dark stubble shadowing the hard lines of his jaw. Sleep doesn't soften his starkly molded features; instead, it lends them a savage kind of sensuality, a darkly primitive appeal.

Even now, there's something predatory, something

wicked in the way his sensuous lips are curved, the way they're slightly parted.

Realizing I'm wasting a precious opportunity by staring at him like a star-struck groupie, I carefully wriggle out from under his arm and creep naked to the door, my heart pounding against my ribcage.

I need to escape, if only to my own room.

I need to put some distance between us.

Last night, at least the portion after the shower, is a blur in my mind, a jumble of darkly sexual sensations and wild emotions. I think I was so stunned by his declaration that I went into a kind of shock, and by the time I recovered, I was already in his bed, with my wrists pinned above my head and him driving into my sore yet perversely eager body.

I don't remember saying no, but I must have. I don't want to believe that I let him fuck me after what he said... or that I came several more times as he took me with unbridled ferocity over and over again.

At least he'd used a condom those other times; I'd be hyperventilating now if it had been bareback.

Reaching the door, I cast a glance behind my shoulder. Thank God he's still asleep. I don't know how I'm going to face him—or what I'm going to do about his marriage threat. And it is a threat. I have no idea how he can force me to say yes against my will, but I know it's within his capabilities. That darkness I've always sensed in him is now directed at me.

As he told me yesterday, he excels at doing whatever it takes to get his way.

Holding my breath, I reach for the door handle and turn it, wincing internally at the faint click it makes. To my relief, he continues sleeping, so I stick my head out in the hallway, making sure it's clear, and then I sprint down to my room, ignoring the twinge of pain in my barely healed ankle.

I get inside without incident and beeline for my bathroom, where I jump in the shower and scrub myself with soap in an attempt to wash away the memory of his rough touch. It's futile—marks of his possession are all over my body, my skin scraped in a dozen places by his stubble, my nipples aching where he'd sucked on them and grazed them with his teeth. The worst, though, is the soreness deep inside me, a reminder of his insatiable hunger for me—and my complete inability to resist him, even in light of the madness he intends.

I turn off the water and step out of the stall, taking deep breaths to control my growing panic. Maybe he didn't mean it. He could've just been upset that I turned down his proposal, and when he wakes up this morning, he'll realize how premature it was.

He hired me just over three weeks ago, and we've spent a grand total of two nights together. How can he be so sure that he wants me for a lifetime, that I'm indeed the one?

Yet no matter what I tell myself, my panic refuses to abate. Despite what I said last night, I know Nikolai. Deep down, I know him—and I know he doesn't say things he doesn't mean. He decided we were fated when I'd been here barely a week, and nothing that's happened since has convinced him otherwise.

What's scarier is he doesn't claim to love me—and I don't think he does. What he feels for me is more of an obsession. With a jolt, I remember Alina warning me about this the night we smoked weed together, telling me her brother isn't my white knight.

"Molotov men don't love, they possess," she said. "And Nikolai is no exception."

Wrapping a towel around my wet hair, I stare at my reflection in the mirror, noting the puffy redness of my lips, still bruised and swollen from his kisses. Near my collarbone is a hickey, and on my hips are faint dark marks in the shape of male fingers.

No, this isn't love. Not even close.

At best, it's a mutual fixation—because even now, as I stand here looking like I've been assaulted, the memories of how each mark got on my body make me throb deep inside.

It's as I'm getting dressed that I decide on the best course of action.

Alina.

She helped me once; maybe she can do so again.

I don't even know what kind of help I have in mind —after my near miss with the assassins, the idea of another escape attempt holds little appeal. Nonetheless, I feel a spark of hope as I knock on the door of her bedroom, and she opens it for me, dressed in her peignoir. Before I have a chance to apologize for waking her up, she glances around the hallway and swiftly ushers me inside.

"Are you okay?" she demands, stepping back to give me a thorough once-over. Her gaze zeroes in on my puffy lips, and her dark eyebrows pull together. "Did Kolya—"

"No, no, I'm fine." My face burns hot, making me grateful my bronzed skin conceals my flush—and my high-necked T-shirt hides the hickey. "He wouldn't— It was all consensual, believe me."

She blows out a breath. "Okay, good. I figured that was the case. It's just... my brother is not entirely sane when it comes to you."

"You can say that again," I mutter under my breath.

She hears me anyway, and her frown returns. "What happened?" Grabbing my hand, she leads me over to her unmade bed and makes me sit next to her. Since she's just woken up, her face is bare, like that fateful time she ambushed me in my bedroom, but her jade-green eyes are clear, clouded only by concern. "What happened? Tell me, Chloe. Please."

I take in a deep breath and brace myself for her reaction. "Nikolai proposed."

Zero response. Not so much as an eyelash flicker.

Did she not hear me?

"He asked me to marry him," I enunciate, in case it wasn't clear. "Last night, he asked me to be his wife."

Now her long lashes sweep over her eyes. "I see."

"Why aren't you more surprised?" I demand, stunned and more than a little disquieted by her calm acceptance. "Did you know he would do this?"

"Know? No. Suspect? Yes." She sighs, pushing back her hair with one hand. "From the moment I saw your keys in his drawer, I figured this is where it might be heading. But of course, Kolya doesn't talk to me about these matters, so I can't say I knew for sure."

My disquiet increases. "I don't understand."

"Chloe..." Facing me fully, she clasps my hands in both of hers. "My brother is obsessed with you. I saw signs of it from the first day we hired you, but I thought—I hoped—it was just a passing attraction on his part, that you'd just be another girl he'd fuck and forget."

"Gee, thanks."

"It's nothing against you. It would've been a good thing, believe me." She squeezes my hands. "Look, Nikolai is... He's a lot like our father. And our grandfather. And from the stories I've heard, other Molotov men before them. Konstantin and Valery— they're a little different, but Nikolai... he's a Molotov male through and through."

"What does that mean?" I ask, frustrated. "He's what? Prone to proposing after knowing a woman for a month?"

She shakes her head. "To the best of my knowledge, he's never proposed to anyone else—or become this obsessed with a woman." She takes a breath. "You're the first, and if I had to guess, the last. Which is how it often happens with the men in our family. Our father saw our mother at a party, swept her off her feet by showering her family with presents, and married her two weeks later. And his father—our paternal grandfather—literally kidnapped our grandmother when she was sixteen, stole her from her village when he happened upon her tending a field with other schoolgirls."

"You're kidding me."

"I wish." Her face is somber. "Our grandmother passed away when I was ten, but I remember the stories she told me about her life with my grandfather, the way he'd control her every move and demand absolute obedience. She was deeply unhappy with him, but she was just a poor peasant girl and he was a powerful, well-connected man, so there was nothing she could do. He wouldn't let her leave him."

I stare at her, my stomach roiling. "And your mother? Was she unhappy also?"

She pulls back her hands, her face turning shuttered. "Not at first. She didn't know what kind of man she'd married, not until much later. It was when she found out that things started to unravel and—" She stops and takes another deep breath. "In any case, that's neither here nor there. My point is, Nikolai possesses that same intense, passionate personality, an obsessive tendency that seeks, and eventually finds, something—someone—to latch on to. Like our father and our grandfather before him, he's single-minded when it comes to getting the woman he wants, and he wants you, Chloe. And he'll have you, at any cost."

I don't know what to say. Struck dumb, I simply stare at her as she says softly, "Also, I don't know if you've noticed, but there's a streak of mysticism within Nikolai, this belief in fate and destiny that he's inherited from our grandmother. Having grown up in a small rural village, she was both religious and deeply superstitious, and she spent a lot of time with Nikolai when he was a little boy. He'd probably deny it—he doesn't consider himself religious in the least—but he's absorbed a lot of her beliefs, including her attitudes about our family and how our very blood carries evil within it... how it was inevitable that our father, her son, would turn out the way he had."

I swallow hard. "Which is how?" And more importantly, has Nikolai turned out the same way?

Alina's lips flatten. "Never mind that. We're talking about Nikolai right now."

"And me. Alina..." It's my turn to grip her hands. "What do I do? I told him I can't marry him, but he's not listening to reason. He insists we're getting married today."

Her face finally displays a flicker of surprise. "Today?"

"Yes, today!" Releasing her hands, I modulate my tone. "Look, I might be freaking out for nothing. I don't know how he can force me into marriage—it's not the Middle Ages. But just in case, can you maybe talk some sense into him? Or help me figure out how to do so?"

She tilts her head, her jade eyes gleaming. "So just to be clear, you don't want to marry him?"

I blink. "Of course not. I mean... I've known him less than a month."

"But you want him, right? Last night and that other time—"

"That's different." My face turns hot again. "That's just biological. He's a very attractive man and—"

"So it's just sex for you?"

I open my mouth to say yes, but the word refuses to come out.

"I see." The gleam in her eyes intensifies. "Do you love him?"

"I..." I swallow against the sudden dryness in my throat. "I don't know. Does it matter? I still can't marry him. He's—that is, he's not..."

"What you imagined as a husband?" she says as I trail off. A wry smile curves her lips. "You know, most women would jump at the chance to marry a rich, handsome man who's crazy about them."

"Would you? Jump at a chance to marry someone like your brother?"

Her features tighten, the smile falling off her face. "We're not talking about me." Standing up sharply, she strides over to the window, her back ramrod stiff as she stares out at the distant peaks.

Confused, I walk over to join her there. I have no

idea what's upset her, but clearly, something has. Cautiously, I touch her shoulder. "Hey, I—"

She turns to face me, her features composed once more. "Listen to me, Chloe. You're right to freak out. If my brother says you're marrying him today, that's going to happen. I don't exactly know how, but he's resourceful. If you really don't want this, your best bet is to delay the wedding."

"Delay? But—"

"Delay," she says firmly. "Outright refusal won't work—it'll only make him more determined—so you have to say yes and then figure out a way to impose some conditions. Maybe you've always dreamed of a particular wedding venue, or a special dress, or having your college friends as bridesmaids. He may honor that, or he may not. Either way, it's worth a shot."

I stare at her, my pulse racing. She's right: I've gone about this all wrong. Last night, until I told Nikolai the truth—that I didn't think it could work between us long term—he seemed amenable to reason, more interested in persuading me than bending me to his will.

Maybe if I agree to marry him at some point in the future, we can go back to a saner dynamic, restore the way things were.

"I'm sorry I can't be more helpful," Alina says, and I can tell that she's sincere. "Anything I say to him will only backfire. It's better if you approach him yourself."

"No, this was very helpful, thank you." I turn to leave when a thought occurs to me. Hopeful, I spin around. "You wouldn't happen to have the morning-after pill, would you? There was a bit of a... memory lapse on our part last night."

She stills, blinking. When she speaks, her voice is strange. "No, I'm afraid I don't have anything like that. And Chloe... you might want to think of a really, really good delaying tactic. Remember what I told you about my brother and accidents? Same thing goes for memory lapses."

I stare at her, my stomach dropping. "You mean..."

"It sounds to me like he's dead set on binding you to him—and is already pulling out all the stops."

NIKOLAI

I wake up with an unsettling sense of déjà vu. Even before I roll over and feel the cool, empty sheets next to me, I know Chloe is not there.

I can feel her absence deep inside.

Logic tells me she couldn't have run away again—the guards are under strict orders not to let her leave the compound—but my heart still thuds heavily against my ribcage as I jump off the bed and get dressed with military speed.

I have to find her. Now.

Before I can exit the room, a flicker of movement outside catches my eye. I step over to the window, and a wave of relief washes over me.

It's Chloe and Slava, standing together on the edge of the driveway, peering into the cluster of trees on the side. As I look closer, I notice a gray-brown ball of fur in front of them—a wild rabbit. I also catch a glimpse of a long, skinny carrot in my son's hand.

The relief merges with a new, purely incandescent sensation, a glowing sort of warmth that fills every crevice of my chest. My son and my wife to be—it feels so right, so perfect.

So utterly fucked up.

I don't deserve this. Deep down, I know that. A man like me doesn't get to experience this kind of happiness, to bask for any length of time in real joy. And Chloe certainly doesn't deserve me. The blood that runs through my veins is pure poison, my nature ruthless through and through. A better man would've let her go long ago, protecting her from the darkest parts of himself instead of seizing this mirage of happiness with both hands.

But I am seizing it. Because I'm a selfish monster. Because when I finally had her in my arms last night, I knew that was where she belonged. And I knew it wasn't enough to simply have her there.

I need the world to know that she's mine, that she belongs solely to me.

I let myself watch her and Slava for a while longer, enjoying the unearned happiness, these stolen moments of uncomplicated joy. I don't know how I'd been able to restrain myself all that time, how I'd managed to hold back and give her the two-week reprieve. Now that I've had her again, I can't imagine spending another night without her, can't even attempt to put the beast back on its leash.

She doesn't want to marry me. So be it. The scorching burn of rage and hurt at her refusal is still there, but it's cooled slightly, hardening into a grim resolve.

It's time Chloe understood with whom she's dealing. One way or another, she's going to wear my ring on her finger.

Tonight, she's going to become my wife.

28

CHLOE

I get through the morning by sheer willpower, going about my lessons with Slava with a smile despite the anxiety shredding my nerves. It helps that Nikolai doesn't show up at breakfast, locking himself in his office with Pavel instead. In fact, I don't see him at all except briefly in the hallway, when he strides past me with nothing more than a heated once-over and a murmured "excuse me, zaychik."

It's as if last night never happened, as if my body doesn't bear the imprint of his possession and my stomach isn't in knots as I try to work up the courage to confront him.

It's not until eleven that the first sign of the changes to come appears. By then, I've grown hopeful that Nikolai has changed his mind, and his threat was empty after all. But no. I walk into my room to find Lyudmila in my closet, grabbing dozens of dresses together with their hangers and carrying them past me without a single word.

"Hey!" I hurry after her as she walks briskly down the hallway. "What's going on?"

She casts a sidelong glance at me as I catch up. "You move today. To Nikolai's room, no?"

"What? No! Give me those." I try to grab the clothes from her, but she proves to be surprisingly agile. Sidestepping my move, she darts into Nikolai's bedroom, then emerges thirty seconds later and beelines for my room.

Fuck.

I run after her. "Don't. Just leave them."

She doesn't listen, snatching another batch of clothes and pushing past me, her matryoshka-doll face devoid of all expression. "If you in my way, I get Pavel to help."

Dammit.

Brimming with anger, I step back and let her do her thing. The alternative—physically fighting her and her mountain of a husband—would be both pointless and stupid. Who cares where my clothes reside? It's what this move signifies that matters.

Nikolai is taking away my room, my private space… my only refuge from him.

I can't hold off on the confrontation any longer. If I don't want to become his wife today, I have to act.

Leaving Lyudmila to do as she will with my closet, I stride to Nikolai's office and knock decisively on the door.

"Yes?"

"It's Chloe." My voice is low and furious, my anger burning away all caution.

The door swings open, revealing Nikolai's large, broad-shouldered frame. Propping a muscular forearm on the doorframe above his head, he rakes his gaze over my body. When his eyes return to my face, they're a bright, predatory gold. "What is it, zaychik?"

"We need to talk."

He takes a half-step back, his sensuous lips curving with dark amusement. "Come in, then."

He's still partially in the doorway, so I have no choice but to push past him. My shoulder brushes against his hard-muscled chest, and I catch a faint whiff of bergamot and cedar, mixed with the enticing musk of warm male skin. A familiar heat scorches my veins, my insides turning soft and liquid despite the fury burning in my chest.

Fucking biology. This is the last thing I need.

Clenching my teeth, I head over to the round table, where I plop down in a chair, my eyes locked challengingly on his face. I refuse to let my body dictate my actions, to have sexual needs decide my fate.

I'm not marrying this beautiful, amoral man if I can help it. No matter how I respond to him in bed.

"So…" He leans back, lacing his long fingers over his ribcage. His voice is brushed silk as he says softly, "You wanted to talk."

I've had all morning to think of the best way to approach him, yet I still find myself tongue-tied, my thoughts in a chaotic jumble. Partially, it's the way he's watching me, with that cynical, mocking half-smile, like he's already looked into the future and knows exactly what I'm going to do and say. But mostly, it's the cool resolve I sense in him. The arguments I've rehearsed suddenly seem inadequate, the very premise of bargaining with him deeply flawed.

"How are you planning to do it?" I blurt finally. It's not what I was going to lead with, but I have to know what's in store for me if I fail. "How can you make me marry you against my will?"

The muscles around his eyes tighten minutely, even as the smile remains on his lips. "Against your will? Is that the lie you're feeding yourself, zaychik? That you are being forced?"

Blood rushes to my face, anger mixing with illogical embarrassment. "What are you saying?"

"I'm saying that I'm doing you a favor." His smile sharpens. "Decisions can be a heavy burden, especially when your ideas of what's right conflict with your actual wants."

My nails bite into my palms. "I don't *want* to marry you. You asked and I said no, remember?"

"Oh, I do." He sits forward sharply, the smile dropping from his face. "Some things are meant to be. One day, you'll see it and be thankful, zaychik. For now, I'll do what I must."

"Which is what? Get some kind of officiant here? And then what? How will you get me to say yes?"

He doesn't reply, just leans back with an inscrutable expression, and my imagination makes the leap.

Staring at him in horror, I choke out, "You're going to drug me, aren't you? That's your plan."

NIKOLAI

My clever zaychik. She does know me, no matter what she claims.

The little vial is already in my desk, the liquid inside ready to be sucked into a syringe and pumped into her veins. It's the mildest, gentlest form of one of our special drugs, the dosage just barely enough to blur the edges of reality and lower a person's inhibitions.

When I use it on Chloe, she'll be aware of what's happening, but she won't object... because deep inside, she also wants this.

I know her by now as well.

Which is why I'm not surprised when she takes a breath and squares her slender shoulders instead of pleading or crying. "Fine," she says, her voice shaking only slightly. "You win. But just so you know, I won't forgive you if you go through with this. It will poison everything between us... just like your grandfather's actions ruined whatever chance his marriage ever stood."

Fucking Alina. I should've expected this, yet Chloe's words still spear me like a fishhook, penetrating deep and snagging directly on my heart.

I lean forward, my tone sharpening. "You're leaving me no choice."

"No. You're trying to leave *me* no choice." She leans forward as well, glaring at me from across the table. "The no-condom thing—that was on purpose, wasn't it? You didn't actually forget."

I hold her gaze, the flare of anger cooling as a peculiar ache bands around my chest. Is she right? At the time, it didn't seem like a conscious decision, more like a primordial directive, an overpowering urge to be inside her with no barriers of any kind. The condom wasn't even a consideration; it's as if my mind had blocked out the existence of such protective measures, much less the need for them.

I don't want more children—or at least I thought I didn't. Then I saw my seed on Chloe's thighs, and all sorts of tempting images flooded my mind: of Chloe growing round with our child, of her nursing a chubby infant... of us playing with a brown-eyed toddler whose radiant smile lights a room.

It was like a montage from some fucking Hallmark movie, except it made me ache deep inside.

With effort, I shut down that line of thinking. Whether or not I acted consciously doesn't matter. The outcome is the same either way.

Forcing my shoulders to relax, I sit back and study Chloe's tightly drawn features. "Tell me something, zaychik... what will it take for you to accept our marriage and be happy? For the two of us to avoid my grandparents' fate?"

She's too smart, too cautious to come in here just to castigate me. There's something she's after, some kind of goal she's hoping to achieve, and I suspect I know what it is.

She stares at me for a couple of long seconds, and I sense the battle playing out in her mind. Continue pressing me on the condom question or move on to her actual agenda?

She must decide on the combination of the two because she sits up straighter and says, "Well, for one thing, unless and until I agree to have a baby, I want us to always use protection. In fact, I want you to get me back on birth control pills right away and get me a morning-after pill today."

"Done," I say, suppressing an irrational surge of disappointment.

It's really for the best; another Molotov is the last thing this world needs. I don't know what came over me last night, but I intend to control myself better in the future. In fact, I did use condoms throughout the rest of the night, so I will chalk up what happened to a momentary lapse of reason.

Chloe blinks, clearly surprised by my easy acquiescence. "Okay. Good. Then how about we discuss the timing of the wedding? I think next summer or fall should be—"

"No." I didn't intend to rush her into marriage, but now that we've gone down this path, I can't imagine waiting a day longer. As impatient as I've been to have her in my bed, it's nothing compared to my burning urge to tie her to me. I wasn't planning to propose until some weeks from now, after I'd dealt with Bransford, but everything changed the moment I saw my seed on her and knew I could've made her pregnant. At that moment, putting my ring on her finger became my top priority—and it still is, regardless of whether or not there's going to be a child.

The mere possibility of it made me realize that nothing less than having her as my wife will do.

She sucks in a breath. "But—"

"No. The timing is nonnegotiable." I know I'm being unreasonable, but I can't—I won't—relent on this. Something irrational in me is convinced that if I don't make this happen now, I will lose her... that I must seize this chance at happiness, illusory though it might be.

She balls her hands as spots of darker color appear on her cheeks. "I thought you wanted this to work, for us to actually be happy in this marriage."

"I do... and we will be. But first, there has to be a marriage. And for that, there has to be a wedding—which is what's happening at five o'clock today."

"This afternoon?" Her voice jumps in pitch. "You realize how insane that sounds?"

I smile grimly. "Sanity is overrated, zaychik. What sane person is ever happy? In any case, you don't need to stress about the logistics. Everything's already been arranged."

For a few beats, she just stares at me, breathing shakily; then she pushes back her chair and launches to her feet. "What about what I want? What I need to accept this marriage?"

"Tell me what it is, and I'll do my best to make it happen—as long as it doesn't result in a delay." Rising to my feet as well, I step around the table and cup her delicately carved chin, tilting her face up to take in her mutinous expression. "Tell me, zaychik. What can I do to make you happy? What is it you need?"

She grips my wrist, her eyes dark with turbulent emotions. "I need you to not make me do this."

I smile and bend my head to kiss the fragile shell of her ear, my body tightening as I breathe in her wildflower scent. "No, zaychik," I murmur when I feel her shiver. "That is precisely what you need."

Someone as innocent as her will never embrace a man like me without worrying about how it compromises her society-imposed morals and feeling at least some form of guilt.

I meant what I said. In my own selfish way, I *am* doing her a favor. This way, she can pretend she doesn't want this, that she's embracing me against her will.

The delicate line of her throat ripples with a swallow, and she inhales raggedly, backing out of my hold. Her eyes are even darker as they meet mine, her delicate features tightly drawn.

"In that case," she says unsteadily, "I have two more conditions. If you can meet them, I will marry you at five o'clock today, no drug required."

Intrigued, I cock my head. "Go on."

"First, I want you to tell me what exactly happened with your father. And second..." Her voice wavers. "I need you to promise not to kill mine. I want Bransford to pay, but not that way."

30

CHLOE

Nikolai's jaw turns to stone, volcanic clouds gathering in his eyes. In a dangerously level voice, he says, "I can do the first, but not the second. Bransford is a threat to you for as long as he's alive."

"Not if he's been exposed and people know what he is. I can go public with my DNA results; with that kind of proof, the media will have to listen."

I don't know when the idea of this Faustian bargain with Nikolai came to me, at which point I decided that since there's no way to avoid losing the marriage battle, I will at least surrender on my own terms. These two matters—finding out the truth about Nikolai's past and getting him to leave Bransford alive—are equally important to me, and I need to use what little leverage I have.

Bransford has to pay for his crimes, but I don't want his blood on Nikolai's hands and, by extension, on my conscience.

"The media?" Nikolai's lips twist. "You do understand what that would entail, don't you, zaychik? They'll be on you like a flock of hungry seagulls. Every bit of your life will be dissected, your mother's death and everything about her past analyzed in nauseating detail. You'll never have a moment of peace again. And while the scandal will likely tank Bransford's political career, there's no guarantee he'll go to jail for your mother's rape; the statute of limitations might prevent that."

"He's also guilty of ordering her murder."

"Yes, but good luck proving that with the assassins out of the picture."

Dammit. He's right. In my haste to come up with an alternative to killing Bransford, I didn't consider that last part. I have no idea what Nikolai did with the assassins' bodies, but either way, dead men can't testify as to the identity of their employer. Worse yet, pointing the authorities to the assassins' graves—or even just disclosing the incident in the woods—could create all sorts of problems for Nikolai. The last thing I want is for him to be arrested for protecting me... or to have the media flock all over him, which they're bound to do if we are married.

With Slava needing to stay hidden from his mother's family, I can't go public with my relationship to Bransford. The very idea is a nonstarter.

Still, I'm not ready to give up. "What if it's not me? I bet there are women besides my mom he's done this to, other girls he's assaulted at some point. Men like that tend to have a certain MO, so maybe we can find his other victims and—"

"Find them how?" Nikolai's tone gentles. "I understand what you're trying to do, zaychik, believe me, but even if some victims were conveniently lurking in the wings, it could take us months or years to find them and persuade them to come forward. By that point, he might be President of the United States, and taking him down will require infinitely greater effort. In the meantime, he'll continue hunting you... and also potentially creating other victims. Have you considered that? If he does indeed have a taste for unwilling teenage girls, then every minute he's alive, he doesn't only pose a threat to *you*. By taking him out, I'll be doing the world a favor."

Ugh. I turn away, rubbing my forehead. He's right again, but I can't accept that assassination is the only answer. There has to be something else we can do. I'd even be down with something shady, like blackmail or—

I spin around. "What if we didn't need to find them, the victims? What if we created them ourselves?"

Nikolai's dark eyebrows arch, his gaze lighting with a hint of amusement. "Are you suggesting paying some women to accuse him? Manufacturing false evidence? You don't find that unethical and wrong?"

"Not when the alternative is killing him. Besides, it's not like he's innocent."

"No," Nikolai says flatly, all humor gone. "He's not."

"So is that a yes?" Stepping closer, I gaze up at him hopefully. "Can we try this, see if it works out?"

He brushes a strand of hair off my face. "No, zaychik. False accusations won't work."

"But—"

"If we're going to create victims, they have to be real... or at least the evidence needs to be."

I blink up at him. "What do you mean?"

"I have one idea, but I need to run it by Valery."

A lightbulb goes off in my head. "Are you talking about Masha?" Whatever age his brother's "asset" really is, she could easily pass for a teenager, so if we got her close to Bransford—

"Exactly." Nikolai walks over to his desk and opens his laptop. I watch with bated breath as his long fingers dance over the keyboard, firing off some message.

Maybe I'm counting the chickens before they've hatched, but it seems like he's on board. He thinks this idea has merit.

"All right," he says after a minute, closing the laptop. "Let's see what Valery thinks, and if Masha would be open to altering the current plan."

"Which is what?"

The curve of his lips holds a hint of irony. "Let's just say the first part of it isn't too different."

I blink. "She was going to seduce him?"

"Just enough to get him to have a meal with her."

Where she'd give him whatever is supposed to result in that fatal "heart defect."

I do my best to keep my tone even. "Okay, so then it

should be easy, right? Maybe she could seduce him just a bit further and take some compromising pictures. Or—"

"Don't worry about the specifics, zaychik." He walks around his desk and stops in front of me, his eyes the darkest shade of amber as he tucks another strand of hair behind my ear. "Your only job today is to choose the dress."

31

CHLOE

Nikolai was wrong. It's not just the dress. After lunch, a pack of fashionably dressed people invades the house, bringing with them everything from a department store's worth of shoes to hair styling tools. Alina directs them all with brisk efficiency, and before I know it, I'm washed, waxed, plucked, perfumed, styled, and made up to the nth degree.

By the time we actually get to the dress selection, I feel like I've been through a mild form of torture, and everything takes on a surreal vibe. My wedding day— just those words are like something out of a book or movie, a fictional tale featuring a girl who can't possibly be me.

Marriage was never my dream. Not the way it is for some women. It was just something I figured would happen in the future if I met the right person and all the stars aligned. Say, if we were both doing well in our careers, liked each other's families and friends, and had tons of interests in common. Also, if we were of a proper age, which to me is late twenties at the earliest.

I never imagined myself getting married at twenty-three—and certainly not to a Russian mobster. Because that's what Nikolai is, whether or not he accepts that label. The Molotovs cloak themselves in high-society trappings, but at the core, Nikolai and his brothers are savages, as violent and amoral as any cartel leaders.

The thought of joining my life to such a man should terrify me, but I feel numb instead, so overwhelmed that everything feels like white noise. Less than two months ago, my only worry was finding a job post-graduation, and then my life went so far off the rails that none of what's happening today seems all that scary or strange.

Or maybe that's a lie I'm telling myself to get through this day. Maybe the enormity of this will hit me later, when I'm better equipped to process it.

The dresses presented to me are stunning, each one a work of art. There are fourteen total, and Alina makes me try all of them on before declaring that number seven—an ivory mermaid-tail number with an off-the-shoulders neckline—is the one.

I don't know if I agree with her—to me, all the dresses are straight out of a fairy tale—but I'm grateful to have her guidance. Whatever she may think of today's proceedings, she's taken charge, running interference with the invading pack on my behalf.

Thanks to her, I don't have to make any tricky decisions, such as what color eyeshadow to apply; she tells them what to do with me and how, and I just have to sit there like a zombie doll while they do all the things, including dabbing some concealer on my neck to hide the hickey and other marks of Nikolai's lovemaking.

It's almost five by the time I'm fully ready, and as the pack leaves, two new cars arrive. One contains two people with fancy-looking camera equipment, while the other belongs to a slim middle-aged man dressed in a black suit with a white collar.

"Nondenominational priest," Alina explains, coming to stand next to me by the window. "He'll conduct the ceremony."

Ceremony, right. My heart gives a panicked thump, some of my numbness fading. This *is* real. It's happening. An actual wedding, with a fancy dress, a priest, and a photographer/videographer team. I have no idea how Nikolai managed to pull this off on such short notice, but I guess when you have enough cash to throw around, you don't need to worry about such plebeian concerns as booking highly sought-after professionals in advance.

"Where's Slava?" I ask, belatedly realizing I haven't seen the boy since our lessons in the morning. "Will he be at the ceremony as well?"

Alina nods. "Lyudmila's been keeping him out of sight, since the fewer people who know of his presence here, the better. But Nikolai does want him at the wedding and in the pictures, so he's taken the appropriate precautions with the priest and the photographer team."

"Precautions? As in, some kind of non-disclosure agreement? Wait, on second thought, I don't want to know."

She flashes me a dazzling grin. "Smart of you. But yes, an NDA is part of it, I believe. Along with some stronger measures."

My heart gives another thump, then launches into an all-out gallop. The reality is descending on me, fast, and with it, a sense of panic.

What am I doing? Why did I agree to this? How do I know Nikolai will hold up his side of the bargain? He still hasn't told me what happened with his father—though to be fair, with all the wedding preparations, we haven't had much time to talk. Which is a problem in and of itself. Everything is happening way too fast, all the decisions out of my hands, all the implications huge. For one thing, it's dawning on me that by marrying Nikolai, I'm not just gaining a husband, but also a son.

I'm going to be a stepmom to a four-year-old.

I must look a little wild-eyed because Alina reaches over to squeeze my hands. "Breathe. It's going to be okay. Just take it one minute at a time."

That's good advice. That's what Mom always told me: just focus on the next step, the next thing that needs to happen. Nobody has a crystal ball when it comes to the distant future, so it's pointless to think too far ahead. In any case, becoming Slava's stepmom is the least scary part of this venture, as I already love the boy and can't imagine not having him in my life.

I take a deep breath to settle my frantic heartbeat. "Thanks. We should probably head down before Nikolai comes looking for us." Stepping back, I give her sea-colored gown a swift once-over. "You look amazing, by the way."

Alina's grin returns. "Me? You're the gorgeous bride."

That may be the case, but she outshines me, as always. On a regular day, Nikolai's sister could pass for a starlet walking the red carpet, but when she puts in extra effort with her hair and makeup, as she has today, her beauty is almost unreal. If I saw a picture of her like this, I'd be sure it was Photoshopped to death, perfected with all sorts of filters. Yet here she is, standing next to me, as real as can be.

"Do you have anyone back in Russia?" I ask on impulse. "A boyfriend or anything like that?"

Despite our growing friendship, Alina's been as closemouthed on that topic as on the subject of her family, and I can't help but wonder why. I've told her all about my ex-boyfriends, but she's never reciprocated with such stories of her own.

If I didn't know better, I'd think she hasn't dated much.

"A boyfriend?" Her peal of laughter sounds forced. "No. There's no one like that."

And we're back to square one.

"Why not?" I ask, unable to leave it alone. Focusing on Alina's love life is vastly preferable to dwelling on where mine is heading. "Surely—"

"We should go downstairs," she says, turning away. "Let's go before we're late."

32

NIKOLAI

"Slavochka…" I crouch in front of my son. "I have to talk to you about something."

He stares at me unblinkingly, unease evident in his expression. He couldn't have missed all the people going in and out of the house, and I know he's been wondering about what's going on. Lyudmila told me he's been peppering her with questions all afternoon—questions she's held off answering, figuring I should be the one to break the news to him.

"It's nothing bad," I say when he remains silent. "In fact, it's something really great. Remember when I promised you that Chloe is going to stay with us forever?"

He nods warily.

"Well, that's what today is all about." I smile broadly. "We're getting married. Chloe is going to be not just your tutor, but your new mom."

His eyes go wide, and his small chin quivers. "My mom?"

"Technically, stepmom, but I'm sure Chloe would like it if you came to think of her as your mom over time."

I expect Slava to react with joy, since he absolutely adores Chloe. Instead, his chin quivers harder, and shiny tears pool in his eyes. "Does that mean—" His childish voice cracks. "Does that mean she'll die?"

Fuck. This again. I feel like someone smashed my chest with a hammer.

If Ksenia weren't already dead, I'd kill her for dying in that car crash and instilling this fear in our son.

I grip his arms tightly. "No, Slavochka. She won't. In fact, I'm marrying her to ensure nothing bad ever happens to her. She'll be safe here with us."

The chin quivering stops, even as drops of moisture cling to his lower eyelashes, making them sparkle. "You promise?"

"I promise."

"She'll always stay with us?"

"Always." Or at least as long as there's breath in my body—but I'm not going to say that, lest he starts worrying about me dying as well.

He rewards me with a beaming smile, and the hammer hits my chest again, the pain reverberating deep. Only it's a different pain this time, one I've learned to welcome. It's hard to verbalize the way my son makes me feel; all I know is I can no longer imagine a life without him, without these powerful emotions that oftentimes feel like they're tearing me apart.

Over the past two weeks, the tentative rapport we've established thanks to Chloe has deepened, our relationship changing to something I never thought I'd have... something that makes me wonder if another child, one with Chloe, would be so bad after all.

But no. I promised it would be her decision—and it has to be, if our child is to have any chance at overcoming the Molotov curse. I don't want him raised by a mother who resents his very existence and tells him that everything he is disgusts her, that evil is a part of him and always will be.

I don't want him to end up like my father.

Pushing that grim thought away, I smile back at Slava. "Let's get you dressed and ready. It's almost time for the wedding."

Standing up, I extend my hand to him, and as his small fingers close trustingly around my palm, I feel more certain than ever that I'm doing the right thing... for myself, for Chloe, and for my son.

33

CHLOE

We take our vows in the glass-walled terrace overlooking the ravine, where the mountain vistas provide an Instagram-worthy backdrop and the late-afternoon sun casts everything in a warm, golden light.

To an outsider, it would look like the most picture-perfect tiny wedding, right down to the music piping in through the ceiling speakers and the adorable tuxedo-clad child beaming in excitement to our right.

"Do you, Chloe Emmons, take Nikolai Molotov... your lawfully wedded husband... and to hold..." The priest's words fade in and out, like a faulty radio broadcast, the white noise effect returning to create a constant hum in my ears. I'm vaguely aware of Alina standing next to me, unofficially playing the maid of honor, and of Pavel's bear-like frame next to Nikolai. Is he his best man? Is that even a thing in Russia?

"I do," I say when I realize the priest is silent and has

been for a while. Nikolai has already said his part, so it's just down to me.

Lyudmila, who's holding Slava's hand, says something to the boy in Russian as the priest smiles and says, "Now exchange the rings."

We have rings?

Sure enough, Nikolai's strong fingers are already gripping my right wrist. Turning my hand palm up, he places a plain gold band in the middle of it, then picks up my left hand and slides a delicate, diamond-encrusted gold circle onto my ring finger.

Huh. I guess we have rings.

Clumsily, I work the plain band onto Nikolai's ring finger and look up. His eyes match the color of the precious metal on his hand, the scorching heat in them chasing away the white noise in my ears and bringing the proceedings into stark relief.

Holy fuck.

We just got married.

The man in front of me is now *my husband*.

"Congratulations. You may kiss the bride," the priest says, and my heart lurches into overdrive as Nikolai tilts my face up and bends his head, a darkly satisfied smile playing on his lips as they descend on mine.

It's a brief, almost platonic kiss, but there's no mistaking the raw possessiveness in it, or in the way he clasps my hand afterward as he turns to face the flood of applause and congratulations coming our way. Even as everybody hugs us, he holds on to me, refusing to let go.

Finally, the adults back off, and Nikolai kneels in front of Slava, my hand still firmly in his grasp.

"Slavochka…" His tone is solemn, his English words carefully enunciated. "We're a family now. Chloe is my wife—and your new mom."

Okay, whoa. I was not expecting this. Shouldn't we be easing into this? I don't want Slava to resent me for taking his dead mother's place. Sure, I'm technically his stepmom, but that doesn't mean he can't continue to think of me as Chloe for now, and later, when the timing's right, we can—

My thoughts come to a screeching halt as Slava gives me the biggest, brightest grin and throws his short arms around my skirt, hugging my legs with all his strength.

"Mama Chloe," he exclaims, looking up at me with an even bigger grin, and it's all I can do to hide my shock at his easy acceptance of this change in our dynamic. Where's the resentment? The wariness at the sudden change in his life? Not that I'm not happy he's so on board. Nikolai must've talked to him at some point today, warned him about what's going to happen. Still, I would've expected at least a short adjustment period. Unless of course—

I stop myself. None of that is important right now. Framing Slava's upturned face with my palm, I give him the brightest smile I can muster. "Yes, darling.

We're a family now. You can call me Mama or anything else you want."

As jarring as it is to suddenly find myself in the role of a parent, I have a feeling Slava is going to be the least complicated part of this marriage, and not just because I feel zero shame in admitting that the child already has my heart.

When I glance over at Nikolai, his expression is warmly approving. Smiling, he brings the hand he's holding to his lips and kisses my knuckles one by one, sending tingles down my spine and making Slava giggle.

"Mama Chloe," he repeats excitedly and bounces over to Alina, chattering at her in Russian.

"Congratulations again," she says as I catch her gaze. Quietly, she adds, "I'm glad to have you as my sister."

Sister. Right. Because that's what it means, to marry. One gains not just a husband, but a family. Like a son, a sister, two brothers, and however many cousins... all the siblings and relatives I never had.

For the first time, I comprehend just how much my life is changing.

I'm no longer an orphan, making my way alone in the world.

The realization is still reverberating through me as the photographer shepherds us outside to take a million pictures on the cliffside, where the summer breeze kisses our faces with pine-scented coolness.

Not an orphan.

Not an only child of a single mother who had no family of her own.

How long have I secretly wished for something like this? In my imagination, it was my father who would come into my life and introduce me to all the cousins, aunts, and uncles I never knew I had, but who turn out to be wonderful. Now, knowing what I know about Bransford, I can't imagine it. Just the thought of meeting someone related to the man who's trying to kill me is revolting. Thank God he has no other biological children—at least none the media is aware of. From what little I've allowed myself to read about him, I know he's a widower who recently remarried. His first wife battled some rare form of cancer for a decade before passing away a few years back, and his new wife has two young children from her prior marriage—a girl and a boy he regularly parades in front of the cameras, playing the role of a wholesome, all-American husband and father to perfection.

If only they knew.

Lost in thought, I obey the photographer's instructions on autopilot, and the next time I look around, the sun is setting behind the mountain peaks, bathing everything in a reddish-orange glow.

"That should be enough," Nikolai says, and we return to the house, where the gourmet spread on the dining table puts Alina's birthday celebration to shame.

There's everything from seafood to traditional Russian dishes to a huge variety of sushi and international delicacies like escargot.

They must've had most of this flown in; there's no way Pavel had time to make even a fraction of what's in front of us.

My stomach emits a growl, and I suddenly realize I'm ravenous. All that picture-taking must've been more energy intensive than it seemed. Or maybe it's the stress. Either way, as soon as we sit down and Pavel makes the first toast to our health, I load my plate with five different types of caviar sandwiches, followed by blintzes, puff pastries, an enormous variety of pickled fruits and vegetables, lobster tails, cured meats, gourmet cheeses, and salads of every kind. Everything is as delicious as it looks, and my dress is bursting at the seams by the time I finally pause to take a breath.

Looking up from my plate, I catch Nikolai watching me with an indulgent smile.

"What?" I ask self-consciously, putting down my fork.

"Nothing. I just enjoy seeing you eat."

More like seeing me pig out. My ears burn, but I grab another lobster tail. This food is just too freaking good, and if there's anything I've learned during my month on the run, it's not to take good food—or any food—for granted.

Two toasts later, however, I have to admit defeat. There's no way I can eat anything else, and the main course isn't even out yet. To distract myself from the

ANNA ZAIRES

overstuffed feeling, I look over at Nikolai, who's explaining something to Pavel in Russian.

I wait for him to finish, and when he glances at me, I say, "Your brothers... Have you told them about the wedding?" It's just occurred to me that I haven't yet met my new brothers-in-law, and they may have no clue that I'm now part of the family.

Nikolai gestures toward the videographer, who's discreetly circling around the table with his camera. "Valery and Konstantin are getting the live feed, and they'll videocall in a bit to congratulate us."

Of course. He's thought of everything. Why am I even surprised? Organizing a wedding in a matter of hours must be child's play compared to planning a high-profile assassination. Not that the latter is happening any longer—at least if Nikolai keeps his word.

With effort, I refocus on the celebration, which reminds me a lot of Alina's birthday, only with all the toasts directed at me and Nikolai. The majority of them are given by Pavel and Lyudmila, who seem determined to outdo each other with well wishes, but Alina raises her glass a couple of times too, first to wish us a long and happy marriage and then to toast to me as "the sister she's always wished to have."

She's had at least four shots of vodka by this point, I know, but her words still touch me, tugging at that small, secret part of me that's always wanted a sister too.

206

Maybe being a Molotov won't be so bad. Gaining a family—even a mafia family—might be worth it.

My tentative enthusiasm lasts through the main course and dessert, fueled by several glasses of wine and two shots of vodka. Everyone around me is happily buzzed as well, with the exception of Slava and Nikolai.

Like at Alina's birthday, I get the sense that alcohol only sharpens my new husband's faculties, that vodka is more like Red Bull or coffee for him. Or maybe it's simply that it strips away some of his polished, elegant façade, the one he uses to veil the potent force of his personality, that dark intensity that simmers within him and seeks to bend everything and everyone to his will.

To bend *me*, molding me into what he wants me to be.

His wife. His possession. His in every way... because the ring on my finger is a cage, one from which there'll be no escape.

The realization should frighten me—and normally it would—but alcohol doesn't act like Red Bull for me. Instead, it paints my world in warm, blurry shades, like the watercolor of a sunset—which is why I don't object when Nikolai pulls me onto his lap, where he feeds me chocolate-covered strawberries by hand while we talk to his brothers on a laptop Pavel brings to the table.

Konstantin calls in first, his lean face so reminiscent of Nikolai's my heart skips a beat when it first appears on the screen. Upon closer examination, however, the differences become apparent. Konstantin's nose is slightly larger and more hooked, his strong chin boasts a cleft, and his eyes are set deeper within their sockets, their striking color hidden behind his black-rimmed glasses. More importantly, his lips lack the cynical, wicked curve of Nikolai's, though they're just as beautiful in their own austere way.

For some reason, it's easy to picture Nikolai's older brother as a warrior monk, transcribing ancient scrolls by hand in between decimating hordes of invading barbarians.

"Congratulations on your wedding," he tells us. His voice is deep, like Nikolai's, his accent perfectly American. I wonder if he also studied here in the States. "I'm happy for you both." His gaze homes in on me. "Welcome to the family, Chloe."

"Thank you. It's so nice to meet you."

We exchange a few more pleasantries as Nikolai feeds me the strawberries, his arm looped possessively around my ribcage, and it's not until Konstantin hangs up that I realize he didn't react in any way to the sight of me being held on his brother's lap and fed like a child. There was no teasing smile, nothing to indicate he'd even been aware of it.

It's as if we've just spoken to an AI instead of a human being—which, given what I've heard about Konstantin's IQ and tech genius, is not out of the realm of possibilities.

Valery is up next, and the vibe I get from him is completely different. If possible, Nikolai's younger brother looks even more like his twin—or rather, his clone, given the four-year age gap between them. But that's where the similarities end. There's something cold and calculated about Valery. The smile on his sensual lips doesn't quite reach his eyes, which scan my face with an unsettling lack of emotion.

A puppet master—that's what he reminds me of, I realize as he congratulates us in a cool, even tone, his deep voice as unaccented as his brothers'.

As with Konstantin, our call with him is short, just a simple meet-and-greet. At the end of it, I have no idea what he thinks of me or our hasty wedding—or anything else for that matter.

"Your brothers are... interesting," I tell Nikolai when we disconnect. "Were you close growing up?"

He brings another strawberry to my lips. "Not exactly." Before I can ask him to elaborate, he pushes the sweet berry into my mouth, then picks up a glass of champagne and hands it to me.

I swallow the berry and take a sip of the fizzy, slightly sweet drink as Nikolai picks up another glass of champagne and waits until everyone's eyes are on us.

"To my beautiful bride," he says, pinning me with his intense tiger stare. "Zaychik... I couldn't be happier to have you in my life, and I will do everything in my power to ensure *your* happiness."

And again, I hear the unspoken "even if you object."

34

NIKOLAI

Two more toasts from Pavel and Lyudmila, and the dinner is over. Sweeping Chloe into my arms, I carry her upstairs to my bedroom.

No, *our* bedroom. Now that she's my wife, she's going to be sleeping in my arms every night.

My heart thuds heavily as I push open the door with my shoulder and carry her inside, where I carefully set her on her feet in front of the bed. She sways slightly and giggles; clearly, all that wine and champagne has gone to her head.

My head is clouded as well, but not from alcohol. It's lust that tangles my thoughts and fills my veins with slow-moving lava. The lengthy celebration was another test of my self-control, one I barely passed.

I wanted to grab Chloe and carry her off to bed right after we said our vows, to seal our bond in the most basic way possible. The only reason I resisted was for the memories.

When we're old and gray, I want to look back at the pictures and videos and recall every detail of this day.

Chloe sways again, blinking up at me owlishly, and I grip her shoulders to prevent her from falling. Then, ignoring the hunger coiling inside me, I look at her, imprinting every feature, every eyelash on my mind. Because the pictures and videos won't be enough. I want to remember all the sensations, from the silky warmth of her skin to the champagne-and-strawberries sweetness of her breath.

My bride.

My wife.

No two words have ever felt so right, so satisfying.

She's especially beautiful today, in this white, ethereal gown that makes my hands itch to rip it off her, baring more of her gorgeous, glowing skin. Her gold-streaked hair is arranged in an artful updo, her plump lips tinted with a rich berry color, her brown eyes made even bigger and softer with smoky makeup. Yet all I can think about is how much I want to see her with her face bare and puffy from sleep, her hair tangled from my fingers.

I want to watch her wake up in my embrace tomorrow morning, and every morning for the rest of our lives.

Ignoring the desire scorching my insides, I cup her cheek and bend my head, dragging her fresh, crisp scent into my lungs as I kiss the tender shell of her ear. As hungry as I am for her, tonight I will be gentle, making up for my ferocity last night.

No matter what it costs me, I will make our wedding night everything my zaychik's ever dreamed of.

35

CHLOE

I expect Nikolai to fall upon me as savagely as usual, but he's excruciatingly tender, slowly unbuttoning the dress and pressing soft, warm kisses to my neck and throat until all the anticipatory tension drains out of my body, leaving warm lassitude in its wake. By the time I'm naked, my very bones feel as if they've melted, even as a different type of tension gathers low in my core, my body heating from the inside out.

Laying me down on the mattress, he steps back to disrobe himself, and I watch with a quickening heartbeat as he removes his black tuxedo jacket and bow tie. Underneath, he's wearing a silver vest over a crisp white shirt, both hugging his muscular, broad-shouldered torso in a way that leaves no doubt they were custom made for him.

Swiftly, he divests himself of both items, followed by his pants and briefs. Unlike with my dress, there's a jerky, impatient quality to his movements that makes me realize he's not nearly as in control as he seems. His erection, hard and massive, curves up toward his ridged stomach, betraying his hunger for me.

Nonetheless, when he climbs onto the bed, he's just as careful and tender, picking up one foot of mine to press small kisses to the top of the arch before moving higher up my leg. My breath hitches as his mouth approaches the V between my thighs, but he skips over it, instead kissing and caressing my lower belly, then my heaving ribcage and my breasts.

The softly lit room spins around me, the ceiling turning blurry in my vision as he latches onto my left nipple, laving it lovingly with his tongue before switching his attention to the other breast as I moan, my hands falling onto the cool silk of his hair. It's the alcohol, I know, but I feel like I'm floating in space, anchored only by the wet warmth of his mouth on my breasts and the gentle stroking of his callused hands over my burning skin.

Our wedding night.

It feels as surreal as it sounds.

My eyes drift shut as Nikolai's lips move higher, kissing my collarbone and my neck before claiming my lips in a deep, sweetly cajoling kiss. It's like a drug, that kiss, an aphrodisiac of the most potent kind. His sensual scent fills my nostrils, mixing with the faint aroma of vodka on his breath, and my arousal grows as his tongue strokes and caresses the recesses of my mouth, feasting on me with tender skill.

Still kissing me, he slips his hand between our

bodies to find my aching clit, and I moan into his mouth as his fingers press on just the right spot, the one that intensifies the ache, adding to the tension growing inside me. A tension that swiftly turns unbearable as his fingers embark on a maddeningly uneven rubbing rhythm while his lips return to my neck, where the damp warmth of his breath sends pleasure chills down my arm.

I'm so turned on I may explode, yet the orgasm is still somehow out of reach.

Panting, I buck against his hand, desperate for a smoother, harder rhythm, and his teeth graze over my earlobe in warning. "No, zaychik," he whispers, and I feel the wicked curve of his mouth against my throat. "You're not ready yet."

Not ready? I'm ready to beg, plead, and sell my firstborn. With each light, circling stroke of his fingers, I get ever closer to the edge, but I can't go over it, no matter how hard I try.

"Please…" I shimmy my hips in desperation, my hands fisting in his hair. "Please, I need…"

He leisurely licks the underside of my ear. "What? What do you need?"

"To come," I gasp, bucking against his hand again. "Please, Nikolai, I need to come."

"Wrong answer." His fingers stop moving altogether. Lightly, he bites my earlobe and lifts his head, his eyes gleaming darkly. "Tell me the truth, zaychik. What do you need?"

"You," I whisper, staring up at him. "I need you."

And it's true. I can't imagine being anywhere else, with anyone else, ever. I need him not just for this orgasm but for him, for everything he is, good and bad, sublime and terrifying.

It must be the right answer because he kisses me again and his fingers return to my clit, bringing me back to the edge, to that elusive, maddening cusp of ecstasy. But sadist that he is, he keeps me at that peak, prolonging the exquisite torment until I'm panting and clawing at his back. Then and only then, when I'm ready to scream in frustration, he lets me go over.

The surge of pleasure is so intense it's like an endorphin bomb exploding in my brain. Every nerve ending in my body lights up with the potent force of it, my vision cutting in and out as my inner muscles spasm. The sensations are so overwhelming I lose myself in them, and by the time I come down to earth, he's already pushing into me, his thick cock forcing apart my tender tissues. His face is taut, his jaw clenched from the strain of holding back, and though he's still being careful and gentle, I'm so sore from last night I can't help wincing.

He stops, letting me adjust, distracting me with more of those deep, sweetly drugging kisses, and when I'm a quivering heap of need, my body wet and pliant, he begins thrusting. His pace is slow at first, controlled, but when I wrap my legs around his muscled ass, pulling him deeper into me, his control snaps and he takes me with all the driving power of his hard body.

I come again, screaming his name as he shudders

over me, and it's not until he withdraws some minutes later that I realize he's kept his word and worn a condom. A condom he disposes of before carrying me off to the bathroom, where he deposits me into an already-prepared bath.

"Thank you," I murmur, meeting his gaze as he joins me in the warm, bubble-covered water, and he smiles, the look in his tiger eyes so achingly tender my heart squeezes in my chest.

"For what, zaychik?"

For you. It takes everything to hold back those words, words that are far too close to an admission of my feelings. Instead, I lay my palm along the hard contour of his jaw and plant my lips on his, expressing with my body what I don't dare say out loud.

Not yet, at least.

36

CHLOE

I wake up still feeling that warm glow, a high that intensifies when I open my eyes and find him lying propped up on his elbow next to me, watching me with a tenderly possessive smile.

"Good morning," I murmur, pushing my hair off my face and fighting the urge to rub the sleep out of my eyes.

How long has he been awake and staring at me like this? More importantly, how much of a hot mess am I this morning? I did my best to remove my makeup in the bath last night, but I'm sure traces of eyeshadow and mascara are still smeared around my eyes, raccoon style, and my breath is not the freshest after all that alcohol.

He must not mind that because he leans forward and kisses me with such hunger I'm certain he's going to fuck me right then and there. But he pulls back and smiles at me instead, cradling my face in his big palm. "Good morning, zaychik. How are you feeling?"

Like this marriage thing might not be so bad. "I'm good," I say, smiling back. It's only been a day, but it's already hard to recall why I got so freaked out when he proposed. Like Alina said, this is pretty much the dream nurtured by every fairy tale: a gorgeous, wealthy husband who's crazy about you.

Granted, Nikolai is closer to the Prince of Darkness than Prince Charming, but pretty much all of the terrible things he's done—or planned to do—were to protect me.

Except the bit with his father.

The unsettling words whisper through my mind, but I push them away. I don't want to think about that this morning. I'm sure there's a reasonable explanation for everything, and soon, I'll learn what it is.

For now, I want to enjoy the first married morning of my life with the man who's looking at me like I'm made of chocolate and starlight.

And enjoy it I do. We shower together, an activity that results in a prolonged, steamy—literally, because the stall is steamed up—lovemaking session, during which Nikolai eats me out as if I were his breakfast and makes me come three times in a row before pinning me against the glass and fucking me so hard I scream his name.

I guess he's decided that taking me just once last night was enough to heal my soreness—and he's right. Of course I'm a little sore after *this* session but so satisfied it's worth it.

Afterward, Nikolai decides we need actual breakfast, so Lyudmila brings us a tray of fruit and leftovers from last night, along with tea and coffee, and we feed each other in bed. Or rather, Nikolai feeds me and I try to reciprocate—only he grabs the fork from me and kisses me until I forget all about what I was going to do. Some honey comes into play as well, and next thing I know, I need another shower and am decidedly more sore.

By the time we finally emerge from our bedroom, it's almost lunchtime, and as we head toward the stairs, Slava runs out of his room, Lyudmila on his heels.

"Mama Chloe!" His tiger-cub eyes are shining as he throws his short arms around my legs and squeezes tight before switching his attentions to Nikolai. Hugging his legs, he looks up at him. "Papa! I miss you and Chloe!"

At the look on Nikolai's face, I melt. There's no other word for it. Instead of a muscle with life-sustaining functions, my heart turns into a gooey puddle, and the rest of me follows suit.

Bending down, Nikolai picks up his son and perches him on his hip with natural-seeming ease. "Slavochka…" His voice is strained as he gazes into the child's face. "We've missed you too."

Lyudmila's eyes meet mine, and I see my feelings

reflected on her normally impassive face. Clearing her throat, she says with a thicker-than-usual accent, "I go help Pavel, okay?" and hurries downstairs.

We follow her at a leisurely pace, with Nikolai carrying Slava on his hip as if he were a toddler. The boy seems glad to be there, though, and I can't blame him.

He's missed out on this for the first four years of his life.

As we join Alina at the table, I can't stop smiling—and she notices.

"Fun night?" she whispers to me slyly while Nikolai is busy filling Slava's plate.

I nod, flushing, and she laughs, causing Slava and Nikolai to look at us askance.

My joyous mood must be infectious—that or everyone is still in a celebratory mode—because the lunch proceeds without any of the usual tension between the siblings. Instead, Nikolai and Alina team up to tell me amusing stories about Russia, everything from how Americans are viewed over there to their family's tradition of wintertime dips in frozen lakes.

"That's horrible," I exclaim when Alina describes how she almost lost a toe to frostbite by walking barefoot across the ice when she was seven. "What were your parents thinking?"

I realize my mistake as soon as the words are out—the last thing I want is to remind them about their father—but to my relief, Alina doesn't bat an eye. "Oh, that wasn't our parents' idea. Our grandmother was the

221

one who believed that cold exposure is good for the body and the soul. And you know what? The latest science confirms it. Same goes for saunas, another Russian staple. They're apparently exercise mimetics, and heat shock proteins released during those sweating sessions do everything from improving heart health to preventing cancer. So if you want to live a long, healthy life, you should partake in both ice baths and saunas—and ideally, both together."

"No, thank you," I say with a shudder, but Nikolai laughs and says that he'll have me try out the extreme regimen this winter.

"We'll get you addicted to it, I promise," he adds with a smile as I process the startling realization that I'll be with him this winter—and every other winter in the foreseeable future.

Because that's what marriage means.

We're together for the rest of our lives.

An echo of my earlier panic returns, but I suppress it. I'm not letting my irrational fears cast a shadow over what promises to be a beautiful day together—hopefully, the first of many.

After all, happiness is a choice, and I'd much rather be happy in this forced marriage.

37

CHLOE

The next few days pass in a similarly idyllic manner. Though we haven't gone anywhere, it feels like we're on our honeymoon. We make love multiple times a night (and oftentimes day), sleep in late, eat breakfast in bed, and go on long walks and hikes, both by ourselves and with Slava. One time, Alina joins us as well, and the four of us end up swimming in a nearby lake, where all three Russians make fun of my reluctance to get into the chilly, spring-fed water.

It turns out Slava is as comfortable being cold as the adults, making me the only wimp.

I do end up swimming, though, and as I'm shivering afterward, Nikolai warms me by rubbing me all over with his big, rough palms. If we were alone, he would've undoubtedly done more, but alas, even he draws the line at making love in front of his young son and sister.

That's about the only act where he does draw the

line, though. We engage in PDA all the time. My husband has zero shame when it comes to kissing me, massaging my neck and shoulders, and pulling me onto his lap whenever the mood strikes. It's like I'm a pet he likes to cuddle. I can't say I hate it; in fact, I not-so-secretly revel in his attention.

It would be different if anyone in the household made fun of it or otherwise made me feel embarrassed. But no one does. Even Alina, with her occasional gentle teasing, takes it for granted that her brother can't keep his hands off me, so much so that I have to wonder if it's one of those legendary "Molotov men" traits.

I'd ask, but I'm afraid it might be too close to the topic I'm skirting, the answers I've been telling myself I want, yet can't bring myself to demand. It just feels so good not to think about the darkness in Nikolai and the terrifying things he's capable of. I haven't even inquired about Masha and the new plan to take down Bransford; each time I think about my biological father, my pulse shoots up and my stomach contracts into a hard, tight knot.

Tomorrow morning, I tell myself each evening. *I'll talk to Nikolai about this first thing in the morning.* But then in the morning, I wake up in his embrace, feeling warm and secure, worshipped and adored, and I can't bring myself to risk the peace, so I tell myself we'll talk in the evening.

I know something is bound to happen to puncture our happy bubble, but I'm reluctant for that something to be me.

We go on like that for three more weeks, during which I bask in the attention he lavishes on me, reveling in both his tenderness and his roughness. Both versions of Nikolai—the gentle lover and the fierce savage— thrill me, which is a good thing, because when it comes to my husband, I can never predict what I'm going to get. In the same night, he might worship my body as if I were made of crystal, and fuck me until I can barely walk the next day. At times, I get the sense that he wants even more, that one day, he might push me further, try to possess me even more completely, but that like me, he's reluctant to do anything to bring any strife and tension back into our life, ending this honeymoon of ours.

Instead, he showers me with gifts, everything from expensive jewelry to accessories and clothing. It seems as if a new dress, or pair of shoes, or scarf, or *something* appears in my closet daily. It's almost too much for me —many of the earrings and bracelets I now own cost more than some people's houses—but he insists that it gives him pleasure to buy me things, so I eventually stop objecting... because having those things gives me pleasure too.

I've never known true poverty, thanks to my mom working nonstop to support us, but I also can't recall a time in my life when I didn't have to count every penny and carefully budget for every expense. Most of my childhood clothes were bought second-hand,

and the only jewelry I owned was of the cheap costume kind. Now, my closet is like Saks Fifth Avenue on steroids, and though it may be shallow of me, I love it. Rich people know what they're doing when they buy all those luxuries—they really can enhance one's life.

Also enhancing my life are the Russian lessons Nikolai has started giving me—with Slava's help, of course. The child takes great delight in my inability to pronounce the Russian phrases he says so easily, while Nikolai delights in a completely different thing: making me say love and sex words to him in bed.

"Say, '*Ya hochu tebya*,'" he instructs me while keeping me on the edge of an orgasm. And when I obey, desperate for relief, he orders mercilessly, "Now say, '*Ya lyublyu tebya*.'"

So I do. I say whatever he wants me to, including phrases so dirty they make me flush all over when I later look them up. But dirty or clean, my knowledge of Russian is growing by the day, which greatly amuses Alina and Lyudmila—the latter of whom finds my pronunciations downright comical.

"You so American," Pavel's wife says, laughing, as I attempt to ask her for *zavtrak*—breakfast—in her native tongue. "Why you even try? Everyone here speak English, even me."

I'd take offense, but she's right. Even her English, imperfect as it is, is a thousand times better than my Russian. I've offered to give her some lessons to improve it further, but she hasn't taken me up on it so far—because she hopes to go back to Russia and not need it, according to Alina.

"She really misses Moscow," she tells me. "She's bored here, with nothing to do and no one to see."

I can sympathize with that. Despite all the modern luxury and natural beauty surrounding us, the compound is a prison of sorts, or to put a more positive spin on it, a retreat from the world. I, too, miss my friends, and often scour social media to catch glimpses of their post-graduation lives. I want to contact them so badly, to reply to all of their messages asking where I am, why I haven't posted on my profiles in months, but I don't dare do so in case that somehow leads Bransford to me, to this compound and my new family.

I can't put them in danger, not even to assuage my friends' worries about me.

I would especially feel terrible if I did anything to endanger Slava. With each passing day, my attachment to Nikolai's son grows, and I feel increasingly comfortable in the role of his mom. Instead of Alina or Lyudmila bathing him and putting him to bed, Nikolai and I frequently do so together nowadays, telling him stories about superheroes and reading from his favorite books until he falls asleep.

The three of us are becoming a real family, and the knowledge fills me with a gentle warmth, a contentment that shouldn't be possible with a dangerous, mercurial man like Nikolai.

Not that everything is perfect, of course. For one

thing, the two of us disagree when it comes to what a not-quite-five-year-old should be allowed to do. As it turns out, Nikolai and his brothers—and to a lesser extent, Alina—were latchkey kids, allowed and even encouraged to play outside on their own and overall be dangerously independent. So while I panic each time I see a steak knife in Slava's hand or find him climbing a tree higher than six feet, Nikolai is annoyingly calm about such things.

"Don't you care that he can fall and break every bone in his body?" I ask in frustration when we go on a hike and he lets Slava scamper up an old oak until his tiny figure is barely visible through the foliage. "Or worse, fall on his head and break his neck?"

"Of course I do." His golden eyes narrow at me dangerously. "You think I don't worry about all the terrible things that can befall him on any given day? The stairs he can tumble down, the illnesses he can catch, the poisonous berries he might find and eat? Sometimes it's all I can think about, so much so I'm convinced I'm going insane. But just as we can't be there to hold his hand each time he takes the stairs, we can't expect to be there for every tree he encounters or every knife that comes his way throughout his life. In fact, there's no guarantee we'll be there for him tomorrow. Life can be unpredictable and brutal, and the better prepared he is to face it, the higher the odds that he'll survive."

"But he's still a child. You have to teach him *how* to survive."

"I am teaching him—by letting him face as many of the dangers on his own as he can. Children his age aren't stupid; they've fallen enough to know that it hurts. He wouldn't climb that high if he didn't feel secure in his strength, and the only way to grow and test that strength is to challenge himself when it matters... when there is no rubber mat underneath. Besides," he adds when I'm about to start arguing, "I *am* keeping an eye on him. If he should start to fall, I'll catch him."

I shut up then, because odds are, he will. The man has the reflexes of a cat. The other day, I accidentally knocked a water glass off the table with my elbow, and Nikolai caught it in mid-air without pausing in the conversation. Another time, I tripped over one of Slava's LEGO pieces and would've faceplanted, but Nikolai had his arms around me before I hit the floor—though he was on the other side of the room a second earlier.

If I didn't know better, I'd think he was one of Slava's comic book superheroes—or more likely, supervillains.

That label fits him as well as anything.

───────────

Later that night, as we enter our bedroom, something occurs to me in regard to our earlier conversation.

"If you're so determined to nurture Slava's independence, why are you so determined to shield *me* from any and all danger?" I ask, sitting down on the bed to watch Nikolai remove his jacket and tie. We're still doing the formal attire at dinner, and I must admit I've grown to like it. Not only do I get to wear gorgeous dresses on a daily basis, but my husband is surreally handsome in those sharply tailored suits he favors.

It's like we alternate between two realms: the daytime one where we go hiking in the wilderness and get dirty, and the evening one where glamour and glitz reign supreme.

"Because you're not a child, and you weren't raised the way I'm raising Slava," Nikolai replies smoothly, undoing his cufflinks. "Your mom, as wonderful as she was, didn't equip you to face assassins, zaychik... or men like me."

I swallow hard, my blood heating up as he rakes his gaze over my still fully dressed body. Ever since our wedding, I've gotten better at reading Nikolai's sexual moods and understanding what kind of night I'm in for. And tonight promises to be one of our wilder ones, the ones when I'm never quite sure how far he'll go.

When I can sense the darkness in him, feel it rising close to the surface.

Not that I'm afraid of him. Not really. I know he won't hurt me, at least not in any damaging way. I just sometimes get the sense that what we have isn't quite enough for him, that his voracious hunger for me remains unsatisfied.

At times, it feels as if he wants to consume me, all of me, and nothing less will do.

He takes off his shirt, revealing beautifully defined muscles, and comes toward me, his movements once again reminding me of a big cat's smooth, lethally graceful prowl.

Maybe he *was* a tiger in another life.

Maybe I was his prey.

Instinctively, I scoot backward on the bed, and his lips take on a wicked curve. As always, he knows what I'm thinking and feeling—and he likes what I'm feeling now.

He likes making me just a bit nervous.

Moving with that same predatory deliberateness, he climbs onto the bed and over me, pushing me down flat before catching my wrists and pinning them above my head with one hand.

My mouth goes dry at the look in his eyes, at the dark intensity within them. I dampen my lips, and his gaze follows the path of my tongue, his face tightening. When his eyes meet mine again, they're filled with such scorching heat I feel like I could burn up on the spot. My heart hammers wildly, my skin flushing all over as he lowers his head and audibly inhales, as if hungry for the smell of my hair.

"Um, Nikolai…" I wriggle underneath him, my pulse surging higher as I feel the bulge pressing against my thighs. Even with the layers of his pants and my dress separating us, I can feel how hot and hard his erection is, how massive. I swallow again. "When you said 'men like me,' what did you mean, exactly?"

His lips brush my ear, the heat of his breath making me shiver as he whispers, "Oh, my sweet, curious zaychik... you're about to find out."

38

CHLOE

A shudder ripples through my body, and he lifts his head to look at me, a dark smile tilting up the corners of his lips. I can all but feel him drinking in my trepidation, sadistically prolonging the anticipation.

I try to move my hands, to twist out of his grip, but it's futile. His fingers are an iron shackle around my wrists, pinning them in place above my head. His smile deepens, the golden gleam in his eyes intensifying as I struggle, and I know that he enjoys this too, seeing me helpless in his grasp.

Dipping his head, he drags in another hungry inhale, then finally lets go of my wrists. Before I can let out a relieved breath, he flips me over onto my stomach and, holding me down with one big hand, pulls down the zipper of my dress. When it's open all the way to my tailbone, he runs a warm palm down my bare spine, the roughness of his calluses scratching my skin pleasantly.

"Have I ever told you how much I love your back?" The soft, dark timbre of his voice is soothing, yet unnerving. "So toned and graceful, like a ballerina's. My favorite part of you, though, is this ass." His palm curves over my cheek and squeezes lightly. "So tight and round and perfect... so fuckable."

My heart jumps again as he pulls me up to a sitting position and props my back against his chest, banding one powerful arm around my ribcage to hold me in place as he drags the dress down my torso. He's handling me like a human-sized doll, and there's something perversely erotic about that, something that appeals to a part of me that I try not to think about... the one that's not put off by the darkness in him but drawn to it.

I'm not wearing a bra, and as he pulls the dress down to my waist, my naked breasts pop free, spilling onto his forearm, my nipples already peaked and aching. A low growl rumbles in his chest, and he bends me back over his arm in that way he likes to do, the one that makes me feel like a human sacrifice, an offering to a fierce, primordial god.

His hot, wet mouth closes around my nipple, and I gasp, gripping his head as he bites down, sending fire streaking directly to my clit. My nerve endings riot in confusion, the pain and pleasure blending until I'm desperate for more. And he delivers more, repeating the treatment with my other breast, alternating between sucking on the nipple and using his teeth on it. By the time he lifts his head to meet my gaze, I'm panting, burning from arousal.

I need him. I need him so fucking much.

Forgetting all about my fears, I pull his head to mine, and our lips fuse in a hard, deeply carnal kiss, our tongues tangling as I respond to the violence of his need, matching him stroke for stroke, bite for bite. I don't care what he does to me tonight as long as I can have more of this dark, dizzying pleasure, more of what I crave.

We're both breathing raggedly by the time he breaks the kiss and lays me flat to work the dress down my hips. It refuses to come off easily, so he rips it at the seams, too impatient to care that he's ruining yet another pricey gown. And I don't care either, not with the tension building rapidly inside me, not when every part of me burns for him.

When I'm dressed in nothing but a thong, he flips me back onto my stomach and stuffs two pillows underneath my hips before working the scrap of fabric down my legs. Then he reaches over to the right, and I hear a drawer open.

My trepidation returns, briefly overruling my arousal. I strongly suspect I know what he intends to do, and I'm proven right when I glance over my shoulder and see the bottle of lube and a small butt plug in his hands. Still, my heart jackrabbits into my throat, my ribcage tightening around my lungs. "Nikolai, I…" I gulp in air. "I've never… that is—"

"Never been fucked in the ass?"

My face heats unbearably, his dirty words further knocking me off kilter. Somehow, I manage a small nod, and his lips curve with primal male satisfaction as he says softly, "Good," and drizzles cool lube between my ass cheeks.

I gasp, clenching instinctively as he presses the plug to my opening, and he pushes my head down on the bed. "Relax, zaychik." His voice is rough velvet and dark heat. "I promise you'll enjoy this."

I want to object—the one time my ex-boyfriend tried to put a finger in, I hated every second—but this is Nikolai, whose mastery over my body is frighteningly total. In his embrace, I lose all sense of self, much less what little sanity I still possess. So I keep quiet and do my best to breathe through my nose as the tapered, rubbery tip of the plug presses in, pushing past the tight ring of my sphincter.

Slowly, it slides in deeper, and I stifle my groan against the mattress, overwhelmed by the strange sensations. As that other time, there's an almost nauseating fullness, a feeling of being stretched and penetrated, invaded in an unnatural, uncomfortable way. But there's also something more, a peculiar type of pressure that makes my pulse soar and my insides tighten—a sensation that grows stronger as Nikolai leans over me, covering me with his big, hard body, enveloping me in his sensual male scent.

His breath warms my ear as he kisses the sensitive

crook of my neck, sending pleasure chills down my arm. At the same time, he wedges one hand underneath my stomach and finds my clit while beginning to slowly fuck me with the toy. Immediately, the pressure intensifies, transforming into an erotic tension, a dark, heated pleasure that collides with the discomfort and somehow grows from it. His fingers on my clit, the toy in my ass, his lips on my neck—it's sensory overload, a seesaw of pleasure and pain that rocks back and forth, each time cresting higher.

With a muffled cry, I come undone, shuddering and shaking, but he's not done with me. Pulling the toy out of my ass with a slick *pop*, he penetrates me first with one finger, then two together, the stinging stretch only bearable because of the evil magic his other hand is performing on my clit. It hurts, it burns, yet the pain once again alternates with potent pleasure, heightening it in some peculiar way. Panting, I orgasm again, my ass clamping down on his big, rough-edged fingers, my vision dappling with spots of black and white as a gasping cry escapes my throat.

Before I can recover, he pulls his fingers out of my still-spasming body, and I feel the broad, smooth head of his cock at my opening instead. I tense, my pulse skyrocketing anew, and he runs a reassuring hand down my spine.

"Breathe, zaychik. You can take me." The words are a soft, deep murmur, as comforting as the gentle petting of my back. Yet the moment he grips my hips and pushes against the tight ring of muscle, the seesaw tips all the way to pain, and I know he's wrong.

I can't do it.

He's way too big for me.

"Nikolai, please, st—" I gasp, the plea catching in my throat as my sphincter gives in under the pressure and the massive head of his cock pops in. All air whooshes out of my lungs, my vision going full black for a dizzying moment. He's so big and thick it feels as if I'm being split apart, and as he slowly works his cock deeper into me, I'm certain I'm going to faint.

But I don't. Instead, I feel every long, hard inch of him, experience every bit of the excruciatingly careful invasion. My stomach twists and churns, my skin turning clammy with cold sweat, yet I can't form the words to call a halt to this, my brain as overwhelmed as my body.

It doesn't help that he's leaning over me again, kissing my neck and murmuring soothing endearments into my ear, his smooth voice rough with need. Nor that his skilled fingers are once again toying with my clit, coaxing out sensations that can't—shouldn't—coexist with this type of pain. It's not pleasure, exactly, but something like it, a mix of agony and ecstasy that winds me up anew, wrenching a tortured climax from my body.

I do pass out then, at least for a moment, because the next thing I register is him gliding smoothly in and out of my ass, each thrust generating a sensation of its own, the seesaw once more rocking back and forth, building the powerfully erotic tension. My body floods with heat, my heart rampaging inside my ribcage, and as I come for the fourth time with a ragged scream, he groans and shudders over me, warm jets of cum bathing my sore insides.

Shaken and shattered, I lie there, too weak to move as he withdraws from me and leaves the bed, returning a minute later with a warm, wet towel. He cleans me off, then turns me over and scoops me up into his lap. I force open my heavy lids to find his tiger eyes on my face, studying me with his signature intensity.

Gently, reverently, he cups my cheek, his voice rough as he murmurs, "I'm never going to let you go, you know. Not even if you beg."

I hold his gaze. "I know."

"Do you hate me for that?"

I should. However nice this honeymoon has been, the truth is, he forced me into marriage, took away my freedom, my choices. In just about every way that matters, I'm his captive, at the mercy of his darker whims and passions. Yet the lie refuses to leave my lips. Instead, I tell him the truth. "I love you."

Because I do. As wrong as it is, I love this beautiful, terrifying, complicated man. I love him even as I fear his relentless obsession with me.

I know that in the bright light of tomorrow, I'll regret this confession, that I'll think it a mistake. Right now, though, in this softly lit room, with his strong arms around me and my body still pulsing with echoes of the agony and ecstasy he's put me through, it doesn't feel like a mistake—especially since the tender smile that blooms across his face is the most beautiful thing I've ever seen.

"And I love you, zaychik," he says softly. "I always will."

39

NIKOLAI

I wake up with Chloe's small body wrapped in my arms and my brain flush with happiness. The glowing, incandescent kind that feels as flickering and fleeting as the burning wick of a candle.

As I have for the past week since we admitted our feelings, I absorb the feel of her, the sensation of her warm skin pressing against mine, of her delicate curves molding against the hard planes of my body, of her breath fanning over my forearm. And as has been the case for the past week, I battle an urge to wake her and demand the words from her again, so I can hear her soft, husky voice telling me she loves me.

It's bad enough I force her to say it to me every night, each time I take her.

Burying my face in her hair, I breathe in her scent, the sweet freshness of flowers shaded with sleep-warmed feminine skin. And as I have for the past two months, I fight off a surge of gut-wrenching fear.

Fear that I'm going to lose her. That the wick will burn out, leaving nothing but ashes.

It's irrational, illogical, but I can't help it. I thought extracting the words from her would rein this fear in, letting me get through the day calm and secure in the knowledge that she's mine, but if anything, the worry has grown stronger, more pervasive. Sometimes it's all I can think about: how fragile this happiness is, how illusory.

After all, in the beginning, my mother also loved my father. Once upon a time, they'd known happiness as well.

I try not to think about that, about how everything went to pieces for them, but there are times when I look at Chloe and see my mother's face. Not bright and healthy, the way it'd been when I was a child, but drawn and pale, deeply unhappy—the look she'd worn in her final years.

Partially, it's that I still haven't told Chloe about what happened that winter night—and she hasn't asked. Despite imposing it as a condition for our wedding, she seems reluctant to hear the full story. I think it's because she's afraid of the truth, fearful of finding out just how horrible of a monster she married. So she skirts the topic, and so do I.

There's every chance she'll hate me for what I've done, that she'll look at me with terror and revulsion.

It doesn't help that I'm aware I'm keeping Chloe like a captive princess in a high tower, completely isolated from everyone and everything. We don't leave the compound; we don't go anywhere. We exist in our own little world, one where she has no choice but to be mine. It's for her safety, true, but it's also for my peace of mind.

If given the opportunity, would she flee again?

If the danger to her were eliminated, would she want to leave?

I don't know the answers, and the questions torment me, so much so I've become even more obsessive about keeping tabs on her. I know she can't leave—and with Bransford hunting her, probably doesn't want to leave—but I still feel compelled to know her whereabouts each and every moment we're apart. To that end, I've installed cameras in our bedroom and every corner of the house with the exception of my sister's room and Pavel and Lyudmila's private quarters, and I check the video feed on my phone with the mindless frequency of a social media addict.

"What are you always looking at?" Alina asks, walking in on me in the dining room one day as I wait for Chloe to wrap up her lesson with Slava and come down for lunch. "Is something going on?"

I put my phone away. "Something's always going on."

It's not a lie. Not only is Masha working on getting close to Bransford and sending me daily updates on her progress, but I've also got men keeping tabs on Alexei Leonov. He's still here in the States, the last few days in Chicago. It appears he's there for business meetings, but I can't help feeling uneasy.

Chicago is that much closer to Idaho, to my compound and my son.

Alina regards me thoughtfully. "Is it the Volkov thing? Konstantin mentioned he's been inquiring about investing in his nuclear venture."

"That too." I'm not surprised she's heard about that. A self-made oligarch, Alexander Volkov is one of the wealthiest—and most dangerous—men in Russia. An alliance with him would be both advantageous and risky, especially given his propensity for business practices as ruthless as our own.

If things go south for any reason, we'll have another powerful enemy, but if all goes well, he could help speed up the approval process for the new technology, accelerating its adoption worldwide.

Alina sighs. "I wish he wouldn't go there, but Konstantin rarely listens. Maybe you can talk to him— unless you think it's a good idea, getting involved with Volkov?"

I shrug and change the subject. The truth is, Volkov and the potential joint venture are low on my list of worries, so I'm content to let Konstantin run with it. Our genius brother may be too intellectual for his own good at times, but he's still a Molotov and thus perfectly capable of assessing the risks for himself.

My priorities these days are Slava and Chloe, and I intend to do whatever it takes to keep and protect them both.

That night, one of my worst fears comes true. Shortly after midnight, the door to our room bursts open and Lyudmila runs in, yelling my name.

I'm on my feet and armed with the gun I keep under the mattress before she can explain—and when she does, I set the gun down and bolt into our closet.

"What happened?" Chloe demands, running in after me as Lyudmila rushes out of the room. Seeing me getting dressed, she starts pulling on her clothes as well. "What did she say?"

Realizing that Lyudmila had spoken Russian, I swiftly explain that Slava has fallen ill. "He's vomiting uncontrollably and running a high fever," I say as I hurriedly throw on a shirt. "He needs to go to a hospital right away."

Chloe's eyes widen. "Oh, no. I'm coming with you."

"Fuck, no." My tone is much too harsh, but I don't care. Fear, sharp and metallic, coats my tongue. My son is sick. So sick I have no choice but to risk exposing his whereabouts. The last thing I need is Chloe also in danger. "You're staying here, where it's safe."

She blinks up at me. "But—"

"I'll call you on the way." Catching her chin, I steal a brief, hard kiss, and then I'm running to Slava's room, my mind solely on my son and the fastest way of getting him to a hospital.

CHLOE

"More coffee?" Alina asks, and I nod, hopping off the bar stool to pace over to the kitchen window. It's pitch-black outside, without so much as a sliver of moonlight visible behind the thick clouds.

They're promising rainstorms tonight—not a good thing, given the speed with which Nikolai, Pavel, and four of the guards are driving down those winding mountain roads in their SUVs. Lyudmila went with them to help take care of Slava, so Alina and I are the only ones left in the house.

The only ones not *allowed* to leave the house.

According to Alina, Nikolai has placed all the remaining guards on high alert, so five of them are guarding the house itself, while the rest are patrolling the perimeter of the compound in case of an attack.

"What attack?" I asked when she told me this. "Slava is just sick."

She gave me a look suggesting I'm a naïve idiot. "There's sick, and there's sick—and we don't know which this is."

"You think he might've been *poisoned*?"

"We can't rule out anything," she replied, making me realize yet again just how different her and her brothers' upbringing had been from mine.

In my world, no one would deliberately hurt a child.

I turn away from the window and walk back to the kitchen counter. "Any more updates from Pavel or Lyudmila?"

"No." Alina hands me a fresh cup of coffee. Her eyes are as tired as mine, but her makeup and dress are impeccable—I guess on the off chance we might get invited to a gala in the middle of the night. "I don't think they've gotten to the hospital yet," she continues as I take a big gulp of my coffee. "Lyudmila said she'll text me when they do."

The hot liquid burns the roof of my mouth, but I drink the rest of the cup anyway, masochistically relishing the pain. It keeps me from dwelling on the most terrifying possibilities—such as Slava having been poisoned to lure him and Nikolai out of the safety of the compound, or their car going off a cliff on some dark, rain-slick road.

To make matters worse, I can't even call or text Nikolai for reassurance, as he's forgotten his phone here.

"This is so not like him," I mutter, glancing again at the device I brought with me after finding it in our bedroom. "He never forgets anything."

Alina nods somberly. "I know. I've never seen him this worried. Well, except for that one time with you."

Right. When I ran, and he had to save me from the assassins—an incident that now feels like a lifetime ago.

Setting down the empty cup, I return to the window, my chest tight and my stomach on fire from nerves and excess caffeine. I've never felt so useless and helpless—or so much like a prisoner. Though I've known all along that Nikolai won't let me leave the compound, it somehow didn't sink in fully until tonight, when he outright refused to take me with him.

Logically, I understand why—he doesn't need to worry about me as well as Slava—but that doesn't change the fact that I can't be with the two people I care about most... that I'm stuck here, no matter what.

"I'll be right back," Alina says and slips out of the kitchen—presumably to use the bathroom. I debate pouring myself another cup of coffee while I wait, but I decide that three cups should be enough for now. Instead, I pick up Nikolai's phone and swipe across the screen on the off chance it's unlocked.

It's not, of course. My security-obsessed husband would never be so careless as to leave an unlocked phone lying around. The device demands either a fingerprint or a passcode, and I have neither.

Sighing, I lay the phone on the counter and begin to

pace. This is torture in the very real sense of the word. I'm so worried about Slava and Nikolai I feel physically ill, a feeling compounded by the occasional distant flicker of lightning and clap of thunder.

The storm hasn't gotten here yet, but it might already be where they are.

God, what if they don't reach the hospital in time? An icy needle pierces my heart. *What if Slava is so sick he dies?* It's a thought I hadn't allowed myself before, but now that it's crept in, I can't banish it, and the sickening anxiety expands, crowding out the air in my lungs.

I should be there with them.

I should be in that car.

"Where you should be is your bedroom, trying to get some rest," Alina says quietly, and I spin around, startled to find her back on her bar stool.

When did she come back? Also, was I talking out loud?

I must've been, because she's regarding me with weary sympathy while cradling another cup of coffee in her hands. Even though she's normally a tea drinker, tonight she's mainlining the real stuff, same as me.

"Do you really think we're going to get attacked?" I ask, ignoring her nonsensical suggestion. "And if so, by whom? My father?"

Alina sighs and rests her chin in her hand. "Or one of our enemies. God knows there're plenty—not that Nikolai or Valery tell me anything."

"But Konstantin does?" From what I've gathered

over the past few weeks, she has a much closer relationship with their oldest brother, the tech genius. The two of them talk at least a couple of times a week.

"Sometimes. When he thinks it won't upset me." Her beautiful mouth twists. "He thinks I'm so fragile I'll fall apart at the slightest hint of bad news. Especially anything to do with—" She stops. "Never mind. The point is, I'm not exactly in the loop."

Neither am I—and I don't have the excuse of Alina's headaches, which Nikolai told me stem almost entirely from her mental state.

"Some people get stomachaches when stressed, she gets headaches. Bad ones," he explained when she didn't come down for dinner because of a migraine one day. "Sometimes they last for several days, and get so painful she has to knock herself out with a whole cocktail of addictive shit. Hopefully, this won't be one of those."

It wasn't, thankfully, and Alina was back to her normal self the next day. But I can see why Konstantin worries—I'll never forget the drugged-out mess she was that morning in my room.

If Alina doesn't already have a prescription painkiller problem, she's not far from it.

"Do you think she might benefit from something like rehab?" I had asked Nikolai later that day. "Or at least therapy?"

"She hates shrinks and refuses to talk to them," he told me. "As to rehab, we've considered it, but it's not clear that she's actually addicted. Her drug use is sporadic, centered around times of extra stress. It starts with more frequent headaches, and then it spirals until the headaches are no longer the main problem. She's always been able to stop the pills after a bit, though, which is why I allow her to continue using them. They're the only way she can escape the crippling pain when it strikes."

"What about pot?" I asked carefully, not wanting to rat Alina out in case Nikolai didn't know about her occasional smoke sessions with Lyudmila. "Maybe it could help as well?"

His mouth quirked. "Sure. Which is why I don't say anything when she comes in smelling like an Amsterdam coffee shop."

So he did know. I wasn't surprised. He sees everything that goes on around here—including the tangled contradictions in my head.

I love him. I have no problem admitting that now, to myself and to him. And he says he loves me. It should be enough, more than enough, yet it's not. Even when I lie in his arms in the afterglow of mind-blowing sex, there's an inexplicable distance between us, words unsaid and fears unvoiced.

It's mostly my fault, I think. For one thing, I still haven't been able to bring myself to ask about his father. Each time an opportunity arises, I chicken out. The darkness in Nikolai is like a two-sided magnet, drawing and repelling me at once. I want to know him fully, to understand his past as well as he understands mine, yet I'm afraid of delving deeper into the part of him I saw that day in the woods, when he dealt with the assassins.

Sometimes when I wake up in the middle of the night cuddled against him, I can hear the tortured assassin's screams, and I want to scream as well.

I also can't forget Nikolai's threat to drug me into marrying him. It didn't come to that, but I know it would've. Because for my husband, love and possession are the same.

He would do anything to have me.

Of course, contradictory mess that I am, I don't always mind his ruthlessness. There are times I'm glad he forced the issue, leapfrogging over the normal stages of a relationship in favor of marriage. And there are definitely times I enjoy his darker side in bed—pretty much all the times he brings it out, really. Our sex life is as blazing hot as it is varied, and as overwhelming as his hunger for me can be, I never go unsatisfied, to the point that I have to question if there's maybe something wrong with me... if it's healthy to lose myself in his embrace so completely.

In the embrace of a man who is, in many ways, still my captor.

Plopping onto a bar stool next to Alina, I grab Nikolai's phone and absentmindedly swipe across the screen again.

Yep, there it is, password requirement.

Whatever. I don't even know why I want to get into it. What I really need is to speak to Nikolai, but I'm sure he's got his hands full with Slava and navigating those tricky roads.

"Why do you keep doing that?" Alina asks as I swipe across the screen again. "Do you want to read his messages or something?"

I push the phone away. "No. Maybe. I don't know." What I want is Nikolai in bed next to me and Slava sleeping soundly down the hall, but neither is a possibility right now.

"Try 785418," Alina says. At my startled glance, she explains, "I have a good memory for numbers, and I saw Nikolai put it in a couple of weeks back. He might've changed it by now, though."

My fingers are already flying over the touchscreen. "I'm in!" I grin at her triumphantly. "*We're* in."

Then the implications hit me.

Alina has just helped me invade Nikolai's privacy in a major way.

All of a sudden, I don't feel right about this.

She must read it on my face. "He's been glued to that thing for the past week," she says, and I hear the frustration in her voice. "He hasn't told me why, but it might have something to do with all the guards being placed on code red—and I don't know about you, but if there's a specific threat out there, I want to know what it is. I'm tired of being kept in the dark."

Whereas I have willingly kept myself in the dark for

weeks, again not even inquiring about the progression of our plans for Bransford.

My discomfort transforms into shame at my cowardice. Steeling myself, I hand the phone to Alina. "Here. You'd know better where to look." I'll apologize to Nikolai for invading his privacy once this crisis is past.

She nods, and I scoot toward her as her red-tipped fingers fly over the screen. The first place she goes is the inbox, where she rapidly scrolls through the subject lines, many of which are in Russian. Opening one message, she skims it, a tiny frown bisecting the space between her dark brows as her eyes move over the Russian text.

"Well?" I prompt when she closes out of the email and resumes scrolling through the inbox. "Anything?"

She looks up from the screen and blinks, as if she's forgotten I'm there. "Not really." Her voice is strange, though, tight and a little choked. So is the smile she directs my way as she adds, "Just the usual bullshit."

"May I?" Not waiting for her reply, I snatch the phone back and skim the subject lines myself. My inability to read Russian is a serious hindrance, though, so I exit the inbox and check the texts instead. Nikolai uses an app I've never seen for that—encrypted, most likely—and most of those messages are in Russian as well.

So much for my grand hacking attempt.

I'm about to set the phone down when an icon in the upper left corner of the screen catches my attention. It's one of only a few apps on this phone, and its prime location tells me it must be something Nikolai uses a lot.

Intrigued, I click on the icon—a tiny house—and a series of images, or rather videos, fills the screen. Each one is too small to see anything in detail, so I click on the one where I spot some movement.

Alina peers at the screen over my shoulder. "Is that—"

"This kitchen, yes." In fact, I'm looking at the two of us sitting huddled over the phone. Frowning, I look up at the ceiling and over at the cabinets. The angle of the video suggests the cameras are high up and to the left of us, but no matter how hard I look, I don't see them.

I close out of the kitchen feed and zoom in on another image, then all the rest in turn.

Living room.

Dining room.

Glass-walled terrace.

Laundry room.

Upstairs hallway.

Staircase.

Slava's room.

My former room.

My heart hammers faster, an unpleasant tightness banding around my chest.

Sure enough, there it is, our bedroom.

"Is my room on there also?" Alina asks, her tone carefully level. She must not have known about the cameras either—and to think that just a moment ago, I felt bad for invading Nikolai's privacy.

I return to the app home screen and carefully examine the collection of tiny camera views. "I don't see it," I tell Alina. "Here, take a look."

She methodically goes through every feed. "None of my room," she concludes, sounding relieved. "Nor of Pavel and Lyudmila's. Which makes sense—it's probably Pavel who installed the cameras. He's good with security tech."

"Installed when?" My best guess is this is an advanced version of a nanny cam, something Nikolai implemented when he decided to place the ad for a tutor. If so, the cameras would've been installed either shortly before or shortly after my arrival, when I was still a stranger and thus not to be trusted with Slava. Although why our bedroom, originally Nikolai's bedroom, would be wired as well is a mys—

"Looks like the app was installed a few months back," Alina says, rooting through the settings. "But there were two updates since: one in July right after your arrival, and another, much bigger one more recently. A week ago, in fact." Her eyes meet mine. "Right around the time I started seeing Kolya glued to this screen."

Also right around the time I told him I loved him.

Maybe it's all a coincidence. Maybe it has nothing to do with me and everything to do with the email Alina reacted to so strangely, but my instincts tell me otherwise.

The cameras are there for me. To watch me.

My husband's obsession with me is growing, terrifyingly so—and because I've kept my head in the sand like an ostrich, I still don't know what he's truly capable of.

41

NIKOLAI

"The tests just came back," the doctor informs me when I return to Slava's room after a brief bathroom break. "Salmonella poisoning."

My breath escapes my tightly clenched throat as a wave of relief crashes into me. They've already stopped Slava's vomiting and gotten him on IV fluids, but until this moment, we'd had no idea what's made him so sick.

Salmonella.

Not some exotic designer poison from which there may be no cure.

Fucking salmonella.

I round on Lyudmila, who has the misfortune of being the only other person in the room. "Did you let him touch raw meat or eggs?"

She blanches. "No, I swear! He didn't even eat eggs today, unless—" Her eyes widen, and she presses her hand to her mouth. "Oh, no."

"What? Spit it out."

"Cookie dough," she whispers, her round face pale. "I think he must've sampled raw cookie dough. Pavel was making those chocolate chip cookies for dinner, and Slava and I came in to get some fruit for a snack…"

Fuck. What awful luck. There must've been an egg that had the bacteria, and of course Slava had to eat that cookie dough. In hindsight, it had to be something like this; I've personally vetted each and every single guard, and with our security being as tight as it is, the odds of some assassin being able to sneak poison into the compound were near zero. Still, I couldn't rule it out entirely—not until these tests came in.

"These poisonings are way more common than you'd think, especially among the elderly and the young," the doctor interjects, discerning the gist of my conversation with Lyudmila despite it being in Russian. "Salmonella is notoriously hardy if it's inside the yolk. You'd have to boil the egg for over eight minutes to ensure that you kill it all, and hardly anyone does that." He sighs. "You wouldn't believe the number of people who land in the ER after your standard omelet or scramble—and I'm not even talking about sunny-side-up or hollandaise sauce and what-not. Those are pretty much a Russian roulette… no offense."

I'm too relieved to be annoyed. "What are the next steps?" I cast a concerned glance at the adult-sized bed where Slava is sleeping, his small face pale and drawn from all the vomiting and diarrhea. He's already looking better from all the fluids, but I still shudder at the recollection of our frantic drive here, during which all I could think about was whether or not he'd make it.

"Normally, we'd just let the illness run its course, but he's got a fever, so we're giving him some antibiotics just in case. Between that and the fluids, he should be feeling meaningfully better soon. I'd like to keep him for observation for another day or so, though."

"Of course." If I'd known it was salmonella, I would've arranged for a medical team to take care of Slava at home, the way I did for Chloe, but I was so terrified that my son had been poisoned or exposed to some exotic neurotoxin that I couldn't risk not having the right specialists or equipment on hand. And now that we're in the hospital, it doesn't make sense to unhook Slava from all the machines and drive back in the storm. For fastest healing, he needs to rest and let the antibiotics do their job.

I just have to hope the Leonovs won't catch wind of our presence here—or that by the time they do, we'll be long gone.

The doctor leaves, and a contrite-looking Lyudmila excuses herself for a bathroom break as well. The two of us have been waiting by Slava's bedside while Pavel and the guards patrol the hallway. Not that I'm expecting an attack in an American hospital—at least I'm not now that I know my son wasn't deliberately poisoned. The compound is probably not in any greater danger either, though I'm not telling the guards to shift down from code red until we're back.

I've forgotten my fucking phone, and though Lyudmila's been texting with Alina and I know everything is okay back home, not being able to watch Chloe through the cameras makes me deeply uneasy.

It's as if someone's blindfolded me—or cut out my eyes.

"Let me use your phone for a bit," I tell Lyudmila when she returns, and she hands it to me before discreetly disappearing from the room.

As soon as she's gone, I call my sister and ask her to get Chloe if she's still awake.

If I can't see my zaychik, at least I'll hear her voice.

"First tell me how Slava is," Alina says.

I swiftly fill her in on his condition—Lyudmila has already informed her about the salmonella diagnosis— and again ask to speak to Chloe.

"Give me a minute." Alina's voice holds a peculiar note. I hope she's not getting another migraine, though I wouldn't be surprised if she were, given the events of the night.

I'm not prone to headaches, yet my temples feel like they're getting pounded by hammers.

I wait impatiently for Chloe to get on the phone. I probably should've called earlier instead of letting Lyudmila keep them apprised of the situation, but I needed to know what was happening with Slava first. The fear was like a boulder on my chest, but now I can finally breathe—and talk like a rational human being.

An hour ago, I was on the verge of ripping out the medical staff's throats with my bare teeth over their attempts to make us wait our turn for admission.

Luckily, money speaks even in this neck of the woods, so as soon as I told the ER receptionist that I will make a million-dollar donation to their children's department if my son is treated *immediately*, things got much smoother, and I didn't have to resort to more extreme measures—like, say, planting bullets in a few of the denser heads.

"Nikolai, hi." Chloe's soft voice is like a warm blanket wrapping around me, lessening the pounding in my head and unlocking the tension in my neck and shoulders. I didn't realize until this moment how tightly bunched they'd gotten.

Turning away from Slava's bed, I walk over to the window to make sure I don't wake him. "Hi, zaychik. How are you?"

"Better now that I know you and Slava are safe," she says quietly, and I hear a small hitch in her breathing. "I was so worried, with the storm and all."

My chest squeezes with tenderness. "We're fine. We made it." Keeping my voice low, I tell her all about the awful trip—how sick Slava had been throughout, and how we had to stop a dozen times for him to throw up and go to the bathroom in the pouring rain. How I kept wishing I were the one whose insides were being wrung inside out, and how terrified I'd been that we'd get to the hospital too late.

"I knew children get sick," I say raggedly. "And I

knew Slava might catch something one day, even though he's strong and healthy. What I didn't know was that it would feel like this... like someone was sawing through my heart with a dull knife, cutting it open one cell at a time."

"Of course." Chloe's tone is soft, gently sympathetic. "Parents always feel that way when something's not right with their children. Mom once told me she didn't know what worry meant until she had me—and then she no longer knew what it was like to exist *without* worry."

I pinch the bridge of my nose. "Great. Just great."

"She also told me she wouldn't trade being my mom for the world." She pauses, then asks quietly, "Would you? Trade being Slava's father for peace of mind?"

"Fuck, no." I glance at the tiny figure on the bed, and the tight, uncomfortable feeling I sought to avoid in the beginning invades my chest again. This time, though, I recognize it as worry. Worry and deep, all-consuming love. A different kind of love from the obsessive passion Chloe awakens in me, but one that's no less potent.

I'd kill for them both.

I'd die for them both.

If I lost either one, I don't know how I'd go on.

"So when do you think you're coming home?" Chloe asks, and as with Alina, I catch a strange inflection in her voice. Not a tightness, precisely, but something slightly off.

"We should be back before the evening," I say,

glancing over at a clock. It's five a.m., almost morning, though it's still dark outside. "Zaychik… is everything okay?"

Chloe's tone is now noticeably strained. "Of course. Why wouldn't it be?"

"You tell me. Is something wrong?"

"No, nothing. Just… come home, and we'll talk."

"Talk? What about? Did something happen while I've been gone?"

"No, of course not." She takes a breath. "It's fine. Everything is fine. Just tired from being up all night, that's all."

She's lying. I'm certain she is lying, and I'm about to press her for answers when Pavel walks into the room.

"Masha's on the phone," he says curtly, handing me his device. "The operation is finally on. He's coming to her place in fifteen minutes."

Fuck. "Zaychik, I have to go. Get some sleep, and I'll call you later today, okay?"

Not waiting for Chloe's reply, I hang up and bring up Pavel's phone to my ear. "You got the cameras all set up? And the live feed?"

Masha's voice is as bright as ever. "Of course."

"Send the recording to Konstantin for edits, and for the live stream, direct it to this phone. I don't have mine on me."

"No problem. Now, about Plan B—"

"Just focus on Plan A." I need Bransford compromised, not dead, as per my bargain with Chloe.

Masha heaves an exasperated sigh. "I will,

obviously. But if something goes wrong and I can't contain him, you still want me to eliminate him today, right? I won't be able to get this close again."

I rub my left eyebrow, behind which the skull hammers are back at work. Valery's asset has been crystal clear as to what she will and won't do on this job, and while she's not averse to having Bransford rough her up a bit for the sake of a convincing video, she won't let him fuck her.

"Just do your best to ensure it doesn't come to that," I say finally. "And if you do have to go to Plan B, use the drug."

Though it will be hard to explain Bransford's death to Chloe, I'll do whatever it takes to protect her.

Even go back on my word to her.

42

CHLOE

I wake up with my mouth dry and my eyes as gritty as if they've been filled with sand. Blinking against the bright light filling the room, I peer at a clock—and bolt upright in bed.

Five in the afternoon.

What the fuck?

Before I can gather my thoughts, there's a quiet knock on the bedroom door, and Alina sticks her head in. "Ah, good. You're finally awake."

I grab a water bottle from the nightstand and chug it to ease the parched feeling in my throat. "What happened?" I croak when every precious drop of liquid is gone. I feel dazed and groggy, as though I've been drugged.

Alina strolls in, looking fresh and glamorous, as if she's just stepped out of a full-service salon spa. I, on the other hand, feel—and probably look—like something the raccoons wouldn't fish out of a garbage can.

"You couldn't sleep the rest of the night, so you went to take a nap mid-morning, remember?" she says, gracefully perching on the edge of the bed.

I look at the clock again, as if doing so would change the time displayed on it. "But it's already five. How can it be five if I went down for a nap in the morning?"

She grins. "What can I say? When you crash, you crash hard." She crosses her long legs. "My brother's called about ten times so far, demanding to speak to you. I told him I'm letting you sleep."

My heart rate kicks up. "Is something wrong? Has Slava—"

"No, no, everything's fine. They're actually driving home already, should get here in less than an hour."

"Oh. Is Slava—"

"Doing much better," she assures me. "The doctor was going to keep him for observation until tonight, but he hasn't vomited once since the morning and was able to eat some chicken soup and Jell-O for lunch, so they discharged him early."

"Oh, thank God." I can't wait to hug Slava and kiss him silly. I only caught a glimpse of him last night as Nikolai ran out of the house with the child in his arms, but his pale, wan appearance has haunted me, making me feel exactly how Nikolai described: as if a dull blade were sawing apart my heart.

I guess my husband is not the only one who gets to

feel like a parent these days. With each passing week, Nikolai's son has crept deeper into my heart, and I'm now at the point where I couldn't love him more if he'd come out of my own body—and would be devastated if anything happened to him.

"Do you have your phone?" I ask Alina. "I want to call Nikolai back."

I want to talk to Slava myself and make sure he's truly feeling better, and I'm also dying to hear Nikolai's voice.

No matter how chilling I find those cameras, I can't help missing him, craving him in the most visceral way possible—which is why the thought of our upcoming conversation kept me from falling asleep last night even after they'd safely reached the hospital and I knew Slava would be okay.

"I don't have it on me, but I can get it," Alina says, getting up. "I don't know if you should call him at this point, though. They'll be here soon enough, and then you can talk."

I hesitate, then nod. "Okay."

She's right. Now that they're almost here, I might as well wait. As brief as our conversation last night had been, Nikolai somehow sensed I was upset, and if it weren't for whatever had distracted him, I'm sure he would've pressured me for answers. That must be why he kept calling throughout the day, and why it's best if I just talk to him in person.

It's time I stopped being an ostrich and learned the truth—and we both laid our cards on the table.

It's forty minutes later and almost dinnertime when their SUV pulls up to the house. I've spent these forty minutes getting ready, both mentally and physically. My hair is brushed and coiled into an updo, my makeup is nearly as perfect as Alina's, and I'm wearing a shimmering white gown with two side slits that show off my legs and my golden strappy heels. In my ears are a pair of diamond stud earrings Nikolai gifted me, and around my neck is the heart-shaped necklace Alina lent me once before, for my first dressed-up dinner here. I was going to wear one of my own pieces, but she insisted that her necklace was what the outfit required.

"Trust me on this," she said mysteriously. "This is precisely what Nikolai needs to see tonight."

I decided to do exactly that and trust her for now, though I'm beyond curious what she meant. If I don't get all the answers from Nikolai tonight, I *will* get them out of her.

No more burying my head in the sand.

I'm done being a coward.

Despite my resolve, my heart pounds erratically as I hurry downstairs to greet my husband and our son.

Slava comes in first—or rather barrels in like the little ball of energy a boy his age can be.

"Mama Chloe!" He runs straight for me, and I catch him mid-leap, staggering back under the weight of his small yet sturdy body as my previously injured ankle wobbles in its strappy heel. He smells like medicine and baby shampoo, and I'm so happy to feel his short arms squeezing my neck that I don't care about the potential re-injury—or my makeup getting smeared as he places wet, loud smooches on my cheeks.

"I puke lots," he announces triumphantly after I finally set him down, and I can't help laughing as he launches into a tale about his hospital adventures in a tangled mix of English and Russian, with the gist of the story boiling down to how gross all the puking was.

"What is this? Shouldn't you be all weak and sickly?" Alina asks with amusement, and I realize she's come down to stand next to me. Grinning hugely, she goes down to her knees and grabs Slava in a big hug of her own while whispering to him conspiratorially in Russian.

"Yes, I am Superman," he declares when she's done, and I laugh again, overjoyed to see him doing so well.

"He slept most of the way here and woke up with all this energy," Nikolai says, his deep voice startling me so much I pivot sharply—and nearly fall as the stupid ankle buckles underneath me, sending a spike of pain shooting up my leg.

I say "nearly" because, as always, Nikolai catches me, his powerful arms closing around me before I hit the floor.

"Easy there, zaychik," he murmurs, his eyes a greener shade of gold as he steadies me against his big, warm body and looks me over, holding me by my upper arms. "One trip to the hospital is plenty."

My heart teleports into my throat as the full impact

of his nearness hits me like a wrecking ball. My knees join my ankle in buckling, and my skin ignites with sensations, each cell drinking in the heat emanating from his fingers, the delicious strength and roughness of his callused palms. Like Slava, he smells of the hospital, but underneath is a seductive hint of bergamot and an even fainter trace of cedar, mixed with that warm, masculine aroma that's all his.

"You're here." It's a dumb comment, but all my neurons appear to have gone out for a hike. All I can do is stare up at his face with its high, wide cheekbones and fierce jawline, transfixed by the juxtaposition of wildness and elegance that makes him such a dangerously alluring contradiction.

My husband.

My protector.

My secret watcher.

Is his love something to crave or fear?

He cups my cheek, his eyes darkening as his gaze drops down to my lips. "I'm here, zaychik." Ignoring our audience, he dips his head and slants his mouth across mine, claiming it in a deep, soul-scorching kiss.

My heart is racing in my chest, my skin overly warm by the time he pulls away. As usual, everyone is ignoring our outrageous PDA. Pavel and Lyudmila have come in as well, and they're talking to Alina in Russian while Slava interrupts with stories of his own.

I look back at Nikolai—only to freeze at the chilling look on his face. His gaze is glued to my throat, a muscle ticking violently in his jaw. What the—?

And then I realize what he's looking at.

Not my throat.

The necklace Alina gave me, the one she said he needed to see tonight.

With sudden clarity, I recall her drugged-out mumblings that awful morning when I fled. Like with so many other things relating to my situation, I haven't allowed myself to think about her actual words in recent weeks, to dwell on them for any length of time. But now they come to me, along with everything else I've heard about this family, about how Nikolai is so much like his father.

If I had any doubts left that my husband and I need to have this conversation, they evaporate in this very moment—because if the suspicion forming in my mind is right, Alina is not the only one dealing with a major trauma.

Pretending all is normal, I turn away from Nikolai and walk over to grab Slava's hand. "Come, darling, let's get you into bed before you crash. We'll feed you dinner there."

"I do it," Lyudmila offers, but I shake my head with a smile.

"Let me. I've missed him."

"I'll join you," Nikolai says, his gaze hooded, and my pulse speeds up further as he picks up Slava and carries him upstairs in front of me.

The two of us bathe Slava and tuck him into bed, where he eats some soup and promptly falls asleep, his burst of energy expiring quickly.

"Is it always like this with children?" Nikolai asks in a hushed tone, smoothing his broad palm over Slava's forehead. His puzzled gaze shifts to me. "When they get sick, I mean? Zero to sixty and then back again?"

I smile despite the turmoil in my chest. "No, not always. Slava's just Superman. Haven't you heard?"

His answering smile sets off an explosion of endorphins in my brain. "Oh, yeah, there *is* a rumor going around."

And for a couple of heartbeats, that's enough—this uncomplicated moment of shared joy, of relief that the child we love is going to be okay. But then Nikolai's smile fades, and my pulse shifts into high gear as the space between us fills with simmering awareness, with that scorching chemistry that feels like a charged wire dancing across my skin. We're sitting just a foot apart, but even that small distance suddenly feels like too much... too much and not enough at the same time.

I swallow as he lifts his hand and curves it around my cheek, his rough-edged thumb stroking over my lower lip, making it tingle.

"Zaychik..." His voice is dark velvet. "I've missed you."

And I've missed you too. So, so much. The words pirouette on the tip of my tongue, ready to take flight. It would be so easy to fall back into his embrace, to forget what I saw on his phone and not rock the boat.

To dive back into our faux-honeymoon routine and pretend there's nothing frightening about a husband who obsessively watches me when we're apart... a killer whose complicated past is still a terrifying mystery.

"Nikolai, I..." I draw in a breath and force out a different set of words, the ones I've been avoiding. "We need to talk. It's time you told me exactly what happened with your father."

43

CHLOE

It's as if a dark shutter falls over Nikolai's face, transforming it into that of a stranger. All warmth leaves his voice as he pulls back his hand and stands. "Let's go then. We'll talk in my office."

My heart hammers as I follow him out of Slava's room and down the hallway. As we walk, a chime sounds in his pocket, and he pulls out his phone and glances at the screen. He must've reclaimed the device immediately upon arrival.

Whatever he sees there makes his jaw go taut, and when his gaze returns to me, his eyes are filled with a peculiar light.

A terrible premonition tightens my stomach. "What happened? What's wrong?"

"There's something you should see," he says, and as soon as we enter his office, he goes straight for his laptop and opens it, bending over his desk. His fingers fly over the keyboard for a second, and then he turns the screen toward me.

My heart leaps, and my knees turn into rubber.

Displayed on the screen is a popular news site, where the major headline reads in all caps, "LEADING PRESIDENTIAL CANDIDATE ASSAULTS WOMAN IN SHOCKING VIDEO."

Icy needles dance over my skin as I grab the laptop and carry it to the small round table, where I sink into a chair and read the article in full.

The story is still developing, but it seems that just under an hour ago, a video of Bransford attacking a young woman appeared on Twitter and instantly went viral. According to the news site, the "graphic and disturbing" footage shows him hitting her in the face and ripping her shirt open while she desperately fights back. After a couple of minutes of violent struggle, she escapes by kneeing him in the groin and running out the door while he screams obscenities at her.

"You can watch the video if you want," Nikolai says quietly, and I realize he's come to stand next to me, his gaze glued to the screen from above. "Konstantin's team has worked wonders with what Masha sent him."

My voice is thin. "This was filmed today?"

He nods, his expression unreadable. "Early this morning, some twenty minutes after you and I talked. She had him swing by her 'dorm' before work to sign off on her internship papers so she could volunteer at his campaign and get credit for her AP American Government class."

"AP?" I feel a surge of nausea. "As in, an advanced placement course in high school?"

"Exactly. He thinks she's seventeen, a junior at a boarding school in the DC area." Nikolai pauses, then adds softly, "An orphan whose parents died in a car accident, leaving her in the care of an indifferent uncle who wants nothing to do with her."

"The perfect bait for a predator," I whisper, my eyes burning. "The most vulnerable type of victim... like my mother."

"Yes. That seems to be his MO. We've located two more women he's done this to over the years." Nikolai's jaw flexes. "He likes them smart, pretty, and way too young—and with no one to turn to."

I suck in a breath, the icy needles piercing deeper. "You found them? Will they come forward?"

"They will now."

I swallow to keep the contents of my stomach down as I return my attention to the screen. As sickening as this is going to be, I need to see this video with my own eyes, to know exactly what kind of monster hurt my mom when *she* was a vulnerable teen.

I'm done hiding from reality.

Finding the video, I click "play"—and my nausea intensifies, my stomach cramping with the knowledge that I share this man's genes.

The recording begins with a short but violent chase, with a tall, fit, handsome older man—unmistakably Tom Bransford—lunging at a petite blonde dressed in a pair of tiny shorts and a cropped top. The camera is at such an angle that only a portion of Masha's face shows, but there's no mistaking the youthful line of her jaw—nor the terror in her frantic movements.

She makes it most of the way across the narrow, cluttered room before he tackles her from the back, slamming her into a wall next to a BTS poster, then spinning her around to face him. Sobbing in panic, she attacks, clawing at him with small, slender fingers, but he slaps her brutally across the face and slams a fist into her stomach.

I tense, feeling the blow as if it landed on me, but the worst is just beginning. While Masha is bent over, wheezing for air, he rips at her shirt, tearing it open at the shoulder.

A delicate, softly rounded shoulder, one that could belong to a young teen or a child.

I know that's not the case—I know with her government background, Masha must be at least in her early twenties—but it's easy to forget that I'm not witnessing an actual assault on an innocent teenage victim.

Or rather, that the assault is likely real, but not the victim.

Either way, I can't help exhaling in relief when, after a few more moments of agonizing struggle, Masha makes a twisting motion that seems to accidentally bring her knee in contact with her assailant's groin. He staggers back with a high-pitched scream, his hands cupped over his crotch, and she makes a break for it again, this time reaching the door and disappearing as Bransford screams, "You fucking cunt! Get back here, you fucking tease, or I'll fucking kill you!"

The video cuts off then, but not before the camera zooms in on Bransford's face, on the handsome, even features twisted into a red mask of thwarted fury, a bulging-eyed visage as monstrous as the man himself.

Shaking, I shut down the laptop and gulp in small breaths in an effort to bring oxygen into my tightly banded ribcage—and stop myself from puking.

To paraphrase Nikolai, one person vomiting around here this week is plenty.

When I'm sure my stomach won't expel its contents, I turn to look up at Nikolai. "How did you do it?" My voice is only marginally unsteady. "How did Masha get him to… you know?"

"To attack her?" At my nod, he says, "I don't know all the particulars, but I suspect it was by doing exactly what he accused her of at the end."

"Being a tease?"

"Whatever you'd call strongly encouraging his attentions, then deliberately withdrawing—what men like that think all women do. Only in this case, Masha *was* actually doing it, just with a different goal than what he thought." Nikolai's upper lip curls. "He undoubtedly figured she'd be so eager to get school credit for volunteering at his campaign, she'd let him fuck her, and when she didn't, things escalated quickly… as we figured they might, given his history."

I swallow down another wave of nausea. "So

everything that happened in the video took place for real? None of the footage was fabricated?"

"It was heavily edited, but not fabricated, no."

"Edited for what?"

Nikolai takes a seat across from me. "To hide her face and highlight his, for one thing. Her anonymity is important to her."

I mentally replay the video and realize he's right: Masha's face never actually appears in it. The angle is always wrong. Even when Bransford has her pinned against the wall and the camera is looking directly at her face, his shoulder or something blocks it, allowing the viewer to catch only a glimpse of her cheek, ear, or jaw—enough to get an impression of youth and beauty but not to capture a printable photograph.

"So she's not going to come forward to testify?" I ask, and Nikolai shakes his head.

"Too risky. We created a false identity for her, but it's not one that'll stand up to any real scrutiny. The video was uploaded to the internet anonymously, from an untraceable server—but of course, they'll blame it on Russian hackers, like so many things these days."

"Only in this case, they'll be right."

His lips quirk sardonically. "They're right in most cases, zaychik. Konstantin and his ilk are a menace, especially for your hapless politicians. In any case, it doesn't matter what they say about the source of the video—or whether they call it fake. The damage to Bransford's career is done, his two real victims emboldened. Once they come forward... Well, let's just say daddy dearest is as good as finished."

Daddy dearest. My stomach heaves so violently I nearly upchuck after all. "He's not my daddy anything." I shoot up to my feet, suddenly blindingly angry. "He's just—"

"Your mother's rapist and killer, I know," Nikolai says quietly, standing up as well. "That's all he is, zaychik. Nothing more, nothing to do with you."

The anger drains away as quickly as it came, and I sink back into the chair, dropping my head into my hands. My skull feels inexplicably tight and heavy, as if my brain has been turned into lead.

Large, warm hands land on my nape and shoulders, strong fingers digging into my tight muscles with just the right amount of pressure. "I'm sorry, zaychik." Nikolai's voice is once again soft and warm. "I know it's a lot to process, but I figured you needed to see this video... to know your mom has been avenged."

I want to melt into the seductive comfort of those massaging fingers, to lose myself in their skillful, soothing touch. To once again postpone learning what I fear and instead let myself enjoy Bransford's misfortune, basking in the schadenfreude of it all. The damage we've inflicted on his career doesn't come close to what he did to my mom or those other women, but it's a start—and hopefully, now that the shine is off his golden image, the wheels of legal justice will turn toward him, their spokes nice and sharp.

Gathering every ounce of my strength, I lift my leaden head and cover Nikolai's hands with my own as I twist around to meet his gaze.

"What about your mom?" I ask softly. "Has *she* ever been avenged?"

44

NIKOLAI

My hands tighten on Chloe's shoulders, her question hitting me like a punch below the belt. The necklace gleaming on her throat should've clued me in as to the direction of her upcoming interrogation, but I still didn't expect her to take this exact tack... to know so much about what happened.

"I guess Alina spoke to you again." My voice roughens as I step back. My gaze falls to her pendant, the heart-shaped diamond taunting me, reminding me of things I've been trying to forget. With effort, I tear my eyes away from it and refocus on Chloe's face. "What exactly has she told you?"

Biting her lip, she stands up. "Not much. She hasn't spoken to me again—it was just that morning, right before I left. She said something like, 'He killed her. And then Kolya killed him.' I wasn't sure whom she meant at the time, but I've been pondering it recently, and I think... I think it has to be your mom." She lifts her hand to touch the pendant, her brown eyes soft and dark. "Did this belong to her? Is that why Alina wanted me to wear it tonight and that other night? As some kind of reminder to you about it all?"

My throat tightens and I turn away, abruptly awash in memories—and the burning rage and grief that come with them. And underneath it all lurks the most horrifying guilt, the knowledge that what I've done is ultimately unforgivable. The toxic cocktail is so close to boiling over that I'm not sure I'll be able to keep my word and tell Chloe the whole story, but then her small hand brushes against mine and her fingers curl around my palm, lending me silent support.

"Tell me," she murmurs, stepping around to stand in front of me. Looking up at me, she lifts our joined hands to press them to her chest. "Please, Nikolai. I need to know."

And so she does. I owe her the truth, no matter how ugly.

Looking into her upturned face, I take a breath and begin.

45

NIKOLAI

"When I was around Slava's age, I thought my mother was a princess," I say, my tone cool and steady despite the witch's brew boiling in my veins. "Tall, slim, always perfumed and made up, she wore pretty dresses, sparkling jewels, and high heels, even around the house, and she insisted that everything around her be as beautiful as we could make it—especially ourselves." The memories press down on me, making me feel like the air is disappearing from the room, but I continue. "Valery was just a baby at the time and Alina wasn't born yet, so Konstantin and I are the only ones who remember those years... the ones when our mother was still somewhat happy."

"Somewhat?" Chloe's upturned face reflects both sympathy and wary curiosity as she holds my palm pressed against her chest. "She was never fully happy?"

"Not in my memory." I extricate my hand from her

grasp and walk over to take a seat behind my desk. I feel marginally more in control this way, less likely to give in to the urge to grab Chloe and fuck her until neither one of us can think straight, much less dredge up the noxious sludge that is my past.

She follows me, perching on the corner of the desk, a vision of white and gold in her evening dress, a captured ray of sunshine that's all mine. "Why? Were they never in love? Or did something happen?"

I do my best to keep my gaze on her face and not her cleavage, where the pendant is winking tauntingly at me. "I don't know for sure, but I suspect it started with Konstantin. My father wanted a son like himself, someone to eventually take over the newly capitalist empire he was building, but even as a toddler, my older brother was different. Crazy smart but different. I don't think he even spoke until age three or four."

Chloe's eyes widen. "Oh. So he's—"

"On the spectrum? Maybe. He's never been officially diagnosed. In any case, that may have been the start of the rift between them... or maybe it was just my mother figuring out what kind of man my father was. Whatever the reason, I remember their marriage deteriorating year by year. Each time I'd come home from boarding school, the atmosphere between them would be several degrees icier, their fights more frequent... my father's mood ever darker."

A frown gathers between Chloe's brows. "Why didn't they just get a divorce?"

"He wouldn't allow it. He wanted her, no matter

what." I remember my mother screaming at him about it during one of those fights, begging and pleading to let her go. Clenching my teeth, I shove the recollection away—it hits too close to home.

"In any case," I continue in a level tone, "the more time passed, the worse it got. When I was twelve, he took several lovers and paraded them in front of her. A year later, he killed a man rumored to be her lover. And a few weeks after my seventeenth birthday, I spotted a bruise on her face." At Chloe's expression, I say, "She denied it, of course, said she fell or some such. I didn't believe her for a second. I went to my father and told him that if I ever saw her hurt again, he'd answer to my fist—and I'd take her away where he'd never find her."

Chloe sucks in a breath. "Did he believe you?"

"He did." My mouth twists. "I was his favorite child, the son who was most like him. He knew that even at that age, I'd find a way to keep my promise."

"So what happened then? How did you…?"

"End up killing him?" The words taste like poison on my tongue.

She nods warily, her gaze glued to my face. "When did it happen?"

"Six—no, six and a half years ago. I'd just returned to Moscow after being away for several years—first for service in the army, then my degree at Princeton. Through it all, I kept tabs on my mother, on her health and mental state." My jaw is clenched so hard it feels as if my teeth are wired together, each word more difficult to get out than the next. "There were no more bruises as far as I could tell, but she was miserable, utterly wrecked by their discord. Yet no matter how many times I offered to help her leave him, she wouldn't go. She said she was afraid."

Chloe swallows. "Of him?"

"Of him. Of being without him. Of all of it. By then, they'd spent almost thirty years together. They'd raised four children, such as we were." I catch my hand curling into a fist under the desk and force my fingers to relax. "Konstantin and Valery tried to get her to leave too, but she refused to listen. The excuses were endless: She didn't want to face the judgement of their mutual friends, didn't want to lose the life they'd built together, didn't want to tear the family apart. But in reality, it came down to fear. Fear of my father and what her life would be like without him... without his toxic obsession with her."

"Obsession?" Chloe's voice shakes slightly.

I nod, grimly aware of the parallels. "For better or worse, she'd been the center of his world for close to three decades, long after whatever love they'd shared morphed into this bitter hate. I think a part of her enjoyed it too, the knowledge that she had that kind of power over him, that ultimately, he *couldn't* let her go." I draw in a harsh breath. "In any case, I kept tabs on her, but what I should've been doing was keeping tabs on *him*. Because as her misery grew, so did his—they fed off each other. He started drinking heavily and, as I learned later, using coke. It helped him stay away from her. In a way, he replaced his addiction to her with a potentially less harmful one—and my mother hated that development. Love or hate, she *wanted* his attention."

"So she what? Did something to get it back?"

"She did. She took another lover—a prominent government official, someone who couldn't be dispatched without serious consequences—and told my father she was leaving. I don't think she meant it— it was supposed to be the equivalent of a red flag waved at a bull. But that's the thing about enraged bulls: They can gore you." My voice roughens. "And that's precisely what my father did."

Chloe's hands lock together in her lap, her knuckles turning white as I continue. "Valery was away for his service in the army and Konstantin was in Dubai for business, but Alina was home for winter holidays, having just finished her first semester at Columbia. She's the one who called me that night when our parents' last fight began." My throat tightens, the memories so suffocating I'm not sure I'll be able to say the next part. Yet I go on somehow, my voice reflecting only a fraction of the pain tearing me up inside. "By the time I got there, the living room was like a scene out of a horror movie, with blood splattered all over the gleaming wood floors and white furniture. Alina must've tried to intervene, to protect our mother, because she was knocked out by the wall, one of her forearms slashed open where she'd tried to stop his knife. And our mother—" I stop, then continue gutturally. "She was barely recognizable as human. He'd beaten her to a pulp before slashing her to pieces. To this day, it's one of the most violent deaths I've ever seen."

Chloe's face is ashen, visible tremors running through her slender body, and I want to stop, to end this tale before the horror in her eyes morphs into terror and revulsion, but I promised her the truth, so I divorce myself from the words I'm saying and the suffocating agony they bring.

"He was crouched over her body, knife still in hand as I came toward him. He'd lost control, he told me. It'd been an accident, he said. I knew better, though. Pavel and Lyudmila were scheduled to be there that evening, but they weren't. He'd sent them away for the night. Them and Alina—except my sister had forgotten something and unexpectedly came back."

"So he—" Chloe's voice cracks. "He'd planned it? It wasn't the coke?"

"It was. He was sky high, his pupils blown wide. But he'd known full well what he was going to do while in that state—a clean-up crew had been notified earlier that evening to be on standby. I know that because..." I drag in air, my throat burning from the acid rising into my esophagus. "Because I called them afterward. After he came at me with the knife."

Chloe's sharp intake of air is audible. "He was going to kill you?"

"Maybe. I don't know. He knew I didn't believe him, knew I wouldn't let her murder slide. So when he came at me, his pupils the size of dimes, I acted on instinct." Looking into my wife's stricken face, I say hoarsely, "We fought, and when I got a hold of the knife, I did what he had Pavel train me to do. I gutted him from groin to gullet."

46

CHLOE

He propels himself to his feet then and strides over to the window, where he stands with his back to me, his powerful shoulders tight with tension, his big body as still and hard as if it were one of the mountains outside.

I stare at him for a few beats, absorbing what he's told me, and then I force my frozen limbs to move. "Alina…"

"She regained consciousness in the last few moments of our fight," he says, staring straight ahead as I come to stand next to him. His jaw looks as if it's been turned into granite, his sensuous lips flattened into a harsh line. "I didn't realize it, didn't hear her scream for me to stop—not until after it was done."

"So she…?"

"Saw me kill him, yes. She watched me slice him open."

I drag in a strained breath, reliving those awful

moments when *I* saw him wield the knife. It was against my assailant, my mom's killer who'd been about to rape me and take my life, yet I still feel sick at the memory. What must it have been like for Alina, who'd been barely eighteen the night she saw her parents die so brutally, one at her father's hand and the other at her brother's?

More importantly, what must it have been like for Nikolai?

What kind of damage has that night inflicted on *his* psyche?

My hand shakes as I touch his sleeve, drawing his gaze toward me. His beautifully carved face is carefully blank, displaying nothing of his feelings. But I can sense the well of anguish behind his opaque mask, can feel the paralyzing torment of his guilt and shame.

"Does Alina know?" I ask unsteadily. "That it was self-defense? That you didn't do it just to avenge your mother?"

His black lashes lower, veiling his tiger eyes. "I don't know. We've never really talked about that night. What would it change? I was twenty-five to his fifty-seven, faster and stronger. I could've wrestled the knife away and pinned him down—I didn't have to murder him."

"Did you not?" I can see the scene as clearly as if it had happened in front of my eyes, can picture the older version of Nikolai I saw in newspaper photos, fit and strong despite his age... dangerous even without being hopped up on blood and coke. And I can see a twenty-five-year-old Nikolai, thrust into that nightmare of a scene, stunned by his mother's gruesome death and terrified for his unconscious, bleeding sister.

What would've happened if he hadn't gotten a hold of his father's lethal knife?

Would his blood have also stained that blade, his body joining his mother's and sister's in an unmarked grave in some Russian forest?

"What are you saying?" Nikolai's voice tightens, his eyes glittering fiercely as his mask slips, revealing the raw, festering wound underneath. "I killed him. My own father. Who cares whether it was in self-defense or not? I wanted him dead for what he did to her. I wanted his blood—*my* blood—on my hands, and I'm not sorry I have it. Because you see, zaychik, Alina's right: I *am* like him. In every way that counts, I am my father."

My heart feels like it's being ripped to pieces, his anguish slicing at me as brutally as any knife. How has he been able to contain all this pain inside him? How has it not torn him apart? "No," I say, my voice steadier with each word. "You're not your father. And I'm not your mother. Their fate won't be ours—not if we don't let it."

I don't know when it was during his tale that I understood what drives him, at what point I realized that Nikolai branded *himself* a monster six and a half years ago—and has since done his best to live up to what he thinks is his nature, to the Molotov blood he views as his curse. Not that there isn't some truth to his belief. My new family is dark and ruthless, a throwback to the times when violence and might made right. Their relationships merit their own chapter in a book on broken family dynamics, and my husband is a product of that upbringing, his character shaped as much by the tragedy of his parents' slowly unraveling relationship as its explosive, gruesome end.

Still, he's not his father. Far from it. And I'm not his mother. She didn't know her husband's nature when she married him, wasn't prepared for a life with a man so violent and ruthless. Whereas I, thanks to my biological father, have been through living hell, and while I can't say I wasn't fazed by seeing Nikolai kill the two assassins, finding out what he's capable of hasn't changed my feelings—much to my initial dismay.

Merciless killer or not, he is and always will be my lover and protector.

"No?" He grips my upper arms, his fingers like bands of steel. "How will we escape their fate? You already hate me on some level, don't you? For killing those men in front of you and bringing you back when you begged me to let you go? For forcing you to marry me?"

I hold his fiercely golden gaze, refusing to flinch at the volcanic turmoil I see there, at all the long-repressed emotions that threaten to spill out in a tsunami, wrecking everything in their way. "No, Nikolai." My voice is soft and steady despite the uneven pounding of my pulse. "I told you, I love you. I don't hate you. I never could, so I never did—and I never will."

His fingers tighten, biting deeper into my flesh. "How can you be so sure? You've seen what I'm capable of, what I'm like... how I am with you. How exactly am I different from him?"

I fight the urge to shrink away from the pain and rage bleeding into his words. Instead, I ask softly, "Did your father love you and your siblings the way you love Slava? Did he truly love anyone except himself? And I don't mean his violent fixation on your mother."

His expression doesn't change, but I can feel the answer in the subtle slackening of his grip on me, so I press on. "Maybe you are like him in some ways, but not all ways. Not the ones that count. For instance, would you ever hurt me? Really hurt me? I'm talking fists and knives, not being rough in bed."

He recoils, yanking his hands away. "I'd sooner gut myself."

"What about Slava? Would you ever come at him with a knife... say, while high or drunk?"

Fury flashes across his face. "Fuck, no."

"Exactly." I step even closer to him, my heart drumming up a storm. "Because you're not like your father. No matter what your sister thinks... no matter what I feared after you saved me."

His nostrils flare as he stares down at me. "Feared?" His voice is sandpaper rough, the words tinged for the first time with a hint of a Russian accent. "As in, past tense?" He grasps my arms again, his eyes a feral golden-green. "You think you're safe with me? Because... what? You now know the full ugly truth? Because you think you understand me?"

"I've always been safe with you." And deep down, I've always known it. That's why I've been able to bury my head in the sand all these weeks, why seeing him kill and torture hasn't made me recoil at his touch—and why being forced to marry him hasn't changed my feelings.

Even when I feel like prey under that intense tiger gaze of his, I know he'd never hurt me.

His jaw flexes violently. "How the fuck can you be so sure? How can you trust me, much less love me, given the poison flowing through my veins?"

"Do you love *me*? Trust *me*, given the poison flowing through *my* veins?" My voice rises as the words spill out, filled with all the anger I haven't had a chance to process, all the self-loathing I've been suppressing. It's as if a dam has broken, and I can't stop the bitter torrent, can't rebuild the mental block that's kept me sane all these weeks. "I'm a child of rape, the result of a two-faced, sociopathic scumbag assaulting my teenage mother. At least your parents wanted each other at some point—at least you were conceived in something resembling love."

He lets go of me, his gaze turning opaque again. "It's not the same."

"Is it not?" I wind my fists in his shirt, not letting him turn away. "Think about it. My blood is tainted, same as yours. My father also killed my mother—not out of twisted passion but cold calculation. And he most definitely would've killed me too. Still might try, in fact. So how exactly are our stories different? How am I in any way better than you? If anything, we're a perfect fit—or as you like to say, fated to be together."

He stares down at me, his broad chest moving in an uneven rhythm, and I can see I'm getting through to him, that he's absorbing this basic truth. A truth I didn't fully comprehend myself until this moment.

I may not believe in fate as such, but *something* brought me here, to this family with all its ugliness and beauty. To this wonderful, lethal, damaged man, who'll never flinch at doing what it takes to keep me safe and slay my demons... as long as I also slay his.

I let go of his shirt and lay my palms on each side of his face, feeling the hard strength of his bones under the warm, stubble-roughened skin. "I love you, Nikolai... I love you and I want to be with you, dark past, obsessiveness, and all. Whatever our fathers did, however fucked-up our parents' relationships, we are not them, and we don't have to follow in their footsteps. I'll never rape a teenage girl—and you will never hurt me, no matter how strong your feelings for me become... no matter what trials we go through in the future."

His chest heaves faster as I speak, his eyes darkening until they're the color of tarnished bronze. "Chloe..." His voice is hoarse as he cups his hands over mine. "Zaychik, you have no idea how strong my feelings for you already are, how all-consuming my obsession with you."

I dampen my lips. "I think I do." The cameras are a good indication. We'll need to talk about them at some point soon, but for now, I have more important things to focus on... such as the way his gaze falls to my mouth and ignites with familiar volcanic heat, the dark hunger that excites me and, on some level, scares me—but only because it evokes an equally potent response in me.

He's not the only one whose love now borders on obsession.

He stares at my mouth for another beat, his hands clenching over mine. Then, with a sharp inhale, he crushes his lips to mine, one hand fisting in my hair while the other grips my ass cheek, yanking my lower body flush against his.

He's already hard, the bulge of his erection pushing into me as he drags me over to his desk while devouring me with a brutal kiss, a kiss that I respond to with equal fervor. We fall onto the hard surface in a tangle of limbs and eagerly groping hands, coming together in a fury of lust and love, in the tender violence of passion.

In the most perfect way for two imperfect people.

NIKOLAI

As the last echoes of the ecstasy fade away, I become aware of the hard surface of the desk under my naked back and the slight weight of Chloe's body draped across my sweat-dampened chest. My brain is overflowing with endorphins, and my heart is thudding in a newly hopeful rhythm in my chest.

I told her everything, and instead of recoiling in revulsion, she embraced me.

I laid bare the worst parts of myself, and instead of running away in terror, she told me that we're fated.

Which we are. I've known it from the beginning, but at some point in the last couple of weeks, I've lost sight of it, begun to doubt whether our relationship can survive the poison festering inside me... whether we're destined to go down my parents' agonizing path.

"We're not," Chloe murmurs, lifting her head off my shoulder, and I realize I said the last part out loud. Smiling tenderly, she traces the edges of my lips with one slender finger, her eyes so soft and warm her gaze is like a physical caress on my face. "We decide our life, our future."

Sitting up, I pull her onto my lap, a surfeit of emotions filling my chest as I inhale her wildflower scent and feel her slender arms wrap trustingly around my neck. Tenderness and possessiveness, love and lust, fear and joy—they battle inside me until it feels as if my ribcage can't contain it all.

Is it possible?

Could Chloe's love for me be more than a sweet mirage?

Could this kind of happiness be real and lasting?

There's so much I want to talk to her about, so many things I want to tell her... another confession I want to make concerning her father's fate. But for now, this is enough. I don't want to spoil this perfect moment by bringing up any sort of contentious topics. So I just kiss the top of her head and hold her tight, content—truly content—for the first time in my life.

48

CHLOE

I want to stay like this, cuddled on Nikolai's lap, forever, but I know that we eventually have to move. Out of the corner of my eye, I spy my dress on the floor next to his shirt—along with the laptop we knocked off the desk in our passion. We should retrieve the computer, make sure it's okay... maybe talk about the cameras as well. Or better yet, about our future overall. But before we get there, there's something I have to tell him.

Lifting my head from his broad shoulder, I pull back to meet his warm amber gaze. "Thank you," I say softly. "Thank you for doing what you did to Bransford. I know it's not a perfect solution—I know that even dethroned, he might be dangerous—but I think—"

A loud banging on the door makes us both jump. "Nikolai!" Pavel's deep voice is tense, the stream of Russian that follows urgent.

"Fuck!" Nikolai shifts me off his lap and jackknifes to his feet, grabbing his clothes and yanking them on in a series of explosive movements.

It's such a sudden transition from the peace we were just enjoying that I'm too stunned to process it at first. But then adrenaline clears my mind, and I leap into motion as well.

"What's wrong? Is Slava sick again?" I scramble for my dress, my heart in my throat as I pull it on.

Nikolai is already by the back wall, pressing his palm against the smooth, white surface. "Slava is fine," he says grimly as a section of the wall slides away, revealing a room full of weapons to my startled gaze. "It's our guards. Arkash messaged Pavel about spotting something strange, and now Pavel can't get in touch with him—or any of our other men."

I gasp, my fist flying up to press against my lips. "You think—"

"We're being attacked? Yes." He grabs a terrifying-looking M16. "And if I had to bet, my money would be on the Leonovs."

NIKOLAI

Chloe's brown eyes are wide with fear and shock as I set my weapon down on the desk and shepherd her out into the hallway, where Pavel is waiting. My heart thuds furiously in my chest, adrenaline pumping through my veins as I order harshly, "Get her, Slava, and Alina to the safe room."

He nods, grabbing Chloe in a bear hug. "Lyudmila and the two of them are inside already."

"Wait!" Chloe cries out as he picks her up and carries her down the stairs. "Let me help. I can—"

I don't hear the rest of what she says because I'm already back inside my office. I can't take the time to calm my zaychik, not when every second brings Alexei Leonov closer to our door. And it has to be him. He has to be the one behind this. Our faces must've blipped on some security camera at the hospital, and his hackers tracked us here. It's the only explanation that makes any kind of sense, the only way they could've triangulated our location.

If it were just Pavel and myself, I wouldn't worry. We're trained for this, prepared to go into battle at a moment's notice. But Chloe and Slava are here too, as are my sister and Lyudmila. It's the thought of them in danger that chills my bones and fills my gut with acid.

I'll tear Alexei Leonov apart with my bare teeth before I let him take my son from me. And if he harms a single hair on Chloe or Alina's head, I will eviscerate each member of his family.

With effort, I rein in my rage and open my laptop to pull up the drone footage and the feeds from the perimeter cameras. What matters now is assessing the situation. Where are our attackers coming from? What are their numbers? My chest tightens as I think of Arkash and our other guards, many of them my friends, good men with families back home. How many of them have already been killed? How many wounded?

No matter what, I have to know.

I grab my laptop off the floor and flip it open.

The screen is dark and silent, unresponsive when I try to manually power it on.

Fuck. The fall must've damaged it.

I grab my phone instead—and feel my blood ice over.

It's the same story. The device is dead, the screen black no matter what I do to it.

I whirl around and hit the light switch on the wall.

It works.

My mind works furiously, leaping from one possibility to another. Could they have sent out some sort of EMP, frying our electronics? Is that why Pavel couldn't get in touch with the guards? Because their devices have also been disabled? But then what about Pavel's phone? Wouldn't he have noticed that it's dead?

Unless it wasn't at the time.

If the EMP was hyper-targeted, it might've hit our guards on the perimeter of the compound first, then struck the house.

I have no idea how Alexei could've gotten his paws on such an advanced weapon, but I do know one thing: Konstantin, paranoid techie that he is, thought an EMP attack wasn't completely out of the question. That's why our backup generator is analog and resides inside a Faraday cage deep underground, and why our key power lines are underground as well, hardened with metal casings.

The fuckers would've loved to cut our power, I'm sure, but they've had to settle for taking out our drones and cameras.

A distant *rat-tat-tat* of gunfire reaches my ears.

Thank fuck.

The guards must still be alive and doing their jobs.

I toss my dead phone aside and yank on a bulletproof vest, then strap on several guns and loop a dozen rounds of ammo over my shoulder. I also grab two functioning radios from the armory—like the metal-lined box with the generator, the hidden room is a Faraday cage.

By the time I'm done, Pavel bursts into my office, armed to the teeth as well. "The phones and radios, they're—"

"Dead, I know. Here." I thrust the second radio device into his hands. "Let's go. It's time the Leonovs learned who they're fucking with."

50

CHLOE

"Stop it, Chloe," Alina snaps, and I realize I've resumed tapping my foot—a physical manifestation of my anxiety that inexplicably annoys her. In general, she's more on edge than I've ever seen her, her own movements jerky and her spine so tense it's a wonder she can turn her neck.

"Sorry about that." I shift Slava so he's sitting more comfortably on my lap. "I'm just worried for them."

I'm holding the child as much to calm myself as to comfort him. In fact, out of the four of us, Slava is the least anxious—probably because he doesn't understand the magnitude of the threat we're facing. Lyudmila told him we're here as part of a security drill, and though I'm sure he's picking up on the adults' tension, he hasn't questioned the explanation.

I wish I could be calm as well, but I'm not. My chest is agonizingly tight, my insides churning like they're on a high-speed cycle in a washer. I'm acutely, terrifyingly aware of the fact that Nikolai is out there, facing down an unknown number of enemies—who may or may not be the Leonovs.

For all we know, Bransford has sent a whole army of assassins after me. It could very well be my fault we're in danger.

I catch my breathing speeding up again, and I force myself to inhale deeper to avoid hyperventilating. The safe room—a place I had no idea existed until Pavel tossed me in here—is carved into the mountain under the garage, and is large enough to be considered a studio apartment, complete with a king-sized bed, two futons, a fully stocked mini-kitchen, a small bathroom, and enough supplies in the pantry to survive a nuclear winter. Theoretically, there's plenty of oxygen here, but I keep feeling like we're running out of air, like the walls are inching closer to me with each passing second.

Nikolai is out there, and I'm stuck here, unable to do anything to help him.

"Can you just fucking stop?" Alina shoots up to her feet. Her face is vampire pale in the white light of the LED ceiling strip, her chest heaving as she glares at me, and I realize I've inadvertently resumed my foot tapping.

Before I can snap back—she's not the only one whose nerves are frayed—Lyudmila says something in Russian. Though her round face is pale as well, the tone of her voice is soothing, and Alina sinks back onto her futon, pushing back her hair with a shaking hand before smoothing it over her red evening gown.

I stare at her, struck by just how distressed she is, way more than when we had the incident with Slava. Does she know something that I don't?

Are we in even greater danger than I'm aware of?

I set Slava down on the bed and walk over to her, the cement floor cold on my bare feet—in the rush to get me down here, my strappy heels were left behind in Nikolai's office. Sitting next to her on the futon, I ask quietly, "Are you okay?"

She looks at me, her jade eyes glittering too brightly.

"Is something else going on?" I press. "You seem unusually agitated—not that you don't have good reason to be."

She opens her mouth to say something, then shakes her head. "It's nothing." Her voice is tight. "I'm getting a bad headache, that's all."

Of course. That's what happens when she's under stress. Poor thing. I cover her icy hand with mine, glad to focus on something other than my own debilitating fear. "Do you have your medication?"

"No."

I glance at the fold-out ladder leading up to the garage. What are the odds I could run upstairs and get it for her quickly?

"Don't even think about it," Alina snaps, reading my mind with her brother's uncanny skill. "If I want it, I'll get it myself. But neither one of us should—"

The ceiling light flickers as a loud *boom* shakes the room, making my stomach seize and sending plaster raining down on our heads.

As one, we jump to our feet, and I rush over to Slava, whose eyes are now wide with fear. "Mama Chloe." His voice is thin as I pick him up and settle his sturdy weight on my hip. "Where's Papa? I don't like this. I want him with me."

I tighten my arms around him. "Me too, darling. Me too. But don't worry. It'll be okay. Your daddy will be here soon. We just need to wait." I hope Slava can't feel me shaking—or see the expression on Alina's face.

She looks like she's been placed on death row, with the execution scheduled for today.

Lyudmila must notice because she steps up to Alina and wraps an arm around her slender shoulders, murmuring something in Russian. I catch the words "Alexei" and "braht"—the Russian word for "brother"—and I wish for the hundredth time that I knew more Russian.

I also desperately wish I knew what's happening up there, whether Nikolai and Pavel are okay. In addition to all the supplies, there's a panel of monitors on the other side of the room—presumably a window to the outside world—but the only thing we were able to see on the monitors when we turned them on was static.

"What do you think caused that?" I ask, unable to stay silent any longer. Despite my best efforts, my voice betrays my agitation, the awful terror gnawing at my insides at the thought of Nikolai getting hurt. Hugging

Slava to me tighter, I steady my tone. "The explosion, I mean. Do you think—"

"Could be an RPG." Alina's voice is flat now, oddly unemotional as she extricates herself from Lyudmila's supportive embrace, and even though her eyes are still glittering with that painful brightness, her features are composed once more. "They could've launched it at the garage to take out our vehicles and eliminate the option of escape. Either that, or they manually planted some explosives at the garage entrance—which would mean they're already here, at the house."

And Nikolai is badly injured or killed.

The nausea that twists my stomach is so severe I have to swallow to hold back vomit. It takes everything I have to keep my voice steady for Slava's sake. "Are there any guns down here? I've been to a shooting range a few times, so I can—"

Alina is already walking to the panel with the monitors, where she presses her palm against the wall the way Nikolai did in his office. And as in his office, the wall slides away, revealing a collection of weapons that would make an arms dealer proud.

"My brother has foreseen everything," she says, picking up a Glock. "They're unlikely to find this room anytime soon, but if they do, we're ready." She loads the gun with swift, sure movements that make me realize she's been to a gun range more than a few times.

In fact, she might be as dangerous with that weapon as her brother—and he is lethal. I've seen him in action. He can handle himself.

At least that's what I tell myself to keep from having a total freakout as I set Slava down so I can arm myself. He immediately grabs onto my legs and stares up at me, moisture pooling in his enormous eyes. "I want Daddy." His bottom lip quivers. "Where is he?"

I pat his silky hair, my chest contracting agonizingly. "I don't know, darling, but I'm sure we'll see him soon. For now, we just need to be prepared, okay? So your daddy knows we didn't fail this drill and that we can take care of ourselves—that we're all strong, like Superman."

Slava sniffles but lets go of my legs and steps back to let me pass.

"Good boy." I glance at Lyudmila to see if she can take him for now, but she's arming herself as well, handling the weapons with the same impressive skill as Alina. Which begs the question…

"What the fuck are we doing down here?" I burst out, forgetting myself for a moment. "We should be out there, helping them!" Realizing I'm scaring Slava, I lower my voice as I pick up a gun and begin to load it. "Maybe one of us can stay down here to watch over—"

Another *boom* rattles the dishes in the kitchen and sends more plaster raining down from the ceiling. The lights flicker several times, then wink out, plunging us into total darkness.

In the silence that follows, there's only my ragged breathing—and the sound of muffled gunfire overhead.

NIKOLAI

My radio crackles to life as I step out of the house. "Kirilov here. Do you read me?"

My stomach unknots slightly. "It's Nikolai. I read you." The guards must've realized what's happening and grabbed the emergency stash of radios from their own Faraday cage armory. "Status report, now."

"Twelve heavily armed attackers on the north side of the wall, fifteen by the gate. We've taken out half of them and are holding off the rest. No drones or cameras operational, and we've lost contact with Arkash and Ivanko by the east wall."

Fuck. That means there's most likely been a breach. "Take whichever men you can spare and get over there. Also send reinforcements to the house—Pavel and I might need them."

"On it."

The radio goes silent, and I pick up my pace. If our enemies are already here, inside the perimeter, there's very little time left to prepare an important line of defense—the bombs I've buried around the house.

The first one is on the driveway, precisely three-and-a-half meters from the front door. Stepping onto the subtly marked patch of gravel, I take out a remote activation fob and type in the pin required to sync it with the explosives underneath. It can only be done at a close distance, so no one can accidentally set off the bomb by grabbing the device from my office safe. Not that it's likely, with Pavel the only other person who knows the code to my safe, but with my son always playing around here, I couldn't risk it.

The second bomb is on the southeast corner of the house, the third by the garage. I sync the remote activators with them both and radio Pavel to check on his progress inside the house, part of which—the heavy-duty metal shutters covering the windows—I can see already.

"All set," he reports. "I'm heading up to the roof."

"I'll join you there in a minute."

With us positioned on two corners, no one will be able to approach the house unseen, and the sniper rifles and machine guns we have stationed there will hold off anything short of an army.

I'm about to instruct Pavel to grab extra ammunition when a flicker of movement to my right catches my attention. Swiftly, I step behind a thick tree —and watch with rage and disbelief as figures in black SWAT-type gear pour out of the forest by the dozen.

NIKOLAI

I count thirty-three invaders before I open fire, aiming at what I suspect to be the gaps in their full-body armor. I have to give Alexei credit—this is a military-grade operation, complete with a full-blown, well-equipped army.

They came prepared for war, and war is what I intend to give them.

I don't think about Chloe, Alina, and my son hidden in the safe room underneath the house, don't focus on what will happen to them if I fail. I can't, not if I'm to succeed. In front of me is a far bigger than anticipated force; as prepared as we were for an attack, it wasn't for one of this ferocity or scale.

I underestimated how much the Leonovs want Slava back, what Alexei is willing to do to take my son —his nephew—from me. Unless... Slava isn't the only member of my family he's after.

But no. That's madness. That betrothal contract has

always been a sick man's joke, a useless, toothless piece of paper.

There's no way Alexei brought this army to acquire Alina.

My bullets take down five of the invaders before they realize where I am and open fire in my direction. I wait ten seconds, letting their bullets tear pieces of bark off my tree, then fire back, not bothering to aim. The goal now is to buy time for Pavel to get to the roof, and for our reinforcements to arrive—assuming they ever do.

Given the numbers we're up against, it's possible Kirilov and his men have already been taken out.

A hail of bullets ricochets off the nearby trees, missing my shoulder by centimeters. Alexei's men are coming closer and fanning out, I realize grimly. If I stay here, I'll be surrounded in no time, but if I make a run for it, their bullets will mow me down even faster.

Reaching a decision, I drop onto my stomach and smear dirt over my face to hide the light hue of my skin. Then I carefully peer out from behind the tree, using the tall weeds around me as cover.

As I suspected, the attackers have split into two groups—one to surround me, the other to continue on toward the house. Eight of the black-clad figures are on the driveway, approaching the front door, while five others are creeping around the house to the garage, presumably to try to get into the house from there.

My heartbeat thunders in my ears, sweat soaking my back as a fresh hail of bullets kicks up chunks of dirt around me, yet I wait, still and silent, all my attention on the threat to my family, to the woman and child who are my entire life.

If I can save them, I'll die happy.

If I can ensure their safety, nothing else matters.

I wait, and when the moment is right, I set off the driveway bomb, and a second later, the one by the garage entrance. They go off with the force of landmines, ripping apart everyone within a three-meter radius and painting the nighttime landscape red.

They also distract the men hunting me, who spin around to see their teammates being blown apart. Two seconds is all it buys me, but that's all I need to jump to my feet and sprint for the cluster of trees by the side of the garage, looping around the line of heavily armed men in front of me. My goal is simple: protect the garage entrance at all costs, keeping them away from the underground safe room.

A bullet whizzes past my ear as I run. Another kisses my bicep with stinging fire.

They're on to me.

It's over.

A peculiar calm descends on me, the certainty that death is coming. My heartbeat slows fatalistically, yet my body keeps moving, my leg muscles pumping with greater effort. Some sixth sense makes me angle sharply right, then left, but a bullet still grazes my right shoulder, leaving another streak of fire in its wake.

The cluster of trees is closer now, a few long jumps away, but even a meter is too far when you're out in the open with fuck knows how many guns spitting out lethal chunks of lead.

On instinct, I tuck and roll, and several bullets whizz above me, exactly where my torso and head would've been. The next set of bullets won't be fooled, I know, but just as I prepare to feel them tear through my flesh, a violent explosion of sound erupts above—and my pulse speeds back to life as I recognize the rattle of a machine gun.

Pavel got to the roof.

I finally have cover.

Sure enough, he mows down the black-clad figures as they scatter back toward the forest, and I make it to the tree cluster and add my fire to Pavel's efforts. Before long, all of our attackers—the ones who can still move, that is—have pulled back, their answering gunfire dying down as they take cover.

The machine gun ceases firing as well.

I wipe the sweat and dirt off my face and bring up my radio. "Kirilov? You there?"

A crackle, followed by static.

Fuck.

I switch channels. "Pavel?"

"Still here. But I think they got most of our men."

I ignore the sharp pinching in my chest. "I know. It's going to be a long fucking night."

As I speak, I scan the forest, searching for any hint of movement. By my count, only twenty-four of our attackers are on the ground, leaving nine unaccounted for—plus however many of their comrades survived the battle with our guards.

I'm so focused on my task I almost miss the dark figure melting out of the shadows right by the garage entrance—and by the time I swing my gun toward it, it's too late.

As the enemy dives aside to avoid my bullets, the garage door explodes into pieces, the shockwave nearly rupturing my eardrums.

53

NIKOLAI

I spring into action before the sound of the explosion fades.

"Cover me," I hiss into the radio and sprint for the burning hole in the garage, ignoring the high-pitched ringing in my ears.

I have to get to the garage before the attacker recovers from the blast.

I have to intercept him before he gets inside and finds the safe room.

As I run, bullets strike the ground around me, kicking up chunks of grass and dirt, but Pavel's machine gun keeps the shooters sufficiently far away to interfere with their aim.

The closer I get to the garage, the more the extent of the damage becomes apparent. The fucker must've glued explosives directly to the bottom of the door, as the force of the blast not only tore apart the heavy metal but left a blackened hole in the floor around it too. And—*fuck*. Those are indeed exposed wires.

The explosion must've knocked out power to the safe room too.

It won't stay out; in a few minutes, the second backup generator will kick in, but I can only imagine how scared Chloe and Slava must be right now. As thick as the ceiling and the walls of the safe room are, there's no way they didn't hear this explosion—or, come to think of it, the bomb I set off nearby.

No matter. I'll comfort them as soon as we're all safe.

Speaking of which, where is the bomb-setting fucker? Is it too much to hope the bastard didn't survive his own blast?

My heart pumps pure adrenaline, my nerves thrumming with heightened awareness as I step through the burning opening into the dark garage, holding my breath to avoid inhaling smoke. It's futile; as I advance deeper, I realize the smoke has filled every crevice of the space, so thick in places it dims the red glow of the flames.

Swearing silently, I tear a chunk of material off the bottom of my shirt and press the makeshift handkerchief to my face to avoid coughing as I step around one of our SUVs, scanning the hazy darkness for signs of movement... listening for someone else's cough.

And then I hear it.

A single cough, followed by a full-blown coughing fit—only it's not a man's deep-throated hacking but a small, high-pitched one.

The cough of a young child.

CHLOE

"Slava? Slava, where are you?" I grope around me in the darkness, my heart pounding sickeningly fast as I stuff the gun into my bodice. "Alina, Lyudmila, you there? Where is he? I can't find Slava."

"He was right next to you." Alina's tone is as tense as mine. "Slava! Slavochka, *ti gdye?*"

No reply.

I whirl around, arms outstretched. "Slava! This isn't a game. We're not playing hide-and-seek. Lyudmila, do you see him?"

"No." She sounds equally worried. "Maybe he hurt. I search now for light."

Right. There have to be some flashlights around here. I squeeze my eyes shut, then open them, trying to get my vision to adjust to the darkness—and to my surprise, it works.

It's not pitch-black around me now. In fact, there's faint light coming from the other side of the room.

The side where the ladder is.

My heartbeat speeds up further as I head toward it, doing my best not to trip. "Slava? Slava, come here!" My panic is growing by the second. Not only is the child missing, but I'm beginning to smell something sharp and acrid.

Smoke.

"Slava!" My voice rises in pitch and volume as more light reaches my eyeballs, filling my stomach with cold terror.

There's no longer any doubt where Slava has gone.

The ceiling door at the top of the ladder is propped open.

NIKOLAI

The terror that seizes me is so absolute that for a moment, I'm certain I misheard, that the child's cough was nothing more than a hallucination brought on by all the smoke.

It can't be my son. He's down in the safe room, where it's fucking safe. Where he's supposed to be with Chloe and my sister.

But no. There's that cough again, followed by an achingly familiar, "Papa? Daddy?"

My stomach is a ball of ice, but I retain enough presence of mind not to yell out that I'm here, in case the enemy is also inside. Instead, I get down and crouch-walk over to where I heard Slava's voice—a move that has the benefit of helping me breathe cleaner air, as there's more smoke higher up.

Still, the urge to cough is growing, the toxic particles filling up my lungs. My chest heaves convulsively, my eyes watering from the effort of suppressing the reflex, and I know I will betray myself before long.

I have to locate Slava ASAP.

"Papa? Where are you?"

Fuck. His voice sounds farther away.

He's heading for the garage door, seeking to escape the smoke.

How the fuck is he by himself? Has something happened to Chloe and Alina?

Staying low to the floor, I hurry after him, my heart thudding heavily as my lungs continue screaming that I need to cough, to expel the contaminated air.

"Daddy?"

Slava's tiny figure is briefly outlined by the glow of the flames, and then he steps through the burning hole, disappearing outside.

Fuck it. Coughing hard, I jerk up to my feet and launch into a sprint.

If I catch a bullet, so be it.

I burst outside, gun at the ready, and I see him.

My son, standing just a few meters away, his small face brightening at the sight of me.

"Daddy!" He waves a knife in the air. "I came to help —like Superman."

My heart thunders with a mix of fear and relief as I start toward him—only to freeze in place as a dark figure melts out of the shadows behind him, gun pointed at me.

"Come here, Slavchik," Alexei Leonov says, pulling off his face mask with one hand to reveal black eyes glowing with the light of the sputtering flames behind me. "You're safe now, kid. Your uncle's come to take you home."

56

CHLOE

Forgetting everything, I hike up the long skirt of my dress and climb up the ladder, my terror growing as I climb through the open ceiling door and thicker smoke envelops me, the acrid smell snaking into my nostrils and making my eyes burn.

"Slava!" I cough, peering through the hazy, red-tinted darkness. "Slava, come back!"

Nothing. No response.

"Chloe, wait!"

Ignoring Alina's cry, I climb out completely and survey the smoky hell that is the inside of the garage. It's like a scene from a disaster movie, complete with plaster-covered cars with shattered windows and flickering flames by the big metal door—a door that sports a giant, burning hole.

My pulse skyrockets and I launch into a run, ignoring the shards of glass and rock-like bits of broken concrete biting into my bare feet. The pain is nothing compared to the dread sawing at my stomach.

That hole is where Slava must've gone.

He must've come up here right after the explosion and run outside, straight into God knows what danger.

At least there's no sound of gunfire now—but that could change at any moment. Coughing, I pull the heavy gun out of my bodice and grip it tightly with both hands, lest it slips from my sweaty fingers.

"Slava!" I run through the hole, ignoring the flames eating at its edges—only to skid to a halt, gripped by horror.

In front of me is a scene straight out of a western: Nikolai and an unknown man, guns pointed at each other in a lethal standoff, with wide-eyed Slava in the middle.

CHLOE

Hyperventilating, I bring up my gun, pointing the barrel at the stranger. "Drop your weapon and back away!"

I mean to sound authoritative, but instead, my words come out in a hoarse, trembling croak, my throat raw from smoke.

The man's dark gaze flicks toward me for a millisecond, but he doesn't move an inch. "*Idi syuda*, Slavchik." His deep voice is eerily calm. "*Bystro*."

To my shock, I recognize the first portion of the Russian phrase.

Come here, the stranger said, using another diminutive of the child's name.

Nikolai's gaze doesn't leave his opponent's face, though I know he's aware of my presence. I can feel the lethal tension emanating from him, see his hard jaw flexing.

"My son isn't going anywhere with you," he growls

in English at the stranger. "Slavochka, get behind me. Go now."

Slava looks confused, his gaze shifting back and forth between the two men. *"Dyadya Lyosha? Papa?"*

Dyadya. I strain my brain for a translation, and then it comes to me.

Uncle, that word means. And *Lyosha* is probably diminutive for *Alexei.*

Nikolai was right. It *is* the Leonovs—or at least one of them.

Slava's uncle.

The gun is heavy in my outstretched hands, much heavier than they portray in movies. My shoulders and neck muscles are beginning to ache, my forearms tiring from gripping the weapon so tightly. Ignoring the discomfort, I keep it pointed at the man, my mind spinning frantically, trying to think of a way out of this fucked-up situation.

After everything Nikolai has told me about the Leonovs, I half expected horns and a tail, and there *is* something demonic in Alexei's harsh features— especially his eyes. They're so dark they appear black, making me think of tar pools in the depths of a volcano, complete with a reddish cast from the flickering flames reflecting in them. Yet the man isn't ugly, far from it.

If Nikolai hadn't set an impossibly high bar for male beauty, I might've found Slava's uncle dangerously attractive.

Not that his looks matter when he's holding that

gun pointed at Nikolai—and *his* thickly muscled arms don't show any signs of tiring. Neither do Nikolai's. Both men might as well be made of steel, their faces taut with mutual hatred.

Slava, on the other hand, doesn't seem to partake in that sentiment. If anything, he appears torn between his father and his uncle, his head swiveling back and forth, his posture speaking of bewilderment at the tension between the two adults rather than fear of the invader.

If the child experienced any abuse while living with his mother's family, it wasn't at this man's hands.

Coming to a decision, I cautiously edge forward. As terrified as I am for Nikolai, I have to get Slava out of the direct line of fire.

"Slavochka..." I make my voice as calm and gentle as I can. "Please come to me. Mama Chloe needs you here."

The boy doesn't move. Somehow, he must sense that his presence is the only thing keeping the violence from escalating.

I risk another half-step forward, and Slava finally moves, dashing toward me. As soon as he's near enough, I grab him by the arm and shove him behind me, blocking him with my body as I begin to back away.

The stranger lets out a rough laugh, his dark eyes flashing briefly to the ring on my finger. "Mama Chloe, is it?" Like Nikolai's, his English is as American as they come. "Sweetheart... if you move another muscle, I'll blow your brains out and then your dear husband's. Congratulations on your nuptials by the way," he continues as I freeze in place. "I'm guessing the wedding was very recent?"

Nikolai's eyes are slitted, his voice deadly soft. "None of your fucking business. Now leave before I paint the ground with *your* brains. Since we seem to be family and all, I'll let you walk away before the guards get here."

"What guards?" Alexei's sharp-edged smile is all white teeth and cruelty. "It's just me and my men here now. And you're fucking high if you think I'm leaving without what I came for. Hand over my sister's son and Alina—and maybe, just maybe, I'll let you and your pretty bride live. Seeing as we're about to be even closer family and all."

I blink. Alina? What does she have to do with anything? And what does he mean about closer family?

Nikolai's voice softens further, a lethal threat in every smoothly spoken syllable. "You have exactly thirty seconds to shut up and back away before I open fire."

"With her and the child here? I don't think so." His eyes cut toward me for another millisecond. "Besides, my snipers have you both in their sights."

My stomach drops, but Nikolai just bares his teeth. "Bullshit. They don't have a clear shot."

"No? Want to bet?" Alexei grins savagely. "Either way, all I need to do is wait, and my men will take down the shooter on your roof—at which point you'll be completely surrounded, and I'll take what I came for."

"Not if you're dead by then." Nikolai's expression is dark ice. "You have twenty seconds left. Nineteen. Eighteen..."

My heartbeat surges, my terror doubling with each second counted. He means it, I can see it—and so can Alexei, whose black eyes narrow as well. The smoke-scented air is so thick with incipient violence I can practically taste the warm, coppery spray of blood as bullets rip through flesh and bone.

One or both of these men will die here tonight.

Nikolai won't let his son be taken, and Alexei won't back down.

I have to do something.

If Nikolai is right about the snipers not having a clear shot, it's two of us against Alexei. If I shoot, maybe—

"Stop!" Like a wraith, Alina emerges from the smoky darkness of the garage, the blood-red of her gown contrasting with the ghostly paleness of her skin and the jet-black curtain of her hair.

Like me, she's armed, but unlike me, she's holding her gun loosely at her side, the barrel pointed at the ground.

"Stop, Alexei, please." She steps through the jagged opening, the glow of the dying flames turning her jade eyes a greenish shade of hazel. "Slava isn't going anywhere, you know that. My brother won't give up his son. And he's not—" Her voice cracks. "He's not the one you want anyway."

I suck in a breath, finally comprehending what's happening. This man and Alina—they know each other.

More than that, he thinks he has some type of claim on her.

"Alina, get back." Nikolai's tone takes on a sharper edge as Alexei's entire posture alters, a terrifying sort of hunger kindling in his demonic gaze as it locks on Alina's face.

She raises her gun, aiming it at his face. "You have a choice," she says evenly. "I know you're an excellent shot, but so is my brother—and so am I. And so is Lyudmila in there." She tips her head toward the dark garage. "Maybe you can take down one or two of us before our bullets find you—and maybe your snipers can help—but nobody is going to walk away unscathed. You might have the advantage of the forces surrounding us, but here, we outnumber you. Besides..." Her voice takes on a sardonic inflection. "What good am I to you dead, right?"

"Alina, shut up and get back inside," Nikolai growls. "You don't have to—"

"I will come with you," she continues, ignoring her brother. "I will honor the betrothal contract. And in exchange, you will call off your men and forget all about my nephew. He belongs here, with his father and Chloe—you can see that for yourself."

Alexei's eyes flash toward me for another fraction

of a second, taking in the child I'm shielding with my body, absorbing the way he's clinging to my legs while observing the proceedings with enormous, uncomprehending eyes.

That's why they're all speaking English, I realize with a distant corner of my mind. They're hoping Slava won't understand everything with his still-limited knowledge of the language—and it's at least partially working. He can see the adults pointing guns at each other, but he doesn't fully get why.

Alexei's gaze returns to Alina, the black orbs burning with even darker hunger. "All right. We have a deal. Lay down the gun and walk toward me."

"Do not fucking do it." Nikolai's voice is whip sharp. "I can take him."

"Maybe." She lays her weapon on the ground. "Or maybe you'll both die. Maybe Chloe and Slava will as well. Think about that."

Nikolai's jaw clenches. "I'm not letting you do this."

A bitter smile touches her lips. "It's not your call, brother. Nor is it mine. That whole fate business you believe in? Well, mine was decided when I was fifteen, and it's time I stopped running from it. You and Konstantin have shielded me long enough."

Nikolai is about to argue further, I can see it, but she forestalls any further discussion by swiftly walking over to Alexei—who grabs her elbow and pulls her to his side as soon as she's within reach.

The possessive way he holds her pinned against him leaves no doubt of his intent, his dark figure looming over her making me think of Hades dragging Persephone down into the underworld.

Nikolai must see the same thing because his face twists with fury and he takes a half-step forward—only to halt when Alexei's finger tightens warningly on the trigger.

"Don't, Kolya." Alina's eyes glitter brightly as Alexei begins backing up toward the tree line, dragging her along while keeping his gun trained on Nikolai. "I'll be fine. Just take care of Chloe and Slava, and I'll see you back in Moscow sometime, okay? And tell Konstantin not to look for me. I don't want blood spilled on my behalf!"

The last words reach us as a shout from the distance, and Nikolai's gaze burns with hatred as he watches his enemy disappear into the darkness with his prize, the shadows closing around them like a lover's fierce embrace.

58

CHLOE

I wake up to a cacophony of drills and hammers in the distance—a familiar soundtrack for the past few days. Ever since the attack last week, both the house and the grounds of the compound have been undergoing major renovations and security upgrades, including a quintupling of our guard force.

Nikolai is determined to ensure that no one, be it the Leonovs or some other enemy of ours, can breach our walls again, no matter how many mercenaries or advanced weapons they have at their disposal.

Opening my eyes, I take in the empty mattress next to me and the faint morning light seeping in through the blinds. It's barely sunrise, so my husband must've gotten up early for the videoconference with his brothers regarding the ongoing search for Alina—if he slept at all last night, that is. Much to my worry, his middle-of-the-night runs have increased in both frequency and duration since the attack, so much so that I don't know when he's getting any rest at all.

The door swings open, and the object of my musings enters the bedroom.

I sit up, my heart squeezing at the bleak expression on his face.

"Nothing?" I ask quietly as he crosses the room toward me.

He shakes his head. "It's like they've disappeared off the face of the fucking planet. Konstantin thinks he's holding her somewhere completely off the grid, but where is anyone's guess at this point."

"I'm so sorry." I reach over to squeeze his hand as he sits on the edge of the bed, but he pulls me onto his lap instead. Wrapping his powerful arms tightly around me, he buries his face in my hair and inhales deeply.

When he pulls back to meet my gaze, some of the tension in his face has eased. Cupping my cheek, he asks softly, "How are you feeling, zaychik? Did you sleep well?"

I turn my face to press a kiss into his palm before bringing his hand down to my chest. "Yes." I smile to dispel the lingering worry in his eyes. "I'm fine, I promise."

To say that Nikolai has been babying me over the past few days would be a major understatement. Though a few shallow cuts and bruises on my bare feet were the extent of my injuries, he's been treating me like I've sustained another gunshot wound—or at the very least, have been severely traumatized. And while it's true that I've been having nightmares again, I'm far from falling apart.

Not that I'm not worried about Alina—I am. Nikolai told me about the betrothal agreement their father made with Boris Leonov when Alina was barely fifteen, and if I still had any doubts that the man deserved his fate at Nikolai's hands, they disappeared in that moment.

No wonder Alexei had acted as if he had a claim on her. By that barbaric—and undoubtedly illegal—contract, he does. I can only hope his feelings for her extend beyond the dark lust I saw on his face that night, and that he isn't as terrible of a man as his reputation suggests.

Nikolai's lips curve in an answering smile as he moves to shift me off his lap, but I wrap my arms around his neck, refusing to let him go. "Lie down with me, please," I murmur into his ear. "I'm not ready to get up yet."

As concerned as I am about Alina, I'm almost as worried about how hard Nikolai is taking what happened. He hasn't had a single decent night of sleep over the past week, and it shows in the darker hollows around his striking eyes, the deeper grooves bracketing his sensuous mouth... his unrelenting obsession with Slava's and my safety.

Not only did Nikolai refuse to remove the cameras from inside the house when I asked, but he's having me and Slava wear tracker bracelets that tell him our exact location and measure our vital signs at all times.

I've opted not to fight him on this for now, as we've had much bigger issues to focus on, including the funerals for the fallen guards—yet another reason for Nikolai's grim mood. More than a dozen of our men were killed in the attack, and several others were severely injured—though, luckily, most of Nikolai's army friends weren't among the former.

Alexei's men pinned them down in a ravine, preventing them from coming to our aid or radioing for help, but everybody except Ivanko survived. Even Arkash, who caught a bullet perilously close to his spine, is expected to make a full recovery.

The other bright spot in all of this is Slava. Once we explained that what he saw was a part of the security drill, and that Alina went on vacation with "Uncle Lyosha," the boy has gone right back to his cheerful self, pestering me, Pavel, and Lyudmila with a million questions about the new guards and the construction going on at the compound.

"Zaychik…" Nikolai's voice takes on a hoarser note as I oh-so-innocently let my lips graze his earlobe. "I wish I could join you, but I have a lot of work this morning."

Of course he does, but it can wait until he gets some sleep. Dropping all pretense of innocence, I wriggle my butt against the growing bulge in his pants and kiss the hard underside of his jaw. "Please… pretty please."

If there's one thing the events of last week haven't affected, it's Nikolai's sex drive—and sure enough, that kiss is all it takes for him to flip me onto my back and fuck me until we're both sweaty, sore, and beyond satisfied. And, as I hoped, exhausted enough to sleep... at least those of us who haven't gotten any shuteye.

I wait until I'm sure Nikolai is deep in the embrace of slumber before I carefully wriggle out from underneath his arm and pad over to the bathroom to shower and get ready for the day.

When I come out, he's still asleep, the stamp of exhaustion heavy upon his beautiful features. Smiling tenderly, I watch him for a while. Then I plop into a lounge chair by the window and open my laptop to check the news, as has been my custom every morning for the past few days.

As we hoped, more of Bransford's victims have come forward since the story about his assault on Masha broke—and not just the two women Nikolai found. Every day has brought fresh, ever-more-horrifying revelations... which is why I've been so addicted to the news.

Every damning headline avenges my mom further.

Opening a browser, I navigate to my favorite news site—only to freeze at the words splashed boldly across the screen:

BRANSFORD COMMITS SUICIDE IN HOTEL ROOM

Stomach churning, I click on the article.

Apparently, some thirty-nine minutes ago, Tom Bransford was found in a Four Seasons penthouse with his wrists slit, the suicide note by his bed leaving little doubt as to what happened.

That is, little doubt for anyone who doesn't know my husband and what he's capable of.

Setting the laptop aside, I get up and walk over to the bed, my heart beating unevenly as I stare at the man sleeping there—the husband I've grown to love more than life itself.

Did he do this?

Did he decide that, even stripped of his political pull and on the verge of being criminally prosecuted, Bransford poses too great of a threat to me?

Did Masha or someone like her slip into that Four Seasons penthouse and set everything up to make it look like Bransford killed himself—same as his assassins had done to my mom?

I should wake up Nikolai and demand the answer to these questions, get him to admit the truth—but I know I won't. Not because I'm still afraid to face the darkness within him, but because I'm realizing that this particular truth doesn't matter to me.

Suicide or assassination, Bransford is gone, and that vengeful part of me—the part I wanted to pretend wasn't there—is happy. No, more than happy. It's downright ecstatic.

Whether at Nikolai's hand or his own, Tom Bransford got exactly what he deserved.

I stand by the bed for a minute longer, absorbing the sheer relief of that knowledge, the lifting of the weight I hadn't realized still sat across my shoulders. I let that sensation filter through as I think about the lethal beauty of my husband's face and the terrible darkness in his soul—a darkness I now realize exists in me as well.

Then, carefully, so as not to interrupt his much-needed rest, I lie down next to him and drape my arm across his chest. His eyes don't open and his breathing doesn't alter, but he turns and gathers me against him, his powerful body curving around me, warming me, shielding me from the world.

My chest expands, my heart so full it feels on the verge of bursting. Just a couple of months ago, I was an orphan on the run from her mother's killers, a woman all alone in the world with a life expectancy measured in days. Now I have my husband and my son, and a future full of possibilities.

Maybe we'll stay here for the next few years, and I'll get a teaching job at a local school—a school that Slava will attend as well. Or maybe we'll go to Moscow, and Nikolai will take up the reins of his family organization again, with all that it entails. Or maybe it'll be something else entirely, a path I can't even imagine at the moment.

Whatever that path is, wherever we go from here, doesn't matter.

As long as I have my dark protector, I fear nothing.

Together, Nikolai and I can take on the whole world.

SNEAK PEEKS

Nikolai & Chloe's story concludes here. If you enjoyed *Angel's Cage*, please consider leaving a review!

To be notified about my future books, including more stories featuring the Molotov family, sign up for my newsletter at www.annazaires.com.

Are you craving more dark, suspenseful romance? Check out my upcoming novel *White Nights*, a collaboration with Charmaine Pauls, telling the addictive story of a dangerous Russian oligarch and the American nurse he sets his sights on.

Do you enjoy laugh-out-loud romantic comedy? My hubby and I cowrite raunchy, geeky romcoms under the pen name Misha Bell. Grab a copy of *Hard Ware*, the story of a snarky sex toy designer, a mysterious potential investor, and their two enamored dogs.

Are you an Urban Fantasy fan? Check out *Dream Walker*, written by my hubby Dima Zales, the action-packed tale of a dreamwalker on a mission to save her mom, without falling in love with the dangerous illusionist helping her.

If you like audiobooks, please visit www.annazaires.com to check out this series and our other books in audio.

Now, please turn the page to read excerpts from *Twist Me* and *Hard Ware*.

Power. That's what I think of when I spot him across the ER. Power and danger.

One of the wealthiest Russian oligarchs, Alex Volkov is as ruthless as he is magnetic. He always gets what he wants, and what he wants is me, in his bed.

He's the kind of trouble every woman should run from. The bullet his bodyguard took for him proves that.

I should stay far away, but for one night, I give in to temptation. Before I know it, he's pulling me deeper into his world of excess and violence, invading not only my life but my heart.

How much trust can I place in a man so dangerous? How much do I dare risk for his love?

Turning away from the sink, I look back at the wounded man, making sure everything is okay with him before I go check on my other patients.

At that moment, I catch a pair of steely blue eyes looking at me.

It's one of the men standing near the victim, likely one of his relatives. Visitors are generally not allowed in the hospital at night, but the ER is an exception.

Instead of looking away, as most people will when caught staring, the man continues to study me.

Both intrigued and slightly annoyed, I study him back.

He's tall, well over six feet in height, and broad-shouldered. He's not handsome in the traditional sense. That's too weak of a word to describe him. Instead, he's magnetic.

Power. That's what comes to mind when I look at him. It's there in the arrogant tilt of his head, in the way he looks at me so calmly, utterly sure of himself and his ability to control all around him. I don't know who he is or what he does, but I doubt he's a pencil pusher in some office. This is a man used to issuing orders and having them obeyed.

His clothes fit him well and look expensive. Maybe even custom made. He's wearing a gray trench coat, dark gray pants with a subtle pinstripe, and a pair of black Italian leather shoes. His brown hair is cut short, almost military style. The simple haircut suits his face, revealing hard, symmetric features. He has high cheekbones and a blade of a nose with a slight bump, as though it had been broken once.

I have no idea how old he is. His face is unlined, but there's no boyishness to it. No softness whatsoever, not even in the curve of his mouth. I guess his age to be early thirties, but he can just as easily be twenty-five or forty.

He doesn't fidget or look uncomfortable as our staring contest continues. He simply stands there quietly, completely still, his blue gaze trained on me.

To my shock, my heart rate picks up as a tingle of heat runs down my spine. It's as though the temperature in the room has jumped ten degrees. All of a sudden, the atmosphere becomes intensely sexual, making me aware of myself as a woman in a way I've never experienced. I can feel the silky material of my matching underwear set brushing between my legs and against my breasts. My entire body seems flushed and sensitized, my nipples pebbling underneath my layers of clothing.

Holy shit.

So that's what it feels like to be attracted to someone. It's not rational and logical. There's no meeting of minds and hearts involved. No, the urge is basic and primitive. My body has sensed his on some animal level, and it wants to mate.

He feels it too. It shows in the way his blue eyes darken, lids partially lowering, and in the way his nostrils flare as though trying to catch my scent. His fingers twitch, curl into fists, and I somehow know he's trying to control himself, to avoid reaching for me right then and there.

If we were alone, I have no doubt he'd be on me already.

Still staring at the stranger, I back away. The strength of my response to him is frightening, unsettling. We're in the middle of the ER, surrounded by people, and all I can think about is hot, sheet-twisting sex. I have no idea who he is, whether he's married or single. For all I know, he's a criminal or an asshole. *Or a cheating scumbag like Tony.* If anyone has taught me to think twice before trusting a man, it's my ex-boyfriend. I don't want to get involved with anyone so soon after my last, disastrous relationship. I don't want that kind of complication in my life again.

The tall stranger clearly has other ideas.

At my cautious retreat, he narrows his eyes, his gaze becoming sharper, more focused. Then he comes toward me, his stride graceful for such a large man. There's something panther-like in his leisurely movements, and for a second, I feel like a mouse getting stalked by a big cat. Instinctively, I take another step back, and his hard mouth tightens with displeasure.

Dammit, I'm acting like a coward.

I stop backing away and stand my ground instead, straightening to my full five-foot-seven height. I'm always the calm and capable one, handling high-stress situations with ease, yet I'm behaving like a schoolgirl confronted with her first crush. Yes, the man makes me uncomfortable, but there's nothing to be afraid of. What's the worst he can do? Ask me out on a date?

Nevertheless, my hands shake slightly as he approaches, stopping less than two feet away. This close, he's even taller than I thought, a few inches over six feet. I'm not a short woman, but I feel tiny standing in front of him. It's not a feeling I enjoy.

"You're very good at your job." His voice is deep and a little rough, tinged with some Eastern European accent. Just hearing it makes my insides shiver in a strangely pleasurable way.

"Thank you," I say, a bit uncertainly. I *am* good at my job, but I didn't expect a compliment from this stranger.

"You took care of Igor well. Thank you for that."

Igor must be the gunshot patient. It's a foreign-sounding name. Russian, perhaps? That would explain the stranger's accent. Although he speaks English fluently, he's not a native speaker.

"Of course." I'm proud of the steadiness of my tone. Hopefully, the man won't realize how he affects me. "I hope he recovers quickly. Is he a relative?"

"My bodyguard."

Wow. I was right. This man is a big fish. Does that mean—

"Was he shot in the course of duty?" I ask, holding my breath.

"He took a bullet meant for me, yes." His tone is

matter-of-fact, but I get a sense of suppressed rage underneath those words.

I swallow hard. "Did you already speak to the police?"

"I gave them a brief statement. I will talk to them in more detail once Igor is stabilized and regains consciousness."

I nod, not knowing what to say to that. The man standing in front of me was nearly assassinated today. What is he? Some mafia boss? A political figure?

If I had any doubts about the wisdom of exploring this strange attraction between us, they're gone. This stranger is bad news, and I need to stay as far away from him as possible.

"I wish your bodyguard a speedy recovery," I say in a falsely cheerful tone. "Barring any complications, he should be fine."

"Thanks to you."

I give him a half-smile and take a step to the side, hoping to walk around the man and go to my next patient.

He shifts his stance, blocking my way. "I'm Alex Volkov," he says quietly. "And you are?"

My pulse picks up. The male intent in his question makes me nervous. Hoping he'll get the hint, I say, "Just a nurse working here."

He doesn't catch on, or he pretends not to. "What's your name?"

He's certainly persistent. I take a deep breath. "I'm Katherine Morrell. If you'll excuse me—"

"Katherine," he repeats, his accent lending the familiar syllables an exotic edge. His hard mouth softens a bit. "Katerina. It's a beautiful name."

"Thank you. I really have to go."

I'm increasingly anxious to get away. He's too large, too potently male. I need space and some room to breathe. His nearness is overpowering, making me edgy and restless, leaving me craving something that I know will be bad for me.

"You have your job to do. I understand," he says, looking vaguely amused.

Still, he doesn't move out of my way. Instead, as I watch in shock, he raises one large hand and brushes his knuckles over my cheek.

I freeze as a wave of heat zaps through my body. His touch is light, but I feel branded by it, shaken to the core.

"I would like to see you again, Katerina," he says softly, dropping his hand. "When does your shift end tonight?"

I stare at him, feeling like I'm losing control of the situation. "I don't think that's a good idea."

"Why not?" His blue eyes narrow. "Are you married?"

I'm tempted to lie, but honesty wins out. "No, but I'm not interested in dating right now."

"Who said anything about dating?"

I blink. I assumed—

He lifts his hand again, stopping me mid-thought.

This time, he picks up a strand of my hair, rubbing it between his fingers.

"I don't date, Katerina," he murmurs, his accented voice oddly mesmerizing. "But I would like to take you to bed. And I think you'd like that too."

White Nights is available for pre-order now!

EXCERPT FROM HARD WARE BY
MISHA BELL

So, my Chihuahua fell in love with a bear. Excuse me, a giant, bear-like dog.

Now the bear's scorching hot owner is on my case, demanding an STD test... for my pet.

Another problem with this doggy love affair? The bear's mysterious owner may be the key to funding my new venture and taking my toys company to the next level. And by "toys," I mean the fun kind, the kind every woman (and man) needs.

If only I could figure out what he's hiding—or get my libido to behave. Because mixing business and pleasure is a bad idea, and Dragomir Lamian may not be who he seems.

NOTE: This is a standalone, raunchy, slow-burn romantic

comedy featuring a confident, toy-obsessed heroine who knows every Russian superstition under the sun, her meet-cute with a hot, mysterious stranger, and two dogs engaged in a love affair of their own. If any of the above is not your cup of tea, run away now. Otherwise, buckle in for a laugh-out-loud, feel-good ride.

Is that a *bear*?

The Kegel balls feel like they're on the verge of escaping my vagina. I squeeze my well-trained muscles to keep the toy inside. The pair of balls are of my own design, so I know if I squeeze them one more time, the vibration feature will activate, and this isn't a good time for that.

The leash jerks in my hand.

"Bonaparte, behave." The sternness in my voice is futile. My Chihuahua keeps tugging, his gaze glued to the bear and his tail wagging so rapidly I half expect him to helicopter into the air like a drone.

To my relief, the bear merely sniffs the fire hydrant, oblivious to the delicious four-pound appetizer a mere leap away.

Digging in my heels, I pull back on the leash. "Seriously, Boner. Do you *want* to get eaten?"

The pulling stops, and my dog looks up at me, a mixture of sadness and indignation in his green eyes. As usual, I can imagine what he'd say if I were a dog whisperer:

"*Ma chérie*, that dog is ignoring me. *Moi*! Unthinkable."

I toss him a biscuit. "That bear clearly has no manners. In its defense, though, would *you* be able to resist sniffing that hydrant? We're next to Central Park. Millions of dogs have peed there. The smell must be heavenly."

With a leap, Boner catches the treat, swallows it without chewing, and returns his attention to his gargantuan quarry.

My own gaze shifts to the man holding the beast's leash, and my jaw drops as my inner muscles involuntarily squeeze the Kegel balls.

The vibration activates, but I ignore it, my eyes hungrily roaming over the tall, athletically built male specimen in front of me.

The bear's owner is hot.

Scorching, panty-melting, uterus-exploding hot.

The kind of hot that I'm going to end up masturbating to.

Wait. Strictly speaking, I *am* masturbating to him— the vibration inside my vagina is building my climax with every passing second. Thankfully, he's not looking at me, so I can gobble him up without shame.

The man checks all my boxes, even ones I didn't know I had.

Thick, silky-looking hair the color of mink's fur. Short, neatly trimmed dark beard that emphasizes his regal nose and carved features. Broad shoulders padded with just the right amount of muscle and a chest to die for, all tapering down to a lean waist and narrow hips. He's even wearing a turtleneck, for fuck's sake—and everyone knows that's the guy equivalent of a sexy black dress.

Oh, and his lips. I want to make a mold of those lips and turn that mold into a sex toy.

Speaking of sex toys, the balls are getting me ever closer to the edge. Though I've been accused of being blasé about such things, even I recognize that coming here and now, in front of a stranger, isn't the most socially acceptable move on my part.

I've got to disable the balls, which can be done if I squeeze them three more times. The problem is, each squeeze also changes the vibration speed, so my situation will get worse before it gets better.

No helping that, I suppose.

I squeeze.

The vibration intensifies.

Twice more to go and—

Boner barks.

The bear's massive snout unpeels from the hydrant, and giant brown eyes zero in on the dog-shaped hors d'oeuvre at my feet.

Finally getting the attention he craves, Boner rapidly wags his tail and tries to sprint to his doom.

I squeeze the balls again, involuntarily. One more time, and they're off. Except the vibration is now on full speed, and it feels amazing. So, so amazing...

Crap. What am I doing?

Have to squeeze one last time.

Except the prerequisite muscles have turned to jelly, and I'm having trouble squeezing.

Is this it?

Am I going to have an orgasm just as my dog gets eaten—all in front of the insanely hot stranger?

Order your copy of *Hard Ware* today at www. mishabell.com!

ABOUT THE AUTHOR

Anna Zaires is a *New York Times, USA Today,* and #1 international bestselling author of sci-fi romance and contemporary dark erotic romance. She fell in love with books at the age of five, when her grandmother taught her to read. Since then, she has always lived partially in a fantasy world where the only limits were those of her imagination. Currently residing in Florida, Anna is happily married to Dima Zales (a science fiction and fantasy author) and closely collaborates with him on all their works.

To learn more, please visit www.annazaires.com.